I WILL GIVE MY LOVE AN APPLE

SUSANNA M. NEWSTEAD

PASTMASTERY PRESS

Cover design and art by matthewryanhistoricalillustrator.com/
Photography by Valerie Drew valadrew@yahoo.co.uk
Editing by Gill Whatmough
Thanks to Toni Louka-Fernandez for help with the Anglo-Saxon

Published by PastMastery Press
Medlar House
Hanover Drive
Brackley Northants. NN136JS UK
sue@pastmastery.com

Early English Riddle song from Sussex.

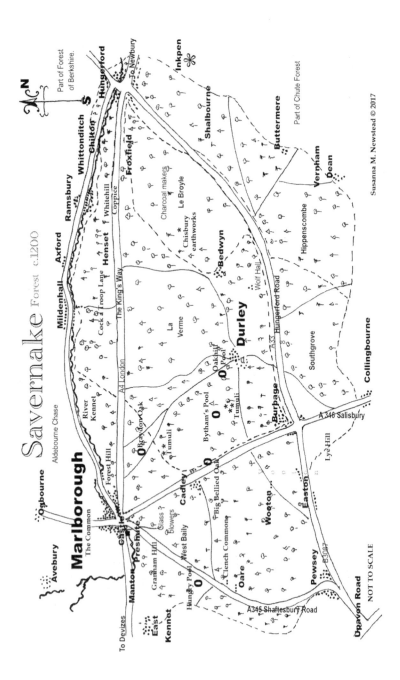

Savernake Forest c.1200

N

S

Susanna M. Newstead © 2017

NOT TO SCALE

Part of Forest of Berkshire.

Part of Chute Forest

To Newbury

Hungerford

Inkpen

Whitionditch

Chilton

Froxfield

Shalbourne

Buttermere

Ramsbury

Vernham

Dean

Axford

Whitehill Coppice

Charcoal makers

Le Broyle

Mildenhall

Henset

Chisbury earthworks

Bedwyn

Cock à Troop Lane

The King's Way

Hippenscombe

Aldbourne Chase

Wolf Hall

Durley

Ogbourne

River Kennet

A4 London

La Verme

Hungerford Road

Avebury

Forest Hill

Oakhill Pool

A338

Southgrove

Collingbourne

Braydon Oak

Bytham's Pool

Tumuli

Burbage

A 346 Salisbury

Marlborough

Tumuli

Cadley

Lye Hill

To Devizes

The Common

Glass ? blowers

Big Bellied Oak

Wootton

Easton

Manton

Preshute

Gramham Hill

West Baily

Clench Commone

Oare

Pewsey

Devon Road

East Kennet

Hungry Pool

A345 Shaftesbury Road

B3087

Marlborough and Savernake Forest c.1200 (1)

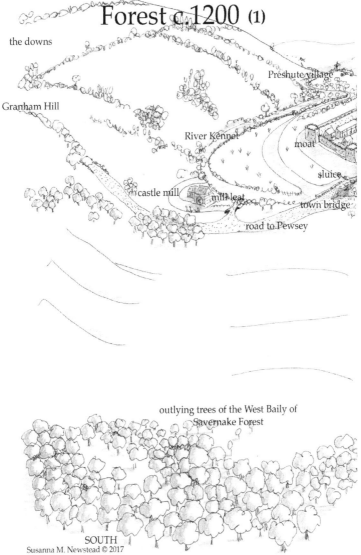

the downs

Preshute village

Granham Hill

River Kennet

moat

sluice

castle mill

mill leat

town bridge

road to Pewsey

outlying trees of the West Baily of
Savernake Forest

SOUTH

Susanna M. Newstead © 2017

Marlborough Town and the forest c.1200 (2)

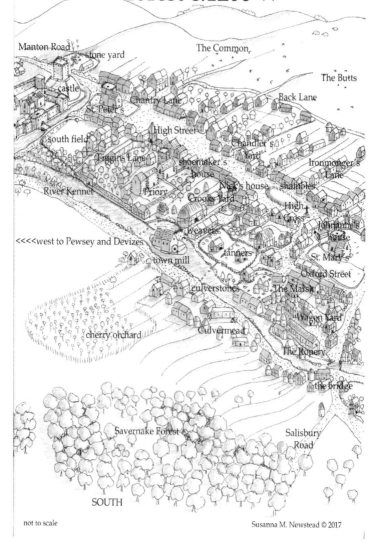

Manton Road · stone yard · The Common · The Butts · castle · Chantry Lane · Back Lane · St Peter's · High Street · Chandler's Yard · Ironmonger's Lane · south field · Figgins Lane · shoemaker's house · Nick's house · shambles · River Kennet · Priory · Crooks yard · High Cross · Johanne's house · <<<<west to Pewsey and Devizes · weavers · St. Mary's · town mill · tanners · Oxford Street · culverstones · The Marsh · Wagon Yard · cherry orchard · Culvermead · The Ropery · the bridge · Savernake Forest · Salisbury Road · SOUTH

not to scale

Marlborough and the forest
c. 1200 (3)

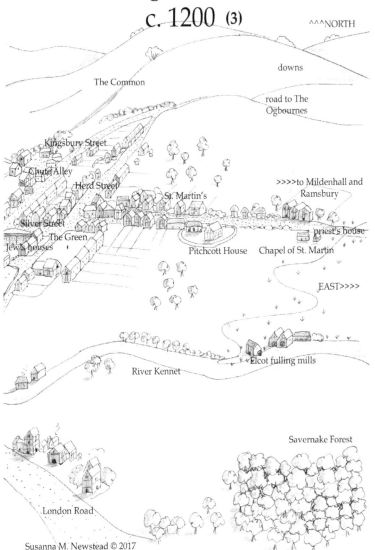

^^^NORTH

downs

The Common

road to The
Ogbournes

Kingsbury Street

Chute Alley

Herd Street

St. Martin's

>>>>to Mildenhall and
Ramsbury

Silver Street

The Green

Jew's houses

Pitchcott House

Chapel of St. Martin

priest's house

EAST>>>>

Elcot fulling mills

River Kennet

Savernake Forest

London Road

Susanna M. Newstead © 2017

Durley Village c. 1200

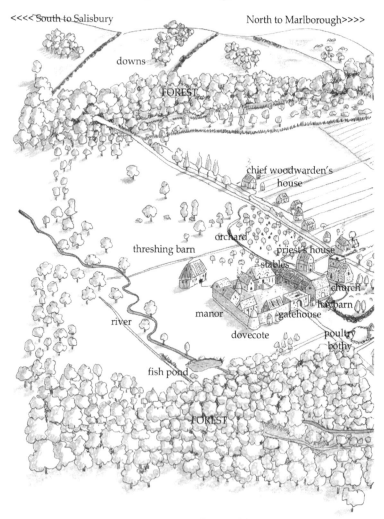

<<<< South to Salisbury

North to Marlborough>>>>

downs

FOREST

chief woodwarden's
house

orchard

threshing barn

priest's house

stables

church

manor

haybarn

gatehouse

river

dovecote

poultry
bothy

fish pond

FOREST

Susanna M. Newstead © 2017

Durley Village c. 1200

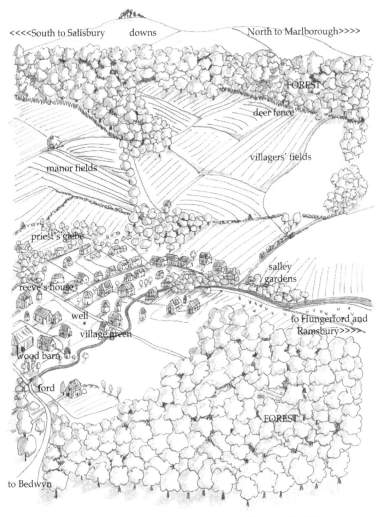

<<<<South to Salisbury   downs   North to Marlborough>>>>

FOREST

deer fence

villagers' fields

manor fields

priest's glebe

salley gardens

reeve's house

well

village green

to Hungerford and Ramsbury>>>>

wood barn

ford

FOREST

to Bedwyn

Chapter One

Snow blanketed the forest from late December, that winter of 1204. It was not deep, but had covered everything, making it perfect and beautiful. I rose just after dawn, that day of December the nineteenth, as is my usual habit and looked from my newly glazed solar windows. The first thing I noticed was the light. How very bright it was. I called over my shoulder to Lydia, my wife of only a couple of months.

"Snow Lydia... it has snowed in the night," excitement in my voice, like a young boy itching to be out playing with his friends.

She turned over in the warmth of the covers and mumbled something like, "How very nice for it..." from the curtained bed.

I smiled and rushed to pile on my clothes, for it was cold and the fire had been covered for the night. I blew gently on the smouldering embers and fed some twigs into them. One of the very best things I had done at my manor of Durley, deep in the Savernake Forest, was to build a modern fireplace with a chimney in my private room. The solar would be warm in no time and the smoke would escape up into the flue and not into the space of the room. When Lydia rose, the solar would be warm. So, how would the snow affect the business of the day? How might we accomplish what tasks we had set ourselves this day, in almost a foot of snow?

I left the solar and descended the steps into the hall. John Brenthall, my chief forester ,was already there, his hands wrapped around a mug of spiced ale. His young son Peter was with him. I think he was wearing every item of clothing he possessed, for he was almost twice his usual size and found it quite difficult to move his arms. His teeth were chattering and his boots were still quite snowy.

"For goodness sake Peter, stand by the fire. Thaw out a little. Hal, is there any of your spiced ale for the lad?"

Hal of Potterne, my senior man at arms, a grizzled veteran of the battles of Henry the second and a man of many talents - one of which was blending a good spiced ale - was standing in front of the roaring hall fire. Here too, in the hall of the manor house, I had built a fireplace, a large one which would take the huge logs from the forest, which I had permission to collect and burn.

"Aye... 'ere you are lad. This'll dry yer boots frum the inside out!" he called.

"Paul my scribe, are you cold, my boy, or is it just that talking about snow has made you shiver? What? You can't hold the pen to write because your fingers are so cold? Oh dear , we can't have that.

If you go to that chest there... yes that one and lift the lid, you will find some felted gloves which have no fingers. Put them on. They will help you. And put some more charcoal on the brazier. We have plenty. We make it, you know, in the forest, right here in Savernake. Oh, I have told you before...oh have I? All right then. Do you, forgive me, wear anything under your habit? A what? Oh is that all? I can see you are wearing boots. I suppose that is allowed in the harsh climate of our country in winter. You may be a monk but you aren't' in the hot desert where most of the religious orders originated, are you? No that's right you're a home grown monk...a Gilbertine.

No, we can't have your fingers seizing up when you are writing about my time as warden of the forest. I can't do it any longer...look at my poor fingers. There once was a time when these hands could hold a broadsword and wield it with deadly aim. Forty years ago now when King John, God assoil him, was on the throne. I could write a good hand too. Now I need you to write for me so, poke the fire a bit, put my blanket round your shoulders... that's better and we shall write down the fourth of our tales of murder and mayhem. We shall write how my good friend Johannes of Salerno, of Marlborough town and I, Aumary Belvoir, Lord of Durley and Warden of the Forest of Savernake, solved yet another mystery and...what's that?

Oh yes, my boy, we were getting quite a reputation for uncovering foul mur-

ders, so much so, that the King had decided that amongst all the other tasks he had set me, he would make me constable of Wiltshire...but that is for our tale. Let's carry on and we shall see what happened...."

Hal had filled a cup for me too and as I walked to the fire to take it from him, John inclined his head towards the table.

"In before dawn sir....these royal messengers are driven folk it seems. Heavens knows when he set out. In this weather too." There on the table was a leather pannier with a royal cipher embossed on the side. I had seen this sort of thing before. Many times at Marlborough Castle. Twice for myself. Once when I had been confirmed as warden, for the duration of my life, and for my male offspring and another when the town of Marlborough had been granted, a fair in August every year, and two market days a week by the King. In this pannier would be a royal document of some import.

I stared at it. " 'Taint goin' to open itself, sir," said Hal with a grin. No, it wasn't was it? I undid the buckles.

Inside was a letter from the king, and a charter confirming me, Aumary Belvoir, as constable for Wiltshire.

"What?" I sat down heavily on the bench. The words were swimming before my eyes.

John and I were childhood friends. I wrote to him regularly, telling him of developments here in his forest, news of import and more personal tales which I know he read, or more properly had read to him, for when we met, he knew all that had been written. He forgot nothing. By the words in this letter, we should be seeing him at Christmas this year. John began by explaining recent events on the continent. His father's empire was almost lost, he said, through the treachery of the Norman barons and the perfidy of the French king. He was returning to England to raise an army to fight back. France and his enemies would rue their falseness.

He wanted me to oversee, in this part of the country, an oath to be taken by all men over twelve. He decreed that, for the general defence of the realm and for the preservation of peace, a commune should be made throughout the kingdom and that all men from the greatest to the very least should swear to keep it firmly. The ordnance to which they swore established a constable in every shire and in every hundred, city and group of small towns, subordinate constables who were to lead the respective communes to the muster whenever summoned by the chief constable, whom they were to obey, " for the defence of the realm and preservation of peace against foreigners or against any other disturbers of the same." If this oath or summons was neglected, it would be an offence of high treason.

Also in this letter he said he had, been thinking about how to overcome the problem of felonies going without proper investigation.

The role of the coroner had been resurrected by his elder brother King Richard some few years ago. In truth it was a Saxon role and Richard had merely dug it up and given it new life. However, the job of the coroner was to pronounce upon the death, not to investigate the murder and gather information. The coroner was intended as a foil to the sheriff of each county of the realm. The sheriff, one to each county, was often an unscrupulous man who used his power to make himself as rich as Croesus. Crowners, or coroners, however, were not paid; they had to be wealthy gentlemen who were able to keep themselves comfortably and so were (it was hoped) beyond corruption. Richard envisaged them almost as tax collectors and used them to screw whatever fine, fee or free gift he could from his people. It worked quite well.

Sheriffs came and went, depending on their loyalty and the king's whim. It was their job, amongst other things, to glean as much information as they could about a crime and try to apprehend the felon. In truth, this happened rarely, for unless the culprit could be caught with the knife in their hand, the sheriff seldom managed to unearth the real perpetrator. He simply did not have the resources or the time. The best ones did their utmost to interpret the letter of the law fairly. The worst simply took the first man they felt would fit the felony, and hanged him. Task complete.

Now John wanted to create a new role, that of constable of the county. It would be the constable's role to investigate and apprehend the culprit, incarcerate them and wait for the justices to trundle along (they were notoriously slow) and pronounce on the evidence. I had damned myself out of my own mouth for I had written to John, detailing the murders in the locality in recent times, which my friend Dr. Johannes of Salerno and I had solved. John had pounced. I was good at it he said. He'd had first hand experience of our skills when we had all been in Rouen in Normandy together, in the spring of 1204. Obviously I was the person for his new role, in Wiltshire.

Oh... John. Dear John. However was I going to manage to juggle all the roles I had been given by him? I was already looking after his forest of Savernake. I had good staff, it was true; wonderfully capable people like John Brenthall, Alan Hart my deerman and all my woodwards, verderers and foresters. I was also under-constable of Marlborough castle. The Lord Hugh de Neville was the constable and chief forester and he relied heavily on me when he was called away, which was quite often. There had been much new building work going on at the castle and for much of it, I had been in charge. It was hard work.

All this and I was lord of the village of Durley and other villages in the forest too. Now John wanted me to take on these new roles.

I would be required to travel about the county, all one thousand three hundred and forty six square miles of it. I would never be at home. No John. I can't do this.

I'm newly re-married, have a five year old daughter whom I would like to see grow and I would like other children too. How am I supposed to achieve that and provide an heir for the wardenship if I am never at home?

John was not a man to be denied. I had heard about his sudden mood changes and tempers though I had never seen them myself. To me, he had always been the best of friends, the most considerate of men. I had always treated him with respect and care and he had repaid me tenfold. How was I going to tell him that I did not wish to be constable of Wiltshire? This might be the first time I saw one of John's tempers! I carried on reading the letter. Mine was a trial. If I could make this work, he would make a constable in every county, sometime in 1205. The document accompanying the letter was a warrant which gave me powers to arrest and restrain felons and to lock them up. It allowed me freedoms to search properties, to sequester goods and livestock, to chase to the boundaries of Wiltshire and to hand on that task to another in a bordering county. I was allowed to pursue any line of inquiry and those who did not help or who hindered me were in contempt of John's authority and could be accused of treason. It was a carte blanche to investigate anyone, anything, anywhere.

It was well known that John was a hard worker and that he expected the same level of dedication to work from his men and officers.

If he found talent somewhere, he would harness it, no matter who the person was. He gave favour wherever he found good men, from the lowliest clerk to the highest ecclesiast in the country.

I wrote to Malmesbury for he told me this is where he would be from the nineteenth of December. I carefully put my case. If he would relieve me of my duties at the castle, perhaps I could manage? The best I could do, I said, under present circumstances, was to become responsible for the area around the forest and for Marlborough and environs, the area I managed for him anyway. If this was his trial, his test, let us see what could be achieved in a smaller area. This I might manage.

I watched the letter travel out of the gate with John Brenthall, nestling in his saddlebag. He would deliver it to Marlborough castle and it would go thence by the heralds along royal channels in dispatches to the king. I would not wait long for an answer.

The manor courtyard was now a churned up grey slushy mess, but beyond the gate, the snow was still quite pristine.

It had taken me quite some time to write my reply for I stopped and started several times and discarded each attempt. Two hours had passed and the manor children were now up and about and playing in the snow. Father Crispin, our priest, was supervising the making of little snow tunnels, his long robe belted almost up to his knees and his boots rising up to his chausses beyond. The smaller manor dogs were being encouraged to crawl through the tunnels and race. Some of the smaller children too, were engaged in racing through them giggling, on hands and knees, their faces ruddy and happy. My daughter, five year old Hawise, and some of the older children, joined by Hal of Potterne, were out by the threshing barn, making snowballs and throwing them at each other. There was much squealing and yelling, laughter and fun. Dysig, a man of nineteen or so but whose mind was that of a three year old, was out with the children, running around and making beautifully perfect, round snowballs which he would lob at the children. It was lovely to see him so happy. He had not had a good time lately and I was glad to watch him involving himself with the village folk. I returned to my office, stoked up the brazier and got on with my manor court accounts. Yes, I could read and write and managed these myself.

Suddenly there was an almighty crash. I looked up. Where had I heard this sound before? Yes, I had heard this sound in the past, when the glass makers had been in the church fitting the windows there and one of the panes had fallen accidentally to smash on the flagstone floor. It brought back memories I would rather leave buried; of poor Piers Pierson, only fourteen years of age, lying dead on the robing room floor of a severe asthma attack. I raced out of the office, through the hall and up into the solar. Lydia was there, staring at the floor. One of the solar windows closest to the threshing barn had been smashed and there on the floor was the culprit. A snowball. I picked it up. It was very solid and quite heavy. Had some child loaded it with a stone and decided to play the Vandal? Had they lobbed it through my expensive glass window pane? I looked out through the space made by the smashed window.

Hawise was remonstrating with Dysig, shaking her head and pointing. Dysig suddenly turned away and ran up towards his bothy which lay on the lane winding through the village from the Salisbury road. We should not see him for a while. Hawise marched round the wall and disappeared in to the sally port, the little door in the manor wall which lay at the back of the kitchen.

Lydia pulled a face. "I'll get a brush to clean it up. It will be sharp..." and she smiled as another memory came flooding back to us both; of the day we met and I caused her to drop a glass slickstone. She had been doing the smoothing of the washing at the house of Johannes of Salerno, who was her uncle and my friend. It too had shattered but not as perfectly as this window pane. I gave her the snowball.

Hawise now raced into the hall and up the solar stairs. Breathlessly she said, "It was me dada...I am sorry. I did not know where it was going to land. I threw it too hard and high."

I put both my hands on my hips and looked at my daughter with a stern eye.

"I will not be cross..."

"You won't?"

"If you tell me the truth."

"But...."

"No Hawise, I know you did not throw the snowball. For a start you could not possibly throw it so hard and high and with such force. Tell the truth."

"I did..."

"It was Dysig, wasn't it?"

My daughter and the halfwit, for some reason, were the best of friends. He was a tied peasant, the son of an unfree man and she was the daughter of a minor nobleman. A more unlikely pairing you would never get but neither of them would say aught against the other.

Hawise hung her head.

"You will not punish him dada...please. He doesn't know what he is doing. He was throwing it to see how high it would go and..."

"No, I will not. It is commendable that you want to take the blame for him but it is a lie all the same and I would rather have the truth."

I thought it was odd that Lydia had said nothing through this encounter with my daughter — the progeny of my first wife, Cecily and myself, for she was as good a mother to Hawise as her own had been. There is no doubt had her attention not been diverted elsewhere, she would have said something to Hawise too. I looked over at her. The smashed glass still lay at her feet. She had not moved to fetch a brush nor ask one of the servants to do it for her, but was staring at the snowball in her hand.

"Lydia?" She came out of her reverie. I watched as she brushed the snowball with her fingers and freed the thing that was inside. She placed it in my hand.

"What is it dada?" asked Hawise, breathlessly. I raised it to eye level and peered at it, turning it in my hand.

"It's an apple."

"An apple? Did we not pick all the apples from the..."

"No, this is not a real apple. It's a pretend one."

"Who would want to make a pretend apple?" giggled Hawise.

The snow was melting from it now, for the fire I had banked up earlier had warmed the room. It dripped from the little thing until the whole of it was revealed; it was the most exquisite little object.

A red apple, a little worn and dirty. It had some lettering around the middle in a band though for the life of me I could not read it.

The whole thing measured about three and a half inches in diameter and it was fashioned perfectly as an apple, with a small stalk a little bent over, and a slightly flattened bottom on which it might sit steady should you set it on a level surface.

The red of the apple was enamel, I thought, the stalk a dull gold and the band of lettering gold also. The whole thing was made up of sections, red enamel separated with tiny gold wires. The gold was dull and dirty but I thought it would clean up.

All three of us stared at the little thing and marvelled. What perfect crafts-manship. I had never seen anything like it. Wait. Yes, I had.

The reliquary which my great grandfather had caused to be made to house the Belvoir relic - a hair of St. Margaret, which he had brought back from the Holy land, was similar. It was a tiny box of enamel and gold just as this apple was, but it was much inferior in workmanship to this creation. I found what I thought was the beginning of the letters. I had no idea what it said. The object had obviously lain in the ground for ingrained in the holes of the lettering were small amounts of soil. I noticed too, that the band around the middle was ingrained with dirt. If we could clean it very carefully, we might be able to see if it opened, like a round box.

What a thing to be lobbed through my window! Where did it come from? I sighed. I would see if anyone recognised it. Ah, no...perhaps it was best kept quiet for the moment.

I swore Hawise and Lydia to secrecy.

First things first though, I would need to ask the glazier to return and mend the window.

Back went the waxed paper in its wooden frame into the 'window' space. This 'snowball' would cost me more than a paltry penny.

*****

That job done, I took my snowball down into the hall, leaving Hawise and Lydia to their morning reading lessons by the solar fire. Crispin the priest had just come in and was banging his boots in the screens passage, freeing them of the snow. I hailed him.

"Crispin, come and look at this and tell me if you have ever seen anything like it." He removed his wet cloak and laid it on a chair-back facing the fire, to dry out. Then he bounced up onto the dais and stared at the apple I held out in the flat of my hand.

"No never. What is it?" He reached and took it and twirled it in front of his eyes, much as I had done. "A very pretty thing. Where did you get it?"

"It was accidentally thrown through the solar window, in the centre of a snowball."

"Ah..." He looked at me. "Accidentally? Surely not accidentally. The person who threw it must have known it was there."

"Dysig..."

"Ah." He said again and the word was full of meaning. "I take it the window is gone?"

"I'm afraid so."

Crispin handled the little apple gently with his long elegant fingers.

"I can't tell you what it says, and if you clean it up a little we shall have a better idea, but I can tell you what the writing is."

"You can?"

"Yes. It's Runic. The script our forefathers used before we started to write the way we do now. The language is Old English...older than that spoken by a few of the old folk nowadays. When the Saxons first came to these shores, this was the language they wrote in."

"Old Saxons...is it so old then, this apple? Many hundreds of years?"

"I suspect so."

"So what on earth was Dysig doing with it?"

*****

I searched for Dysig and ran him to ground watching the work being done in the threshing barn. As soon as he saw me he turned to fly, but Walter Reeve had him by the collar before he could exit the building.

Dysig was not a mute but today he chose to be so. He sat on the barn floor and shut his lips.

Where did he find the little apple? How did it come to be in the snowball? Did he know the thing was inside the snowball? He obviously expected a beating. I told him that I wasn't going to beat him for the accident. I just wanted to know where he found it.

Periodically he would shake his head. I took this to mean he would not tell me anything. Finally, I threw my hands up in defeat and marched off to find the one person who would probably be able to get the story from Dysig; Agnes Brenthall, my right hand man John's wife.

Agnes was the manor housekeeper and could often be found in the undercroft looking after the stores, but today it was too cold in the stone room under the manor house and she had gone up into the buttery and was chatting to Henry my manor steward.

She bobbed a curtsy and he bowed as I entered the room.

"Agnes...I need your help with Dysig." I told her the story of the little apple and the broken window. Off she went to find him and Henry and I spent a profitable amount of time discussing the arrangements for the Christmas festivities, rapidly to be upon us.

Agnes was one of the few people in whom Dysig confided. His great aunt, Old Joan, was another, Hawise, naturally and strangely, my wife Lydia too had a way with him. All women. His best friend, the person who had watched out for him and had been a close neighbour, one of my wood wardens, Hamon Deerman, had been murdered only a few short weeks ago. Dysig had rather drawn into himself after that and was very wary of men.

Agnes came bustling back in, smiling. She warmed her hands over the brazier of charcoal we kept in the buttery.

"Ooh it's raw out there and the wind is rising. I think there's more snow to come."

"I wouldn't be surprised," I said.

"So what did our innocent malefactor say?"

She laughed at that. "He didn't know it was there. He just scooped up the snow and made a ball and threw it but it went the wrong way and...well you know the result, sir."

"Where was he when he scooped up the snow?"

"He and Hawise and a few of the others were down by the manor pond. They were running up and down the river bank, just where it loops. He chased

Hawise with the ball, apparently, all the way to the back of the manor wall by the barn and threw it there. 'Twas a good job it didn't hit her."

"So the snow actually came from…?

"Well, from what he said, sir, I think it came from close by the river bank."

*****

We had the promised snow and the wind blew fiercely all afternoon. John Brenthall came back from the town a frozen man and we thawed him out in front of the hall fire. I watched from the upper windows as the wind eddied out in the unprotected places and between buildings and blew the snow into peaks which resembled the sharp beaks of the falcons which hunted in the forest. The trees gathered the snow to their northern sides and again the familiar landscape was blanketed in white. The paths were obliterated, objects were covered and their edges softened. The fish pond began to ice over and was completely whitened with snow. The river edge too, iced over and as the snow continued, there was little left to tell a man where the edge lay. I spent the afternoon in my office with the little apple. I carefully swabbed it with tiny amounts of sheep's wool dipped in warmed water and then wrung out. I didn't want to get it too wet for I didn't know what damage might be done to it if I did. I remember once, when chatting to a goldsmith in Marlborough about some gems I wanted to sell, that he had said the best thing for dealing with tiny objects like jewels, where you did not want to scratch the gem or mark soft gold, was a thorn. The thorn was sharp enough to reach into tiny corners but gentle enough to remove ingrained dirt without scratching.

Where was I to find a thorn? Outside the manor house steps, growing close to the wall was a tree. An elder, if I was not much mistaken. It had volunteered when I was a young man and there it had prospered. I left it as cover and roosting for the little house sparrows who abounded in the courtyard. Next to it, my first wife Cecily had planted a rose. A rose with quite large thorns.

I donned my boots again, threw on my winter cloak which I grabbed from the peg on the back of the office door as I passed, and went out into the wind. I opened the main door and an icy blast hit me in the face, even though the door faced east and this was a north wind.

I struggled down the steps. I slipped twice, and felt for the wall on my left hand side as I tip-toed my way down the twelve or so stone steps. There was the rose bush, now denuded of leaves. I cut off a few stems, those full of thorns, with my knife, and turned to rise up again. My cloak was whipped up, I grabbed it back, shivering and battled up the steps. Reaching the top I looked back over the courtyard.

Tomorrow, or when the storm abated, I would trudge across the yard and visit my manor carpenter, Alfred Woodsmith and ask him to make a railing to go around the top and down the steps. It was only a matter of time before someone fell to their death there in icy weather.

Back in my office, I blew on my cold hands and threw the handful of sticks onto my table.

I drew the candles nearer and carefully, holding a twig between my thumb and my forefinger, began to scrape the dirt from the tiny patches of enamel with one of the thorns. They were somewhat flexible which meant that they yielded slightly under pressure, allowing me to avoid undue stress being applied to the pieces. Gradually, the soil and debris of hundreds of years was lifted. I blew it away and gently washed the piece with water again. The gold came up shining; the red enamel brighter.

I drew a piece of birch bark paper to me and wrote down the unfamiliar letters which circled the apple. They did not look like letters at all but little drawings; one like a three branched tree, another like an arrow pointing up. There was one which resembled the thorns with which I had cleaned the apple and another which looked for all the world like the shears with which my shepherds sheared my sheep.

Lightly, I grasped the apple in two hands and tried to part it around the band of lettering, for I was certain that this little thing was a round box made to contain...I knew not what. I tried to pull it apart. More work with the thorn and the warmed water freed the gold band which held the two halves together and slowly, to my surprise, the little globe loosened and began to turn.

Working inch by inch, nay quarter inch by quarter inch, I turned the top of the apple away from me and the bottom towards me. No box I had ever seen opened in this way. Suddenly it came free. I was right. This was a container.

Inside, to my surprise, was another perfect apple, this time of gold and as pristine as the day it was made. I buffed it with a dry cloth. Then by the light of the candles, I looked at it carefully.

More lettering, only marginally smaller than the outer case. Here though, it had been set with stones, tiny garnets in a rim around the words, if words they were. Still, I had no idea what they meant.

Something my young half-brother Robert, now deceased, had said echoed in my brain. Once the two of us had found a ciphered message and had puzzled over it, finally managing to decipher it through trial and error.

"The English used ciphering a lot. They were very fond of riddles," he had said.

Might it be that this was what we had here? An English riddle. Perhaps it was an incantation. After all, they were pagans.

Now, I needed someone who could tell me what these strange letters meant. When the snow stopped and I could ride into town, I would take my little apple to the priory and see what the monks might be able to tell me. They could read and were learned.

Firstly though, I would show it to my friend Johannes of Salerno. He would know what to do with treasure trove. For this is what my little apple was and it was best to keep its finding a secret for a while.

Chapter Two

"I'll go sir."

I had called the young village-men to the hall and had asked for a volunteer to go to the glass-blowers who had a permanent camp in the West Baily of the forest and call Master Glazer back to the manor. I had been told by the master glazier that the making of glass required two things in particular; wood ash - and beech wood was the best to burn for this - and river sand. The clean stream of the Kennet river bed would provide the sand which was of uniform grit size and the forest could provide the wood. Beech trees grew well on the thin chalk soil and over in the West Baily, beech trees were more common than in the rest of the forest.

When King John had decided to update and enlarge the castle, he had given permission for wood to be taken from the Royal Forest of Savernake for the making of the glass for the windows. Indeed, Master Glazer said, this type of glass was known as forest glass for it was always made in places where forest and stream ran together. He, though, hailed originally from The Weald of Kent where glass making was an established art. He had as a master, brought his skill further west and when he heard that John wished to add glass to the castle and chapel at Marlborough, offered his services.

Out in the forest, the glaziers had built a furnace where they could heat the ash and the sand together. This required very high temperatures and was an exact art. When the glass was molten it could be taken out of the furnace and blown into a cylinder. It would then be opened out and flattened to make a pane for a window. The master glass fitter would then cut the pane carefully and fit it to a wooden or metal frame and the whole thing would be sealed with a mixture of linseed oil and ground chalk, called putty.

Johnathan Reeve, the youngest son of Walter the reeve and one of my foresters, threw up his hand immediately.

"You know that I have been courting Phillipa Woodward, sir..." There were several good humoured sniggers and jokes passed round. "I can stay overnight with Philly and her parents, if that's all right with you. It's close to the glaziers' camp."

That indeed would be fine and I sent him on his way. The snow had stopped mid afternoon and the wind had dropped. It was hard going underfoot, so I told him to take one of the sure footed ponies from the stable, to make the journey easier.

I watched him go. The little black and white wagtails, who always seemed to be about the manor courtyard, come rain or shine, flicked their tails and with a 'tissick' looped over the outer wall and went with him. I looked up at the sky. It was a muddy brown grey, the colour of a river in spate. More snow no doubt but not necessarily for us, for it looked as if it might pass over and tip the load onto some other unfortunate place.

Then I went to discuss the making of railings with my manor carpenter, Alfred.

When I exited his small workshop by the manor wall; (we had a larger one out in the village where bigger projects were made and stored), the snow-full sky had moved on and afternoon was setting in.

Delicious aromas were funnelling into the courtyard from the kitchen close by the manor hall. I stepped carefully up the stone steps and into the warmth of the building and set to with gusto to demolish a meat pudding lovingly made by my cook, Matthew.

The following day dawned cold and crisp with bright sunshine from the first. The snow had frozen hard. No longer was it powdery and suitable for the making of snowballs. Now, you would find it quite difficult to scoop it up at all. As you walked on the white surface you did not sink as you had on the day before but crunched and slid your way on ice and compacted snow. Johnathan came back in with Odin, the pony, at midday, having delivered his message. The glazier would be with me by dinner time. He would stay, as he had done before, in one of the small rooms I had had built around the inner wall of the manor to house guests and workers and would work on cutting and fitting the glass to my broken window from there.

We were not quite prepared for the burden he brought with him.

*****

The glazier's cart trundled through the gate two hours after midday. One quick glance and all looked normal. Straw covered the back of the cart and glass wrapped in sheep's fleece lay flat on the bed. All the paraphernalia of a glass man's trade was stored away here, in boxes and baskets fixed by ropes to the body of the cart so that they should not disturb the fragile panes. Lying in the back of the cart close by the driver on his platform at the front, was a man.

"I found him on the turn of the Salisbury road sir," said Perkin Glazer. "At first I thought him dead, caught out by the snow storm, but then I noticed the gash in his head. Looks like a nasty swipe with something really hard and sharp."

Perkin Glazer was a small compact man of some forty five years with a shock of dark blond wavy hair curling onto his collar. He wore a small moustache but no beard and his eyes were a startling ice blue. His hair showed no trace of grey and his face was surprisingly soft and unlined. His hands and forearms, however, were peppered with old scars of the burns and cuts he had received from plying his trade as a master glazier.

I called for men to come and haul our stranger carefully from the back of the cart. With him was a pack. A large pack, the sort which is worn on the back.

"I think the man's a peddler sir," said Glazer. "Here's his staff." Once in the hall, folk crowding round, we got the man to the warmth of the fireside. He moaned at that, as if the warmth seeping into him suddenly had made his frozen body ache with coming back to itself. We laid him down gently on a palliasse. Once more I asked for a volunteer.

Who would go to Marlborough town and bring back the doctor?

Our man was in a very sorry state. His fingers and no doubt his toes were frostbitten. If expert help was not forthcoming soon, the man would lose them, if not his life. We washed his hurts, bound his gashed head, made him comfortable and Tostig Frithson wrapped himself up against the cold and took another pony, one called Freya which we usually used as a pack animal, and trotted out of the gate in the direction of Marlborough town, some three miles away.

I looked down at our injured man. He too was blond, with wavy hair, though he wore a full beard, clipped to the chin, as was mine. He was quite well dressed for a peddler with a good brown wool cloak and sturdy boots. His head had been covered with a green hood or capuchon; the kind which rose from the shoulders and over the head in one swoop. This garment, I thought, had protected his head from the blow he had suffered, for it was quite thick. Had he not been wearing it up, surely he would be dead. As it was, the blow had been fierce and the wound had bled profusely, as head wounds do. How long had he been lying unconscious out in the snow?

We eased off his boots and set them to dry on the hearth and covered him with a rough blanket. One of the manor widows, Janet, the eldest daughter of Walter Reeve, tried to get some broth into the frozen man but he was too far gone into himself to eat.

His breathing was becoming noisy and I remember Johannes telling me that this was often an indication that the brain inside the skull had been damaged.

"Janet, will you make sure that he can breathe properly. You may need to tilt his head so that his throat is opened out." She nodded and tucked the blanket closer to him.

I moved away and folk trickled off to their own places or bedded down for the afternoon in the warmth of the hall. I caught Glazer's eye and motioned for him to sit with me on the dais. He came doffing his brown cloak and pulling off the green hood which had covered his head.

"There are several things I want to talk to you about, Glazer," I said. "Not least about my damaged window."

"Yes, m'lord?"

"But I shall begin with our unknown man." I nodded to the scene by the fireside. "Tell me again what you know."

Glazer stretched out his legs and took a deep breath. He let it out in a long sigh.

"As I said, I came upon him just where the Durley Lane branches off from the Salisbury road."

"Where in the road was he exactly?"

"Not quite in the middle. I think he had crossed from the far side of the main road and was setting off to come to Durley."

"We don't know him. He has to my knowledge, never been here before.... Hal!" I called to my man at arms who was sitting by the door whittling a stick. "Have we ever seen our injured peddler before, do you think?"

"Nah m'lord. 'Tis a new face to me."

I thanked him. Hal was an amazing source of village knowledge, having been here for many years. His job, that of keeping the manor safe and secure, required him to take notice of things others would pass over.

"Which way was he facing? Had he come from Marlborough or had he journeyed from Salisbury, Glazer?"

Glazer took a swig of his ale pot and smoothed down his moustaches. "Salisbury I think. He fell with his head towards Marlborough. Though if he looked behind him as he fell, Heaven knows how we would know which way he had been travelling."

"So we think he was struck as he crossed the road. Was he on his back or front... or?"

"Front. I didn't see him at first, covered with snow as he was and no face showing. He was just a lump in the road. It was his pack and his cloak which has fallen from him, a little way off which I saw first and then, as I said, I thought him dead till I heard him moan. I turned him over. Then I saw the wound to his head...or rather I saw the blood seeping into his hood and into the snow."

"Why would someone hit a total stranger on the head? Not for his pack, nor his clothes. It doesn't seem as if anything has been taken. If it were masterless men, they would steal everything he owned. He'd be dead of exposure to the cold by now."

I scratched my head. "Were there any footprints about? No, that's a foolish question. You wouldn't know. It had snowed too hard. All marks would be obliterated."

"Aye m'lord. The only tracks were my own....my cart. I had thought to come on horseback but felt the cart was more useful. Little did I know." He gave a sardonic chuckle.

"Well, all we can do is wait for the doctor and pray that our man lasts the night." I sat forward and leaned with my arms on my knees. I lowered my voice, though there were few within hearing distance.

"There is another thing I want to talk to you about, Glazer."

The man's eyes narrowed. He had noticed my change of tone.

"This is not the first year you have been visiting Durley Manor, is it?"

Very slowly he put down his pot on the oaken table top.

"What do you mean by that, m'lord?"

"I mean what I said. You came this year to Durley to do a job for me but it's not the first time you have visited this village, is it?"

He blinked. "I might've been here before....yes."

"Twenty odd years ago perhaps?

"Maybe. I've been coming to Marlborough since I was a young man just out of my apprenticeship, then I decided to stay. It's natural I've been to a few places here and about. My work takes me to...."

"Oh no. This wasn't for work, Perkin."

Glazer sat back on his stool, his face expressionless, though I'm certain he had an inkling of what I was about to say.

"One of my father's tied women, an unfree peasant, Herleva Brooker...

does the name mean anything to you?"

Glazer reached for his ale cup again, "I don't recall...."

"Very pretty, then aged about fifteen or sixteen, blonde hair, blue eyes, lived by the stream in the village. You still don't recall...?"

He shrugged.

"She died of dock fever years ago, leaving two small children, twins born out of wedlock.

They were brought up elsewhere on the estate by a couple of my father's people, both dead now. When they were fourteen, they began to fend for themselves and moved back to the family home."

At last Glazer said "What are you trying to say, my lord?"

"That these two were your children, born before your legal son Harry."

"I wouldn't be the first man to have children he didn't know about, would I?" He took a large swig of ale and wiped his mouth on his sleeve. "If they are mine of course and I'm not saying they are."

"No, it's true. Not every man acknowledges his bastards or even knows he has children."

"There you are then, sir."

"Well..." I leaned back. "You have no son now, since you chose to slough off Harry as a snake does its skin."

He paused, the cup to his lip. " 'Twas his choice not mine."

"So I heard."

"You're not wanting me to acknowledge these Brookers after all this time m'lord?"

"No, I just want to know to satisfy my own curiosity. Did you know that you left Herleva pregnant?"

Glazer stood and put down his empty ale cup on the oak board. He looked down at me.

"I may have been to Durley as a young man, it's not a crime...I may have met and courted your girl Herleva. It's possible there may have been offspring as a result but I shall not admit it, to you or to anyone." He nodded. "I'm off to work on your window now m'lord. After all, it's what I'm here for."

I watched him go. It wasn't important now, the Brooker twins were gone. I had said I'd asked the questions for my own curiosity and it was true. The family were my responsibility once my father had died and I came into the manor. However, there were no Brookers left now in Durley. Perkin's only legal child, Harry Glazer, was apprenticed in the town to my good friend Gilbert Cordwainer, a fine man who treated his indentured people like family. Harry I felt, was better off a cordwainer than a glass maker.

I had wanted to ask Glazer too, to make a window of glass at the top of the kitchen stairs for it was as black as charcoal there and Agnes had already pitched down it, albeit that she had been pushed by a vicious murderer but I did not call him back. Another time would suffice. Glazer disappeared out of the hall door and passed Johannes of Salerno coming in.

Johannes bowed his head to the master glazier, the taciturn Glazer nodded to the master surgeon and then he was gone. Johannes put his bag on the floor and swung off his snow speckled cloak, shaking it as he did so.

"Still snowing, Johannes?"

"Yes...I think there's much more to come from the look of the sky. I have prepared Little Agnes for my non return, just in case I get stuck out in the forest." Agnes was Johannes' diminutive housekeeper who lived with him in his house and work-place in front of St. Mary's church and behind the market cross, just where Kingsbury Street met the High, in Marlborough Town. I ran down the steps at the side of the dais. "Here's our mystery man. We have done what we can but he is sore in need of your skill."

Janet got up from her place by our patient in the rushes and spread out her skirts, picking stalks from the weave and brushing the dust from them with her hand. One side of her face was pink from the warmth of the fire but I swear as she nodded to the doctor, the other side blushed to match. Here was my friend doing it again. All the women fell for him, young and old and he was mostly oblivious of the fact.

My brow furrowed. "How did you get here so quickly? Alfred has been gone less than an hour."

"I met him on the road. I was returning from Cadley and we met at the lane end. Sprained ankle, thought to be broken but it was not, in Cadley village."

I tilted my head in a questioning gesture. Who in Cadley had an injured ankle?

"No...not one of your main men. Young lad by the name of Will, one of your herdsman's sons. Sliding on the ice and fell, silly boy. He'll be right as the adamant come Monday. Mother is a bit of a worriter."

"I hope this one will be all right," I said. He's not come to yet and is, I think, quite far into himself."

Johannes pulled off his sheepskin mittens, one of them with his teeth and set to examining our peddler with a broken head. I answered his questions as well as I could. Gently Johannes undid the bandaging, probed and felt and then re-wrapped. He lifted the man's eye-lids. He listened to the breathing, felt the pulse in his neck and laid his ear to the man's chest to listen to the life beat of his heart. He picked up his hands and carefully moved the fingers about. He looked at the toes. At last he stood and brushed his knees and asked for warm water.

"Warm mind...not hot!" Janet ran off to the kitchen. "I'll need some sheep's wool - just a little and some linen to tear up for bandage strips. Hal located the rest of the linen we had used to bind the man's head, on the hall table and handed it over; I ran to the office for the little bits of sheep's wool left over after I had used it to clean my enamel apple.

Slowly Johannes immersed the peddler's fingers in warm water. He gently massaged them until they were pink again. The toes likewise. The smallest toe on the man's right foot would not come back to pinkness and Johannes tutted and said it would have to come off if it didn't improve soon. Everyone standing around watching groaned or sighed. We all knew how dangerous an amputation was. Even a small one. If things weren't just right, gangrene could set in and life would teeter on the very edge. However, I trusted Johannes; he was a fine doctor.

He was a tall man, muscular, for one who was not a fighting man, though I know he had once wielded a sword, for he had been out in the Holy Land on the crusade with our last King, Richard Plantagenet. He had shoulder length brown hair, now greying a little at the temples, scrupulously clean and shining, which he often wore tied back in a queue. He was clean shaven, unlike myself who went with the current fashion for a small clipped beard. His eyes were an amber brown, clear and direct of gaze and he had a fierce intellect. He had learned his doctoring in Salerno in Sicily, the best school of learning in the world for doctoring, he assured me, and though he had some odd ideas as far as the rest of the profession believed, he lost fewer patients and cured more people than they could ever hope to find to send their bills to. Cleanliness and orderliness were paramount to Johannes. All in the town, wealthy and poor, knew that he would open his doors to them and would do his utmost to help them. He was a wealthy man, having made his fortune in The Holy Lands. That fortune he now deployed for the good of the poor and sick of Marlborough.

"As to his head, you did well." He nodded to Janet who had been the one to bind this wound. She blushed and curtsied. She was a pretty woman of about thirty five with dark blonde silky hair kept back in a tight cloth and chestnut brown eyes which she kept demurely to the floor. Her husband, one of my woodsmen, had died about two years ago, crushed by a falling tree.

Johannes had been unable to save him, though he laboured hard to do so, I remember. These two knew each other already. Ceneric Woodsman had taken almost three weeks to die.

"I think he will come to the surface soon. The wound is nasty but there is naught but bruising and bloodiness with a little unknown damage to the brain beneath. The head bleeds so. His ear has taken some of the blow. We might find that becomes a problem later but we can save it. He may have some deafness as time goes on but that we may do nothing about. As long as there is no seepage of brain matter or fluid, he will mend."

"I think his hood.." I gestured to the bloodied green capuchon lying by the palliasse, "I think that took a lot of the sting out of the blow."

Johannes picked it up. "Thick felt. Yes....I think you're right, Aumary. We keep him warm, and still and we bandage his feet with snippets of sheep's wool between the toes to keep them separate - same with the fingers. He must not be allowed to stand on them... his feet I mean."

Janet giggled. Johannes looked at her quickly and beamed.

I left them to their bandaging with a "see you in my office when you've finished?" I crossed the hall and unlocked my office door.

After lighting the brazier and stirring the charcoal into life, I went to the chest where I kept the valuables, unlocked it and took out my ancient apple. I placed it reverently on the table top. Johannes came in a few heartbeats later, wiping his hands on a loosely woven thin linen rag. He dropped it into my brazier where it sizzled and was gone.

I nodded to the apple, while lighting more candles.

"Have you ever seen anything like that?"

Johannes lowered himself to my joint stool and gently reached for the apple. He looked down at it, in his strong but gentle hands.

"An apple like I have...no...never seen before."

I shut the office door and sat down on my chair. "Crispin has identified it as being Saxon work... he has seen such fine craftsmanship like it before on reliquaries and ecclesiastical boxes and the like, in the Salisbury Bishopric. He has no idea what the writing, if writing it is, says around the middle but he tells me they are runes. Symbols which our ancestors used to write in." I lifted my head. "Open it."

Johannes looked up from the apple in perplexity "How...?"

"Twist it. Take the top in your right hand and the bottom in your left and turn opposite ways."

Johannes looked puzzled but he did as I asked.

"The left towards you the right, away."

The contents fell into his lap. "Oh… my! What beauty," he said. He took the little gold apple and lifted it nearer to a candle. "More of the same and decorated too. Garnets. Oh, it is a feast for the eyes. So perfect but so tiny. The top fits into the bottom by a screw mechanism. I have seen this sort of thing in the Holy Land, but not as fine as this nor in lines. There, they use a screwing system to fetch water from the rivers, to arid areas. I have also seen masons use this sort of thing to secure things together but again, not linear." His face took on a puzzled expression and he screwed up his eyes. "How tiny are the symbols."

"I was wondering if the priory might help us decipher it. Have they do you think, a book which might tell us what these symbols mean?"

"I'm not aware of anything but even if we could write the words down in our own script, we would have no idea of the words or what they mean."

"No, that's true. But surely English cannot have changed so much. There must be words which we recognise. We have two very old men in the village....."

Johannes put up his hand to forestall me.

"I know, what you are about to say, they cannot read. No, they cannot but they might know something of the old language and they certainly understand that which we speak. If we could translate the words, they might know what they mean," I said. "You remember we found all those little ciphered messages belonging to Old Quimper years back?"

Johannes nodded. Many years before, my brother Robert, Johannes and myself had discovered that Robert's tutor, Quimper, was sending messages by pigeon to the king's enemies in Brittany. He disguised his notes by encrypting them in code. We had spent a deal of time, the three of us, deciphering them by trial and error.

"We could unravel these in the same way, I think."

Johannes fitted the little apple back together again and placed it on the table top. "Why?"

"Hmmm?"

"Why would we wish to?"

I leaned back. "Because I would like to know what it says."

'Why?"

"Because it's a puzzle and I can't resist a puzzle and truth be known, neither can you..."

A smile played around the edge of his mouth.

"And it might lead us to something absolutely splendid."

"It may not."

I shrugged. "We have little to lose."

Johannes sighed. "Even if we find that splendid thing you speak of, it will belong to the king and not to us. All treasure trove belongs to John and you know his love of gems and jewels and beautiful things."

"I know....but still....."

"So tell me. How did you find it?"

And so I told him the story.

*****

The wind blew all day. The snow came down in relentless gusts and banked up on road and hillsides. Some small village bothies were buried completely and their inhabitants had to dig their way out to feed their animals and themselves. I sent some of the older children and young men out to check that people were safe in their homes or that they had been able to dig themselves out. All folk were present and correct in their tithings. In the outlying forest they would have to fend for themselves or make their way to us at Durley. Most chose to stay put. The men went out into the courtyard and shovelled the snow to the base of the walls, so that we might have a clear space to walk in. There was little chance of Johannes or the glazier reaching their homes and so we bedded them down with us to ride out the storms.

Crispin, supervising a few of the village men, dug a path through the snow from the manor gate to the church so that we might celebrate the Nativity in our usual fashion, in our own church of St. Mary.

Tomorrow was Christmas Eve. We struggled up the icy steps with our Yule log and rolled it into a corner ready for the ceremony of the lighting of it.

Matthew and his staff were busy in the kitchen. I asked him to make a good large cauldron of soup in case it was needed by village folk who could not, because of the snow, fend for themselves. The Christmas Mummers, a band of village folk who every year performed a silly little play for us, had been practicing since the end of November. Their womenfolk had been making and mending costumes and they were all stored now in the buttery, against the time when they would disguise our players and the story of St. George and the Dragon would be played out on the dais in the hall. The whole forest usually turned out to watch but this year the audience would be smaller as many would not dare to brave the weather.

On Christmas Eve, Master Glazer came to say that he had finished the window. I paid him and watched him walk through the snow to his lodging on the north wall of the courtyard.

Suddenly there was a rushing sound and a rumbling and several barrels which had been stored by the stables for Christmas drinking rolled inexorably towards the glazier. He turned and would certainly have been mown down by the large and heavy barrels, if my head groom, Richard Marshall, coming quickly out of the stable, had not thrown himself at the man and pushed him out of the way. He rolled safely away himself in hard icy snow which had been shovelled to the edge of the courtyard.

Glazer picked himself up slowly.

"Thank you man...."

"Richard, sir."

"Richard... I'm a bit slow nowadays."

Richard shook off the snow and ice from his tunic as best he could.

"Woe Sakes sir! That was a close one," he said and then yelled as he put his foot to the floor.

"Aw cocks and robins!"

Hal of Potterne had now joined them and he took off his coif and scratched his head as he viewed the carnage. Two large barrels had split and one was leaking.

"What in the name of all the Beezulbubbies? 'Ow did that 'appen?"

He replaced his hat and righted the leaking barrel with stretched arms.

"That's our Christmas ale that is. I for one am not goin' to be lickin' it off the damned floor!"

"Everyone all right?" I yelled from the top of the stairs.

Hal looked up and waved. "Aye sir, though 'ow them tuns got free of them ropes....well, I'll be buried in Burbage 'fore I know the answer."

I shouted down at my head groom. "Richard, you have probably pulled a muscle - get Johannes to look at you."

Glazer was rubbing his left arm.

"Let Johannes have a look at that too Perkin, it must be bruised," I said. "You know he's in the room next to you."

Glazer waved his thanks and was off to the doctor's room. Richard hobbled after him, on Cedric Groomsman's arm.

With the help of some of the grooms, Hal rolled the whole barrels back into place. Then they set about recovering the splintered staves and seeing what, if anything, could be salvaged. Hal picked up the ropes which had secured the barrels together. As I returned to my office, he trotted up the steps and followed me, the rope dangling from his hands. He threw the pieces onto my table.

"Well I'll be bug.... buried in Burbage....sir. Them's ropes were cut.

Chapter Three

I picked up the rope. The ends had been cleanly severed with a very sharp knife.
"That wasn't an accident, sir" said Hal. "Thems rope's from Marlybro,
Timothy Roper, he dun't make a baddun sir. They never fray. That's bin cut."

"So I see, Hal." I caught my lip with my teeth as I thought.

"Who was in the courtyard when the glazier was passing through, Hal?"

Hal sucked on his teeth. He was the best of witnesses, being responsible
for security at the manor.

"Cedric, goin' from one bit o' the stable to another. Middle doors stuck.
Took up too much moisture an' now it won' open. 'As to come out to go in."

"Yes, we have that trouble every winter. I must get the woodsmith to look
at it."

"Wyot, at the gate." Wyot Porter was my gatekeeper. He had rooms in the
gatehouse.

Hal fingered his long grey beard which he wore in two points like his
Viking ancestors of old.

"Young Peter Brenthall a talkin' to Henry the steward. Then a' corse after,
loads of us came out."

"Thanks, Hal." He nodded, pulled down his saffron coloured tunic and then
shook his head again as he tripped out on light feet and shut the door.

Henry came in a moment later. "Sir, we have a problem."

"Another one, Henry?"

He smiled. "It's Richard…."

"He's all right, I take it?" I looked up with a worried expression. "He looked
fine to me."

"Dr. Johannes has said he has badly broken a bone in his foot, sir."

"Oh dear….so he'll be out of action for a while."

"The worst thing is he'll be out of action for the mumming sir. Can't stand, can't fight and certainly can't caper."

The mumming play was a very important thing to the village. Roles were mostly handed down from father to son. The guisers, as they were usually known, for they wore masks to conceal their blackened faces, or strips of old rags over their heads, were supposed to be unknown to the village. It was bad luck if anyone named a guiser, though in truth we all knew who they were. We just never mentioned it.

"This means, Henry?"

"We are short of a pagan sir."

I smiled. "Oh dear....cannot one of the others...?"

"We don't have any others. We have a pagan playing the dragon as it is. Our second pagan last year was Edmund Brooker."

"Ah. And he's dead."

I was trying hard not to smile. I passed my hand over my face. "Are you asking me, Henry, to be a pagan?"

His face took on the most horrified look. "No sir...you can't do that. That would be ... most irregular."

"I suppose I could if I had to...I've seen the play more than twenty five times."

Henry took a step back, "No sir....the Durley guisers would not allow it."

"Ah well."

"Could you ask the glazer sir, this once? He was in the doctor's room with Richard and he has just asked him if there is any way he can repay Richard for saving his skin. I heard him. He has a good voice. He doesn't have much to say, just fall down dead. We've a little time to practice. If you asked him sir...he couldn't say no, could he?"

"Henry, Perkin Glazer is a man unto himself. He can say no to me if he wishes. And I have no doubt he would, if he wished."

I chewed the side of my thumb nail. "Tell you what, you go up to the solar and ask Lady Belvoir to ask him. Now he probably won't refuse her. You know how she has a way with her."

And so he did.

*****

Christmas Day morning dawned clear and cold but with no more wind or snow.

We trooped from the manor to the freezing church for the service and Father Crispin went through it as fast as he was able, at the last with a chattering of teeth.

We piled back into the warmth of the hall for spiced ale and little honey cakes.

Folk went to their homes to eat their early dinner. They would be back later for the mumming. The ale casks were broached and pots went round and songs began to be sung.

Then after dinner Walter the reeve came into the hall from the screens passage door.

He stood in the middle of the hall, as he had done countless times before, and banged his stick on the wooden floor. There was silence.

"M'lord there are strangers at the door, guisers come to entertain, we know them not but shall I allow them in?" It was the old form of words which had been spoken since I was a little lad and long before. And the answer always had to be, "Aye, let them in, even though they be strangers. If they bring luck and good fortune and if they bring us laughter, they will be welcome."

In trooped the guisers. I glanced around for Richard Marshall who by rights should have been amongst them and saw him, sitting with his foot bandaged and up on a stool, nod in approval. The mummers costumes entirely covered them from head to foot. Seven figures, some with black faces under their rags, others with grotesque masks.

Only one was without a costume of tatters. Saint George, the hero of it all. He wore a flat topped helmet, an old one of my father's I believe, so we did not see his face. He carried an old broadsword, blunted for the purpose of the play. Over his long tunic was a white surcoat with a huge red cross painted on it. The paint was old and flaked and in places it has run where it had been damp but still it drew hushed appreciation from the crowd as they settled to watch.

The guisers all walked round in a circle and then one of the lads broke off and capered up onto the dais which we had vacated for the performance.

"We are the Durley guisers. We've not been here last year." There was a lot of laughter. There was every year this line was spoken. "We bring you joy, we bring you luck and if you care to watch our play we'll bring you much good cheer."

Everyone hurrahed at that. I looked over at my wife Lydia and my daughter Hawise, their faces glowing in the candlelight.

"Good sirs and madams, we'll tell our tale. How brave Sir George," (I always wondered how he could first be a lord and then a saint...but...). Sir George raised his sword and we all cheered. "Did vanquish evil spirits, so they did show their tail!" One of the evil spirits then capered onto the dais and showed us his bottom, by upending his tatters. Naturally there was much laughter and shrieking.

And so it went on. In silly doggerel, some slightly changed from the year before, and the year before that, so that much of it was complete gibberish. We laughed till we split our sides at the princess, so coy behind a thin veil borrowed from Lydia. I remember one of the previous years, a manor dog had run off with the last veil and we found it a while later half eaten by the reeve's goats. I thought I saw the demure face of Peter Brenthall under that veil but I couldn't be sure. She repulsed the advances of the first pagan, tripping him, beating him about the head with a wooden spoon, hitting him in sensitive places and laughing whilst he pretended great hurt. Eventually she let him have one kiss and he fell down dead in ecstasy.

Now it was the turn of the wise man to come and revive him. We all knew he would.

"I am a quack, a quack so rare..." I saw Johannes, leaning on the wall by the fire, laugh and fold his arms over his chest.

"I've travelled from Quacksalver. My famous ale it cures all ills, I've never known a failure." Everyone cheered. The wise man then began to pour his 'ale' over the dead pagan and... Lo, "He rises see, he rises live. For this I'll have coins, silver, five!"

The pagan shook his head and capered a little just to make sure he was alive. He turned a somersault.

"I live, I live, do give him money. For bein' dead, it isn't funny."

Everyone howled at that and hats and bits of food and all sorts of rubbish were thrown at him. He retired from the dais and poked out his very pink tongue; pink in the blackness of his face. The wise man retired too, most indignant that he had not been paid.

On came St. George. I always thought his lines arrogant and proud but then....he was a saint I suppose.

"I am Sir George, Saint George the bold,

I'll fight you young, I'll fight you old

I am the best in all the land

And when I win I'll have the hand

Of this fair maiden, she'll not refuse

For killing the pagan, I'll have my dues.

My face is handsome, my heart is gold,

No one can better me I'm told."

He strutted, he capered, he posed and the crowd lapped it up. His voice was loud and issued well from his helmet with a slight tinny nasal echo.

On came the second pagan. In a good bass voice, Perkin Glazer said,

"You churl, you dog. You spiny black hog. I'll fight you till you die. I'm not afrit, I'll slice you thick and put you in a pie!"

I could see Matthew my cook yelling in amongst the laughter, in good natured banter, "Aye, and I'll bake him for you!"

George and the pagan began to fight.

There was a lot of waving of swords and grunting and posturing. The pagan was often hit on his rump with the flat of the sword and yelled in a wonderful falsetto.

"You mealy fool. You cheat you do."

I noticed he was quite careful with his left arm. It must still pain him.

Eventually there was a great swipe and the pagan fell down dead with a rather good twitch.

Then naturally we called for the quack again. The wise man was off stage paring his nails with a huge dagger, far too big for the job. He was called and called and because he took no notice, the crowd joined in. Eventually he came swaggering up onto the dais and was asked to revive the pagan. No, he would not. He hadn't been paid the last time. And then he asked for twice the amount.

All the other players made great show of cobbling together the money from their purses and at last, his ale was poured on the poor pagan.

With a great roar, the pagan revived. "I'll show you how a pagan fights. Just you get ready to lose your lights. I'll fight you till you're dead and then I'll fight you till you're dead again."

And there was more silly fighting.

This time the pagan succeeded in wrenching the sword from Saint George. Saint George called upon God to re-arm him.

And the wise man's ridiculous knife was procured and handed to him by one of the guisers.

There was more silly posturing and tripping and rolling on the floor. Everyone was in fits of laughter.

Then with a great and final gesture, Saint George plunged the knife into the side, (truly, between the side and the arm of the pagan). The pagan died beautifully yelling and gurgling until at last he lay still.

Saint George stood up tall and paraded around like a Roman gladiator. "Enough, enough, bring me my bride. I have deserved her well. I've slain the pagans. And in my pride.... I am the glorious winner..."

There was a huge roar off to the side of the dais.

" 'Tis a fearsome dragon.....come to eat us all," said the first player. "He means to make us dinner..."

Then Dysig Herlevason, our lackwit, who was standing close to the action screamed and pointed.

Perkin Glazer was struggling to sit up. There was blood seeping from his side and blood on the boards of the dais. I saw Saint George falter and turn to look. He dropped the knife which he had hitherto been brandishing in a warlike fashion. The edge was bloodied.

The dragon totally missed his cue and just stood stock still, the horns, made from pared down goats' horns, leaning at a comical angle. Had the guisers perhaps decided that, in the name of reality, the pagan should bleed from his wounds somehow? I couldn't remember them ever doing this before.

I saw Johannes push himself from the wall and leap onto the dais. Crispin was fast behind him. Hal jumped up on the dais and took charge of the fallen knife.

"For God's sake...give us room there!" yelled Johannes as he lay Perkin Glazer down again.

The rest of the guisers stood back for him, but not one of them doffed their costume.

I pushed my way through the throng to the base of the dais and stood by a shaking Dysig, throwing my arm over his shoulder. "What's happened?"

Perkin took a shuddering breath. "The knife...was a real one, a sharp one," he said between clenched teeth.

"Shh." said Johannes as he tore the costume from Glazer to get at the body beneath. "Let me look."

" 'Twas not so at practice yesterday," said Glazer as he gritted his teeth again." 'Twas blunt then."

Johannes called for water and linen. The hurt wasn't great and hadn't pierced the Glazer's body too far.

It had gone in between the tatters of the costume and bounced on a rib and out again with no real damage to anything, but it had sliced a long thin flap of skin from the glazier's side.

I looked up at my mummers and frowned. They were all, including Saint George, now standing in a semi-circle at the back of the dais. George had doffed his helmet. He was sweating profusely and worriedly ran his arm over his forehead. George was my blacksmith and farrier, Hubert Alder.

I came up to the tableau on the dais.

"Harm done Johannes?"

He looked up. "No, he'll be sore, but no, no real harm. Could have been though."

I looked back at my mummers and counted.

Now there were only six.

*****

"I swear I counted seven when they entered the hall," I said to Henry later in the confines of my office.

"There should only have been six this year, sir," he said. "Pagan one, who is also the dragon this year, pagan two, George, the wise man - he doubles as the hand of God usually; this year we changed it. The maiden, the speaker who does the capering at the beginning and moves the action on. We have a spare set of rags in case something happens...." He tailed off looking worried.

"Your spare set was used then, by someone who wanted something to happen."

"And returned to the buttery afterwards," said Henry.

We had broken up the party. Folk had gone off to their homes in the village and those who slept in the hall were sitting round the table with brimming ale pots, no doubt embellishing the tale of the seventh mummer.

Poor Perkin Glazer had been carried to Johannes' room and they were now making him as comfortable as they could.

"No one noticed him?"

"No sir, each is immersed in their own role and well, frankly, we can't really see very well through all those rags."

Henry was the wise man and he had taken off his hat to which the said rags had been attached, and was standing in front of me in just the ragged costume he had worn for the play and with his face blackened. His bright blue eyes seemed oddly more blue in the dark of his face, rimmed with red.

"And when you are playing, no one would be looking for an extra body would they? You don't see what you don't expect."

"No, sir."

"Well, in the light of what happened today with the ale tuns, and now this we had better keep a watch on our glazier. Someone is very angry with him."

I dismissed Henry and he passed Lydia as she came through the door.

"Johannes will see to him tonight Henry, but we'll need to organise a guard for the next few days while he's incapacitated."

"Yes, m'lord, shall I use Stephen and Peter?" I nodded and he shut the door. I called him back. He peeped around the door.

"Send Hubert to me will you Henry? Oh… and when you had charge of the knife, as the wise man, was it the blunted one?"

"Aye sir…it was."

"Is the glazier all right, Aumary?" asked Lydia when the door had closed once more.

"Aye…the damage to his ribs isn't great, though Johannes is stitching him now. It was more shock, I think. He is a tough man and has had many more accidents with sharp edged glass in his professional life than you or I can imagine. So this will be naught to him."

"I suppose not."

"He'll mend soon enough."

"You think, by the sound of you, that someone in the village has a grudge against the man?"

"Well, it is the only explanation I can conjure up. Unless we are looking at pure coincidence."

I picked up the rope still lying on my table top.

"No, the barrels were meant to roll and if not kill him, injure him badly. See how the rope holding them together has been severed?"

There was a scrape at the door and Hubert Alder, now divested of his costume and helmet, poked his head around the door.

"You wanted me m'lord?"

"Aye...q uickly Hubert...who handed you the knife with which to slay the pagan? Who was the hand of God?"

"Shoulda been ..." and then he stopped. "Ah, sir... I can't tell you the name of a guiser, it's bad luck."

"Hubert" I wiped my brow with the back of my hand. "I know you are George, I know the glazier was the second pagan in place of Rich and I know that Henry is the wise man. I know he should have given you the knife but didn't't this year. There are only three left."

He disappeared from the doorway then came in and shut the door. He realised that my wife was in the room.

"The Lady Lydia will not breathe a word, will you, Lydia?"

"Oh no...not a syllable." She smiled sweetly at my farrier.

" 'Twas Thomas Potter sir. The mumming king or the speaker, some call him, that's he as does the story telling sir, the other pagan is Phil Wheelwright the younger and then the last one,

"Is Peter Brenthall?"

Hubert's face fell.

"You knew, sir?"

"Aye, I knew. Thank you. I'll speak to Tom later." He backed out bowing all the way and quietly closed the door.

"What can the glazier possibly have done to a villager, that they must try to kill him, Aumary?" asked Lydia.

My eyebrow flew up into my hair.

"You haven't heard the rumours about the man?"

"No." She sat down expectantly on my joint stool. "Tell me."

I chuckled. "You must be the only woman in Durley who hasn't then."

She blinked.

"I suppose your station as my newly wedded spouse gives you a certain immunity," I said.

I too sat.

"It's said that Perkin Glazer is a womaniser... always had been. His son has fallen out with him because of it."

"Oh!"

"There are few women who haven't been charmed by him...or at least felt an attempt to charm. I'm almost certain that twenty odd years ago, he seduced Herleva Brooker here in the village, and got the Brooker twins on her. How many others I don't know."

"They were his children?"

"He won't admit it, but when you look at young Harry, his son by his legal wife, well, the likeness is uncanny. You know who I mean, don't you?"

"The cordwainer's lad?"

"Aye, him. Harry Glazer," I affirmed.

"It's said that Agnes Brenthall sent him packing last time he was here. Almost boxed his ears."

Lydia laughed her tinkling laugh. "She would, I'm sure. She has eyes for none but John."

"Then there was Phillipa Forester. According to Johnathan Reeve, she too sent him off with a slap to the cheek."

"For a seducer, he isn't very successful then," she laughed.

"Ah, but we don't know the number of women he has managed to charm, do we? Just you be on your guard whilst he's here," I said in devilment. "A swift knee to the cods is what's needed."

"I doubt he'll be fit for any nonsense for a while with his wound," said Lydia. "Besides, like you say, I am your wife. I don't think he'd dare."

"You aren't tempted by the older man then?"

She reached over the table and pinched my arm. "I've had one thank you, as well you know." Lydia was the widow of an older man, the Lord of Wolvercote near Oxford.

"And I wouldn't exchange the old crock I have now for all the hay in the hay barn!"

I stood and was round the table in a splice. "You cheeky madam," I said. "Old indeed..I'll show you who's old" and I made a grab for her.

She retreated round the table's end, laughing.

And so it was the first day of Christmas ended in fun and frolics after all.

"What's that Paul? Oh yes, I think there still are some of his children in the town. None in the village though. And his grandchildren. And great grandchildren for all I know. I know that Harry married and had two children. Oh... you mean the glazier's children; children out of wedlock... well... who's to know, eh?"

I spoke to Tom later in the day. No, the knife had not been on the table where it should have been waiting for him.

He'd looked for it but had guessed one of the others had taken it upon themselves to be the hand of God. They had argued apparently, over who would perform the role this year. The blunted knife was later found under a bench by the fire. The sharp one was its exact copy. Nothing special about it, just a plain knife. There were many such in the village.

*****

The Christmas season went on in much the way it had started. There were more flurries of snow and the cold seeped into the ground which would make it impossible to dig or work the soil. Folk sat idle round their fires. Food stocks began to dwindle. If this kept up, no planting for the spring would be done, nor could it be and the seed which had already been planted, was likely to die in the ground.

There would be famine if this continued.

"But I race on ahead Paul; there are more things to happen before we get to famine and fevers. We must gloss over the twelve days of Christmas and come to Twelfth Night, January 5th."

We usually had a feasting celebration on Twelfth Night but no one really had the stomach for it. We had to conserve our foodstuffs. It was the topsy turvy time, when servants were served and masters did the serving, within reason of course.

It was a time to appoint the master of the revels, the Twelfth Night King, and again, the same as last year, the village appointed the butcher, John Kellog, a genial man in his forties with a loud voice and a sense of humour as black as his butcher's apron. He was the perfect master; irreverent enough to make it fun, deferent enough not to go too far as to make everyone uncomfortable. He sat on the dais in his parchment crown and an old robe of mine which had definitely seen better days. It just fitted around the butcher's large frame. In his hand he held the mummer's sword and a sceptre of sorts which Hal of Potterne had, years ago, fashioned from a curly branch of hawthorn. It looked ridiculous and it was meant to. Anyone he touched with this item had to do his bidding or pay a forfeit. The night usually deteriorated into mayhem and although Henry Pierson and Walter Reeve were there to keep order, Lydia and I, with Hawise and her maid Felice, would retire before it got too rowdy. This year the feast was no feast and drink was watered. Our water supply, the river and the well in the village had iced up and so we boiled snow to cook and to drink. There was plenty to drink....it was just not of the intoxicating kind and it dampened the festivities into a quietness.

I sat with the common folk later in the evening, talking quietly to Hal of Potterne, the much recovered glazier on my left.

Hawise, looking very tired, came up and climbed onto my knee and leaned against me, staring out at the dancing which was taking place in the centre of the hall. I cuddled her fiercely to me. She soon nodded off to sleep and after a while Hal ruffled her lovely copper locks.

"C'mon my gel," he said. "Think 'tis time you were abed. Yer da would like his arm back."

She murmured softly and allowed him to lift her. He nodded to me and I nodded back. He would take her up the steps to the solar and hand her over to her nurse Felice and to Lydia at the solar door.

Then he threw her over his shoulder and jog trotted through the dancers, scattering them and twirling around with them whilst Hawise giggled and screamed in joy. The dancers laughed and twirled around them.

I smiled. How Hal of Potterne loved my daughter and had done so since she was a small creature creeping around in the rushes. There was nothing he wouldn't do for her... or with her.

They appeared at the top of the solar steps and he bent to kiss her forehead. She tugged his beard and I saw him dip a hand into his scrip and fetch out a tiny thing and press it into her hand. It was a jointed doll about four inches high and was meant as her Twelfth Night present. I had left mine on her bed. Four marchpane mice. She loved marchpane. Then she disappeared through the door. The glazier nodded in his direction.

I smiled again. "Hal is so good with all the children of the manor. It's a gross pity he never married and had any of his own."

"Aye, I've noticed he's often to be found with them, playing games and making stuff for them and suchlike."

"He is. He has the patience of Job with children. Adults now...well....he brooks no nonsense"

"Suffers no fools eh."

"He is consummate at his job. I would be lost without him." I nodded towards my two men at arms, who were dancing in the centre of the hall. Stephen Dunn was kicking up his legs and smiling inanely, Peter Devizes was sedately swinging Agnes Brenthall round by the waist. "Those two too, have served me well the time of my lordship here."

"I've seen them about town, have I not sir?"

"Aye, you have. They are mostly at the castle where, as you know, I'm under-constable. I keep them there in case I am called to arms by the king. I bring them back to Durley for the festive season each year. At other times too."

Glazer nodded. "I thought, when I was working the castle chapel windows, I'd seen them about in the bailey."

"Aye, they're a busy pair. There's always so much to do and they are more than willing to do it. They are worth every penny I spend on them. I am very lucky with my folk." I turned on my seat to face him,

"Which brings me to a question I have wanted to ask you since the Christmas Day mumming."

Glazer put down his pot of ale.

"Who here in the village might have a grudge against you, enough to set a few barrels loose at you, and make another plunge a sharp knife into you?"

Perkin Glazer shook his head slowly.

"I know of no one with whom I've been at loggerheads, if that's what you mean."

"No one whom you have wronged..." he bridled at that; I put up my hand. "Or who thinks they have been wronged, by you?"

His eyes, those bright and cold ice blue eyes, searched my face. "No m'lord. No one."

I was silent a heartbeat watching him. He seemed unperturbed.

"All right then. I don't think you'll be returning to Marlborough or your glass kilns in the forest quite yet. Just watch yourself whilst you're here, that's all."

Hal rejoined us and looked into his empty ale cup. "Ah... " He tipped it up and looked at the bottom. "Mus' 'ave an 'ole in it. I'm sure I left some ale in it 'fore I went."

I slapped him on the back. "No Hal....it was already empty. Here...'tis Twelfth Night. My turn to fill it for you." And I took his cup and lifted my leg over the bench and trotted to the barrel in the corner.

When I returned I heard Perkin Glazer asking Hal about something which had been found on the manor, something old and beautiful. Hal was professing not to know anything. He caught my eye over the head of the glazier and winked. I knew he had said nothing about my little apple.

"It's just I hear 'twas made of glass."

Both Hal and I were silent. Who had told him about my apple? Very few knew and they were sworn to secrecy.

"Who told you that?" I asked.

"I think it was your little lass. You have just the one don't you, sir?"

"Aye, I do. Hawise. You have just seen her."

"Aye it was the Lady Hawise. I met her playing in the snow out the back and she was searching the river bank. I asked her what she was looking for and she said, 'apples.'"

Hal and I exchanged glances. He was one of the people who knew about our little apple. He had to; he was responsible for the precious things on the estate.

"Well, I laughed and I said 'you won't find apples where there are no trees and in this season....' said Glazer. He took a swig of his ale. "Then of course she said it wasn't real apples she was looking for, it was precious glass ones." He chortled. "Who-ever thought of that eh? Then I set to thinking."

I sat turning my ale cup in my hands for a few heartbeats.

Then, "Yes," I said. "We did find an apple. It is, I think, a form of glass."

His eyes widened. "Well, I have never seen anything like that in all my days as a glassmaker."

"Would you like to?"

"I would, m'lord...very much."

I touched Hal on the arm as I passed him. "Come with us, Hal."

*****

The glazier lifted the apple to the candle light and his face glowed. "Oh. 'Tis a very fine piece. A master craftsman made this." He turned it this way and that. " 'Tis beautiful." He traced the lettering with his finger. "Gold, enamel, niello, such fine work."

I sat at my table. "It came through the window wrapped in a snowball causing the damage you saw, to the window. Dysig, our halfwit threw it accidentally. You are a master in glass Perkin, can you tell us anything about this piece?"

"It's old, that I can say. The English had such skills. Few nowadays could attempt such work. The French have a word for such stuff, they call it cloison. It's very hard to make."

"So how is it made...was it made?"

The glazier sat down on my joint stool and rolled the apple in his fingers. Hal leaned against the door.

"See here, these little gold bits. They are thick pure gold wires fitted to the top. Soldered. A little depression is created by adding more and more. The cloison..is the word for these little patches, small depressions like a tiny aumbry. Now, you can add precious stones if you like to the little cells, but this here...this is made from something called vitreous enamel."

"Vitreous as in glass...?"

"It is. You make your glass, see, in the usual way, then you make it into a powder; grind it up. Then you heat it hard, so it flows...that takes some time and a great deal of skill, I can tell you."

"Glass is see through, well almost...how do you get it to be coloured like this... so bright.? Do you paint it with something?" I asked.

"No, when the stuff is melting you can add certain other stuffs to it and turn it different colours. These are minerals you find in the ground. Copper is one, silver another. You can make it coloured from a violet to grey almost but your apple is a good red. They use gold to get it this much red - it's beautiful."

"Open it by twisting it, Glazer," I said. He looked at me puzzled, much as Johannes had.

"There's another inside."

Once the little gold apple was free, he balanced it in the palm of his hand.

"Oh that is beautiful...see here's what I was talking about....the gems, garnets, have been put into the little cells made by the wires. Also you have something here called niello."

"What's that then?" asked Hal, coming away from the door to look.

"It's a black stuff made of copper, silver and lead. You see here where the little patterns are, the niello has been oh so skillfully added to the band. What you do...."

The master glazier's eyes glowed with passion for his subject. "You make the patterns with something called a burin. It's a sharp tool which will scratch into the metal, into the gold. You do it in reverse..."

"Wait a moment..." said Hal, taking off his cap and scratching his head. "Yer score yer gold with this 'ere burring.."

"Burin..yes."

"Then you 'as to 'ave it back to front to make the patterns."

"That's right" said Glazer. "The little patterns..."

"We think they are words, Perkin."

"Aye, they might be. You need to do it in reverse. It's called repoussé. French again. Then when you turn it the right way round, your 'words' if words they are, will stand out proud, the right way round..."

"AH! I see" said my man at arms. He had only just been getting to grips with words and reading as he accompanied my daughter at her lessons, some days. He was fast learning to read himself, just by being with her.

"Then you dribble your niello into the gaps you have made and it outlines the words, in this case. Makes the patterns much easier to see."

Hal whistled softly. "All that work...jus' to make the words easier to read."

I smiled. "Thank you for that, Perkin." I held out my hand and reluctantly he handed the two parts of the apple back to me. I fitted them together.

Hal put the apple back into the chest, locked it and gave me the key. I slipped the chain over my head and dropped it down into my shirt.

"How is your wound now?"

"Mending, thanks," said Glazer.

"Good."

"A corse.....where there is one beautiful object like that apple, m'lord, there may be others just waiting for you to find them."

"I have thought of that Glazer," I said. "And so, obviously, has my daughter."

Glazer stood and took a deep breath.

"Aye well. Ah...I meant to ask. How is the fellow I found in the lane?"

"Mending as are you Perkin. He is in the room next to Johannes', the other side of you. Go and sit with him. He is conscious now but he remembers nothing. He doesn't even know his name. In fact he hardly speaks and when he does...his mouth will not form the words. Dr. Johannes has every faith that he will recover his speech though, in time."

"So what happened to him is still a secret then?"

"Yes...it is."

I then swore him to secrecy about the apple, too.

Chapter Four

The next day I gave permission for villagers to break the ice on the fishpond and on the larger pools of the stream, to dabble for the fish which had gone down into the deeper and warmer waters. I watched as they struggled over the piled snow, pickaxes over their shoulders and laid lines of bait out on the whiteness. It was a Tuesday but fish would last in this weather till Friday, a fish day. They moved on and opened up several holes in the ice along our little river, for any who wished to fish.

I crossed the courtyard later in the day, about to look in at my horses. I was concerned, particularly for my newly acquired race-horse, given to me by a grateful father for solving the murder of his son. Fitzroy was apt to become restless if he wasn't ridden but in this weather it was difficult to take him out and give him his head. Huge potholes lay unseen under the snow and it would only take one false step to break his leg.

I was talking to Cedric Groomsman who looked after him, when there was a shout and a slipping and sliding sound. A great gout of snow which had lodged on the roof of the furthest stable plunged to the ground. I raced outside.

No real damage done. Some people were laughing and dusting themselves down having been showered with snow.

I saw Hal move towards the shed where we kept the shovels. It would be a matter of moments to clear it. I yelled to him. "Hal...to save this happening again, can we ask a few folk to get the snow off the roofs. It's heavy stuff...the thatches might col..."

No sooner had I said this than the roof of the middle stable began to creak and crack. We all looked back. Edward was quickly bringing out Fitzroy. We had decided to walk him round the village slowly just to give him a change of scenery.

Two other grooms hastily followed with the pack horses and one mule. It was fortuitous that they were clear, when the whole of the middle stable roof sagged and bowed and the thatch came tumbling down with the weight of the snow, breaking beams and crushing the walls.

I shouted over the noise, "No one in there?"

"No, sir. All out."

"Good."

When the noise had subsided, I said, "Organise a party to sweep the snow from all thatched roofs. Every one. There's little else to do today anyway. Ropes will be needed to drag, brooms to sweep. Shovels to dig. All able bodied men and older boys. John, can you marshal folk for that job?"

"Aye sir, I can," said John Brenthall and he ran off to confer with Walter Reeve and Hal.

Suddenly, there was a wailing. Felice came running across the courtyard. "No..no..she can't be..."

I turned and caught her as she tried to run past me. "What, Felice?"

"Hawise sir..."

"Calm down ,woman and tell me properly. What about Hawise?"

"Oh no... I can't... she… she… she was in there, in the stable with her pony." And she began to cry.

*****

I left her and speedily pushed my way through the damaged doorway of the stable. Hal of Potterne, drawn back by the noise, followed me. We were both calling Hawise's name over and over. Spikes of roof spars stuck out at odd angles from the fallen snow, many of them still settling. Some of the partitions of the horse stalls had fallen almost flat. I lifted them just in case Hawise was trapped beneath; they were very weighty.

Hal took one of the large brooms used in the stable and brushed the snow carefully from the top of a huge pile. We saw a tiny glimpse of blue cloth. I tried to picture what my daughter had been wearing that day. My man at arms got down on his knees and with his bare hands scraped away the snow. I joined him. There was a further rumbling and creaking as what was left of the roof above us shifted a little more under the weight of the snow. Neither of us looked up; we kept digging. Eventually the cloth came away with a final tug and we realised it was a piece of rag used to polish the tack. It had always lain draped over the side partitions. Fool! I thought...fool, you have wasted precious time on a rag!

Hal got up and frantically began to search the snow piles again. Some of the roof beams had splintered and had become deadly spikes with jagged ends. I imagined one of those piercing my daughter's little body.

I must have groaned, for Hal looked up at me and said, "Don't you worry lad - we'll 'ave 'er right out in no time. 'Ale and 'arty."

We dug and moved debris with our bare hands. Others had now joined us. I saw Peter Brenthall and Phil Wheelwright pulling on the larger beams, trying to free up the spaces beneath. Phil's father was peering into the dark space for any sign of life.

Others, headed by Crispin the priest, were digging the snow away with shovels and piling it outside the ruined building.

"Hush!" I shouted suddenly for I had thought I'd heard Hawise's voice calling me. I did hear as plain as day Lydia's voice calling my name, from across the courtyard.

I moved back and listened. Hawise's voice strong and clear came up to me and Hal turned to the wrecked doorway.

"Sir!" He pointed and then took off his cap and threw it in the air.

There accompanied by Perkin Glazer, came my daughter. She shrugged his arm from her shoulder and came running across the courtyard. Lydia was a few steps behind her having descended the hall steps.

"Hawise!"

"Dada!"

I went down on one knee; my chausses were already soaked through, and she ran into my arms. I hugged her close.

"Oh my sweetling, I thought you were in the stables buried under the fallen roof." I was close to tears.

Hal came up and ruffled her hair as he was wont to do. "Aw little mistress," he said, "We were awful worried 'bout you."

I glared at Felice who had stopped snivelling. She thew up her hands. "She was there, I saw her, m'lord."

"Where was I dada?" mumbled Hawise into the folds of my cotte.

"In the stable with your pony."

"I was but I took him out and walked him about a bit round the walls..... look there's Cedric - he was with me. He'll tell you."

I rose from my knee. Cedric came walking the pony, Felix, through the gate and round in a tight circle prior to returning him to the stable. He stopped dead with a jingling of tack when he saw the damage.

"Christ's Bones!" he said. "What's 'appened?"

I didn't't answer him immediately.

"Well, we are all very happy that you are safe, Hawise. We were really worried. We thought that you were buried under the ruins of the stable roof."

I turned to Cedric, "The weight of snow on the thatch has caused the roof to collapse. It's an old building. The horses will all have to go into the threshing barn or the haybarn until we can repair the damage here."

I hugged my daughter to my side and looked over her head. Lydia was standing in the courtyard white with shock.

"All is well lady," I said. "No one is hurt."

She let out a huge breath as if she had been holding it in since she shouted my name heartbeats before.

"Oh Aumary, I thought as you did....that someone was..." and she came running to me. I now had Hawise under one arm and Lydia leaning on me cradled in the other. Their arms locked together.

"Hal, can you organise please for the stables to be made safe so there are no more falls. Be very careful how you go about in there...one false step and the rest may come crashing down around you."

"Right you are, sir." He turned to go but then swivelled back. "We 'ave some long lengths of timber stored in the undercroft; maybe we can use those to shore up stuff?"

"By all means Hal. But be careful."

"Lydia, Hawise, Felice...off you go into the warm. I'll be up in a minute."

I called together all my stable staff. Two of them, the brothers Ben and Bill were now homeless, for their rooms were above the horses' accommodation, snug in the apex of the middle roof. "Can we double up boys? Until we get it sorted. Mind you, before we do anything we must make sure that the two end blocks of the stable are safe and aren't going to cave in like this one, or you'll all lose your homes. We will see what we can salvage of your possessions as soon as we can."

They all nodded. Hubert the farrier and Phillip Wheelwright senior took it upon themselves to check the safety of the further buildings and ran off to fetch some hayforks from the barn to pull the remaining thatch from the stricken roof.

Peter and Stephen, my men at arms, came trotting in the gateway with a large rope with which they proceeded to sweep the snow from the thatched roofs. There was only one more fall of roof timbers before it all settled and I was satisfied things were under control. Then and only then did I make my way wearily, for the shock of believing Hawise crushed under the weighty timbers of the stable had taken its toll of me. I took some burntwine, not something I like, just to steady me, once I was back in the hall.

Hawise was sitting demurely on a bench before the fire with Lydia. They had their heads together and were murmuring conspiratorially. Leave them, I thought. They are happy enough. I heard Hawise say "I don't like him," but I didn't't hear the answer my wife gave.

Sitting shakily on a bench at the other side of the fire on a cushioned chair and wrapped in rugs, was our mystery man. I filled another small beaker with burntwine and sauntered over to him. This would be the first time I'd had the leisure, since he had awoken, to speak with him.

"Good day my man," I said, in the absence of a name. "How are you today? It's good you are up and about." I held out the beaker. He smiled a lop sided smile and took the wine. In a slurred voice he said, "I'm not sure I like this stuff, but thank you kindly, I'll take it and try it m'lord."

I smiled and sat on the edge of the bench which ran the length of the large oak table in front of the fire.

He sipped the fiery liquor and coughed. "MY! It's powerful stuff."

I leaned forward rolling my own fiery stuff in the beaker between my hands.

"Aye, but it's good for shock and damage. To your continued recovery my friend." And I tossed the remainder of my burntwine down my throat.

He smiled again. His was a very open face. Tanned with years of weather and sun. He was a man of about forty-five; wrinkles were beginning to crowd his eyes and there were pronounced lines across his forehead. His curling fair hair was parted in the middle and just above his ear, Johannes had secured a new bandage which made the waves of it stick out oddly. The bandage was a lighter one than I had seen on him a few days ago. No blood had seeped through.

Johannes obviously thought he was mending for our man looked less trussed up than heretofore. Someone had tidied his beard since I had last seen him and he looked clean and well cared for.

"Have you regained any of your memory at all? You have any notion of what happened to you."

He did not shake his head for I think the action would have pained him. "No, I know not who I am, where I come from, nor what happened to me."

"How are your feet?"

He wriggled his toes. He wore soft shoes, my old soft indoor shoes I thought.

"Whole, thanks to your doctor. He is a good man. I must thank you for taking me in. I would be dead else, sir."

"You will stay as long as is needful. No need for thanks. Though if thanks is needed anywhere, it's to the master glazier who found you and brought you to us."

"Aye, I have spoken to him and given him my heartfelt thanks. It was his quick eye which spotted me at the side of the road, I think."

"It was. And he bundled you up in his cart and brought you here, to Durley."

"I don't think I have been here before. I don't even know where I was headed when the snow overtook me."

"My guess is the town of Marlborough, in the Kennet valley."

"It's terrible… terrible…." He wiped the spittle from the corner of his mouth, "I can't even recall if I know that place either."

"I'm sure it will all come back to you. It's only a matter of fifteen days or so since you were brought in near to death."

I shifted on my bench. "Johannes tells me that sometimes memory will come back if someone suggests things to the forgetful person. It would be helpful if we knew your name at least."

"My lord," he said smiling. "You are more than kind to spend so much of your valuable time with a humble peddler, for peddler they tell me I am."

"Aye, you have a pack stuffed with good things. I am sure when you are well and fully recovered, there will be plenty of opportunity to sell to the folk of my manor." I patted the rug on his knee.

"And as to me spending time… well… I love a puzzle. It's well known and you sir, are a puzzle, and I can't resist a puzzle." I smiled heartily. "I have little to do at present for the weather keeps us penned up. Let's see what we can do about your name."

He looked perplexed at that but indulged me. "I shall go through the letters and think of as many names as I can, slowly mind, so you have time to think and remember if you can."

He slowly and carefully inclined his head.

I saw from the corner of my eye, Perkin Glazer come though the hall door and head for the pot-board where the ale jug was kept.

"Here is your saviour. Perkin! I shouted, "Join us…Sit. We are about to play a game and three heads are better than one."

Perkin Glazer sat on the bench next to me but a deferent distance away. Hawise turned her head and I thought I saw her glare at him.

"M'lord......Peddler," he said.

"I shall begin with the name of our first man."

"Adam," said the peddler.

"Well, that is good...for you remember this much." I smiled. "Now for more names beginning with A." Slowly we went through all the names we could think of, from Adam to Alfred, Adelmar to Athelwine. We then went through B. Glazer entered into the game with gusto.

We had reached L, when Hal joined us.

"A word sir...?"

"Yes, Hal, I turned round to look at him.

"The stable will need a bitty more work to make it safe but we'll need to cut some more timber or go out to the store at the carpenter's shed in the village, and work on some that Martyn says we 'ave there."

"Yes, do so, Hal. Whatever is needed."

"Martyn says 'es bin savin' some big bits in the shed seasonin' nicely. You know what Martyn's like sir...'es a man as likes to be prepared."

Our mystery man gave a cry. "Martyn....Martyn. Yes..."

"Peddler?"

"Yes, that's it!" He sat up straight in the chair.

"My name is Martyn. It is. Martyn. Martyn Summersete!" And he beamed.

*****

I left Martyn being congratulated on regaining the memory of his name by several of the manor folk, and looked in on Johannes in his room on the north wall of the manor courtyard.

"Our peddler has a name at last, Johannes. Martyn, Martyn Summersete. You were right, a little mental jogging did him no harm."

He put down the parchment he had been reading and got up from the bed on which he had been reclining.

"That is excellent news. I feel sure the rest will follow, though I am not so sure his hearing or his speech will ever be quite the same again."

"No, well it's very early days as yet."

Johannes nodded and combed his long locks with his fingers and retied his queue.

"That was an unholy mess this morning at the stables, Aumary. I was out in the village. You have a new addition to your Durley family by the way. Peter and Marian Ash have added to their brood. Number five I think. A boy. I was told of your disaster when I came back in."

"I wondered where you had gone."

"Aye. The midwife couldn't get here because of the snow, so I did the job. They have only called him Johannes after me." His eyes leapt up to Heaven.

I smiled. "Johannes Ash has a good ring to it. I hope he will be as good a forester as his father is." I sat down on the stool which had been neatly stored under the table. "Aye, the roof of the middle stable collapsed with the weight of the snow. None hurt, but for a moment, we thought that Hawise was trapped inside."

"No!"

"She wasn't. She was out with Cedric walking her pony around the walls but I don't mind telling you - it was Geoffrey all over again for a fleeting moment."

"Aye it would be."

My five year old son Geoffrey had been killed five years earlier by falling masonry from the newly built gatehouse. Even now, it was a raw wound.

"She's fine and she and Lydia have their heads together in the hall. I'm sure they are up to something."

"Then let us go and see."

Hawise was playing hopscotch on the hall floor when we entered. The rushes had been swept back and the hopscotch frame had been shakily scratched onto the flagstones with a piece of chalk. Lydia sat perched on the edge of the table, her turn obviously over. The manor dogs, those who came into the hall, sat watching in fascination as the rhymes were played out and Hawise jumped, holding her skirt up to her knee. I looked up and saw Perkin Glazer watching her carefully. Was he wishing he had a daughter? He didn't even have a son now he had disowned Harry.

"Uncle Johannes, will you play with me too?" asked Hawise. Johannes chuckled. "I haven't the balance, my chick," he said, "I'd fall flat on the floor."

Hawise giggled at that and grabbed his hand. "I'll show you," and she proceeded to take him through the moves of the game. First one foot, then two.

I laughed and turned to my wife. "Are you all right after your shock earlier?"

"Yes....it was all so sudden and Felice worried me with her certainty that Hawise was inside the building."

"She had gone round the walls with Felix and Cedric."

"Yes...." Lydia's face took on an odd expression.

"Something Hawise said when she got back has puzzled me, Aumary."

I guffawed as Johannes jumped and lost balance as he said he would and had to windmill his arms to stay upright.

"Hmmm?"

"She said that Master Glazer followed her out of the gate and round the walls. He then went off to the river side and walked up and down. Eventually he rejoined her and came through the sally port with her. He sent Cedric off alone round the north wall to bring Felix back in by the main gate."

"And?"

"He was asking her about where the apple was found and would she show him, down by the river?"

"Was he indeed?" I turned to find the glazier, a way off sitting at the table, his arms folded onto the flat of the board, staring at the antics of my daughter and my best friend.

"And she said?"

"My father has asked me to tell no one about the apple and I am not going to tell you."

"A true Belvoir!" I answered.

"What was the master glazier up to, Aumary?"

"I suspect he is as fascinated by the little apple as we are. I showed it to him. After all, he is a glass-maker and the thing is made of glass. I learned a lot from him, last evening about how the thing was made and with what. He is a very knowledgeable man. It's his special field, after all. I expect he is hoping to come across something else of a similar ilk, by the river, if he searches in the right place and for long enough."

"But Aumary...that would belong to you," said Lydia in a horrified tone.

"No, Lydia, strictly it belongs to the King. It's treasure trove and all items found so belong to him. We shall have to give it up eventually. Whatever we find. Which reminds me, John said he would be at the castle over Christmas. If he could, he would have been here for Christmas Day perhaps or at the very least Twelfth Night. The snow has prevented him. When we can we shall have to go out and see if he's still at Marlborough Castle. I don't want to miss him altogether. I want to discuss this idea of his about constables in every county. We can take our apple with us, as a Twelfth Night gift. That would please him no end! He adores things like that."

"Let us keep in on his right side then," said Lydia.

Crispin came in through the hall door. Hawise abandoned Johannes to his return jump and leapt on our priest. "Sir Crispin...come...you are really good at hopscotch I know. Come and show Uncle Johannes how to do it properly."

Crispin laughed, belted his robe higher and threw himself into the game. I laughed long and hard. Until it was my turn.

"What Paul? Oh yes...I have had to play hopscotch. I'm quite good actually. Couldn't do it now though. Pah!"

That night the wind howled around the manor like a wailing demon from hell. The snow fell and once again, it was whipped into furious churning by the gale. All our digging and piling would be to no avail. We should have to do it all over again.

Sleep was hard to come by that night for the noise of the storm was relentless and I tossed and turned, the events of the day playing over in my head. At one point when I was on the cusp of sleep, I have no idea of the time, I thought I heard a shutter bang followed a little later by a cry out there in the cold and dark. In my stupor, I decided it was probably the cry of a mating fox. In the languid time between sleep and awake, the shutter continued to bang, but eventually sleep overtook me. The little sparrows, roosting in their tree outside the solar window, woke me with their chattering later in the morning. It seemed as if they were trying to calm the gale with their loud and incessant twittering. I reminded myself to throw out some crumbs for them, for they would find it hard to forage in this weather.

I threw on my cloak and padded to the window and cleared the glass of ice. The window glass fogged up as soon as my breath met it. I rubbed it with my hand and peered out.

White on white. Nothing but white. I could just make out the far wall of the courtyard. I crossed to the other wall. Even whiter here and the shape of the threshing barn loomed grey in the whiteness. The snow had speckled the stone wall and it was so pale that it was hard to make out.

Someone had, thankfully, lit the solar fire. I dressed hurriedly in front of it, shivering as my flesh came into contact with cold clothes.

Lydia was in the far room with Hawise, encouraging her to get up. Hawise wanted to stay in the warmth of her bed. I didn't blame her. I called a good morning and descended the solar stairs.

A few people were milling around in the hall. Palliases were being stored, benches replaced and Hal was stoking the fire. People were reluctant to store their blankets and were throwing them over their shoulders for extra warmth.

Matthew my cook, came up from the kitchen with a huge pot of watery soup. His wife followed with a platter of bread. We all took out our bowls and spoons and set to. This would keep out the cold, for we had much clearing work to do this morning.

Indeed, the morning was spent clearing paths through the courtyard. I shovelled the snow from the hall steps once more and wondered what I could do to make them safer. Alfred Woodsmith had installed his wooden railing and they were less dangerous than they had been but the freezing night had made the surface like polished glass. Johannes' slickstone came to mind, as I recalled the day Lydia and I had met. She had been smoothing shirts on his kitchen table with a hot glass slickstone and I had surprised her and made her jump so that she dropped it. I smiled. It seemed a long time ago but it was barely months.

I stood staring at the steps for a while, a germ of an idea forming in my head. Hal came down the steps and stood half way up.

"Sir...can I 'ave a word?"

"Surely, Hal."

I shrugged my cloak back onto my shoulders and followed him as he descended and took me around the end of the hall, past the kitchen building to the little door in the rear of the west wall. This was the small door, always left open during the day in times of peace; the door Hawise had entered yesterday on her return from her walk around the manor with her pony.

"I locked the sally port sir, as I always do every night when I make me rounds. Bolts it and locks it every night I do."

"I know you do, Hal...you are most diligent."

" 'Twas wide open this mornin' m'lord, when I comes to unbolt it."

"Someone was up before you and went out, Hal?"

"Nope, sir, I don't think so. No prints, see. The snow stopped fallin' before dawn. I was up about then. I found it when I was makin' me rounds early this mornin'. If they'd a bin up and out afore me, there would'a bin prints."

"I see what you mean, Hal. If they had gone out after the snow stopped they would have left foot...." I stopped.

"You all right, sir...?"

"Aye...just something I remember last night, Hal. Banging. I thought it was a shutter banging in the wind. Now, I think it might have been the sally port. I can hear it as I'm the nearest to it up there," and I pointed to the solar window, "save those who sleep in the kitchen."

"Aye sir...someone went out in the night."

"Then they are a fool!" I laughed. "The storm was as fierce as a unicorn."

"It did die down a bit arter midnight - I went to piss in the big pot..." he chuckled, "too much watered ale. The wind had gone and the snow stopped. Then about an hour later it were fiercer than ever. They must'a gone out then. And they din't return."

"No?"

Hal shook his head. "Wyot says no one came back through the wicket, and the sally was open all night. Whoever went out never came back agin to shut it."

We stared at each other.

"Oh dear."

"Can you ask folk to look out for everyone else and see who might be missing? Get everyone into their tithings. We might have to organise a search party."

Later on I struggled against the wind, out of the gate, through the party of men clearing a path round the walls to the church and on into the village proper. I was heading for our large carpenter's barn-like workshop.

Martyn Carpenter and a few other men were there sorting out the long lengths of wood needed for shoring up the wrecked stable. These would be re-used when we re-built the place.

"Morning lads," I said. They all took off their coifs.

"No... please... return your headwear." I chuckled. "It's too cold on the ears to go without."

They all chuckled in their turn and went back to work.

Martyn Carpenter finished hefting his large piece of wood onto a couple of saw benches and then came over to me.

"Martyn... I must thank you for the care you have taken in storing the wood so well. If you hadn't been thinking ahead, we might not have had enough to do repairs." I squeezed his shoulder.

The poor man squirmed at the praise. I remembered he was a shy fellow; a man of few words. "Oh no, sir.... I'm only doin' my job. That's what carpenting's about, sir. Gotta think ahead." He would not meet my eye.

I smiled. "How are you now?"

"I'm fine, sir," he said and turned away.

Martyn, a freeman, lived by the workshop, close by the reeve's house. Sadly, he had lost his wife and daughter in the autumn of 1203. His wife was a Cadley girl and she had been interred in the churchyard there with their little girl, who was nine. Madelen had been fostered out in the town of Marlborough to learn the role of lady's maid to the town reeve's wife, Felicity Barbflet. For all I knew she had been happy there.

Maggie Carpenter had died of a sleeping disease. She had complained of headaches and a heart which pounded, and a large swelling grew on her neck. She would fall asleep at a moment's notice and was always tired. One day she just did not awake.

Her daughter Madelen, who was nine, it was thought, missed her so much, she went into a decline and died of a lung disease after about a month or so. I know that Nicholas Barbflet had engaged Johannes' services but he could do little to prevent her slipping away. She had refused much food and water and had dwindled to death. Martyn too, had wasted away and it was only his work, the support of his friends and colleagues and the vigilance of Walter Reeve and his wife, his near neighbours, that had kept him alive on this earth. He too would have joined his wife and daughter in Cadley churchyard.

"So then," I rubbed my cold hands together. "How are we doing here?"

Martyn took me to the pile of timber stored at the back of the barn. "Plenty to repair the stables."

I looked round. I saw the Sylvestres, father and son, busy making hurdles at the other end. These two were my bonded men, tied peasants who worked the land in return for their own strip and men skilled in the making of hurdles, the woven panels used as animal fences. I nodded to them. They knuckled their foreheads and carried on.

I raised my voice. "If this wind keeps up Sylvestre, we shall have great need of new fencing come the spring." I shouted against the noise of the wind whistling through the huge space.

"Aye m'lord," said the elder man. "And up on the sheep fold in the downs."

I mentally pictured my sheep which I farmed high up on the downs near East Kennet. I trusted my shepherds to keep them safe in this weather, but understood well the battle they must be waging with the snow and wind. I hoped they had all made the large barns and sheep folds scattered over my land up there.

First opportunity I got, I would go up to the sheep pastures and see how everything was faring.

"Martyn, can we keep the shavings and dustings from the cutting - perhaps in a barrel. We have a spare broken one in the courtyard. It's going to be hard work finding kindling for fires under all this snow."

"Aye sir, we can."

I nodded, all was well. "You live in the village centre, Martyn. How is everyone faring? I hope none are suffering too much with the weather?"

"Not yet, m' lord, though like you say, if it goes on long..." he tailed off and shrugged.

"Yes,...well, I'll tell Walter to keep an eye out for need and difficulty. Two uncomfortable bedfellows eh?"

Martyn Carpenter smiled one of his rare smiles, "Aye sir, almost as bad as sorrow and hopelessness."

Profound words from a man of so few.

"Aye, and you'd know Martyn," and I clapped him on the back.

As I turned I heard him say, "And you too, m'lord."

Everyone seemed present on the manor and in the village. Families counted their members and pronounced them all present. People were bustling about clearing snow, fetching and carrying and of course, there was much work to-ing and fro-ing in the courtyard with the mending of the stables. In the late morning, I took a long pole from the carpenter's barn with which to steady me and went out to the river bank with a large bucket. Hal followed with a pickaxe and a shovel. Hawise decided she would come too. The river bank was a draw for her now that she knew the little apple had been found there but I had forbidden her to go there alone.

Wrapped up in her thick red winter cloak she stuck out brightly like a holly berry against the pure white of the snow. She trailed behind finding it difficult to balance in the depth of the snow.

"Step in our footsteps Hawise. Like hopscotch," but she could not, for our stride was much longer than her own. I set down my tools and went back, hoisted her up and set her down in safety.

"Now...you madam, will stay in sight and you will keep away from the edge."

"Where is the edge dada?" she asked.

I swept my long pole across the snow and drew a rough line.

"This is river ice and this is snow on the bank...I think."

Hal hefted his pickaxe. Two blows and he broke through to water. "Aye that's it, right enough."

Our little stream was barely fifteen feet wide here, where it looped between two alder trees. We could see where earlier the fishermen had opened up holes to let in their rods. There were two deeper pools here; one on the far bank and one on our side. The ice was thinner where the holes had re-frozen overnight and they were covered with a dusting of snow. I cleared a patch for us.

"Now what we are going to do, is this."

When I had been looking at my icy hall steps earlier, it had come to me that gravel would be safer to walk on than the glass like stone. Our little stream trickled happily over a bed of gravel, as it wound its way on to the confluence with the Og. We would scrape up some gravel into a bucket and sprinkle it on the steps. We were standing where the stream was just over two feet deep, gravel would be easy to shovel up from the stream bed.

Hawise wandered off downstream a little with my pole, making patterns in the snow and scooping up handfuls to build a tower. I kept her in my view which was easy with her bright scarlet cloak.

Hal broke the ice and I stepped down into the freezing water and shovelled up the gravel.

Before we had a chance to be frozen to the core and our boots were too soaked, we had a pail full and were scrambling back on to the bank.

I heard Hawise squeak and looked up. She had taken my pole and was hunkered down sweeping it flat on the ground, making semicircular patterns on the snow. In her playfulness she had strayed out onto the frozen stream.

I shouted. "Come back Hawise..."

She turned and as fast as she could run through the snow, falling a couple of times, she came up to me, dropping the pole.

Her eyes were huge and her face almost as white as the snow surrounding us. She took my hand and I felt her trembling through her felted mitten.

"What is it sweeting?" It was almost as if she could not speak. She took my hand and pulled me towards her handiwork by the stream bed.

Hal followed, setting down the bucket on the path we had forged through the snow earlier. Hawise pointed but would go no further than a few feet from the bank of the stream. Hal pushed past me and gingerly, for he weighed a lot more than Hawise and the river was deeper here where the bends had cut into the bed, he stepped out onto the now uncovered ice.

"Ah," he looked up at me. "I think we may 'ave discovered who went out of the sally last night sir."

I pointed at my daughter and like a dog I commanded her to stay, and I too went out on to the river. There, looking up at the leaden sky with ice blue eyes, his long fair hair all about him, was Perkin Glazer.

"Poor bastard, beggin' yer pardon sir, musta fallen in and freezed to death," said Hal, pulling off his coif and clutching it to his bosom.

"Think again, Hal," I said. "This is one of the holes made yesterday by the fishermen, yes. However I think someone took advantage of the fact that the ice was clear here and dumped him in. The ice reforming did the rest."

Hal screwed his cap back on his head. "His 'ead has been stoved in... I can see the blood now." He looked up at me suddenly.

"Same as Martyn Peddler, side o' the 'ead. 'E's in the river to be makin' sure he wasn't goin' to recover like the peddler did."

"Get the man out, Hal," I sighed. "Get a few people out here and get him out."

I looked back at Hawise. She was shaking uncontrollably and had fallen on her knees. "I'm taking Hawise back to the hall," and I ran back and scooped her up.

I explained to Lydia what had happened and Hawise was chivvied up the solar steps like a chick by a hen. I watched them go and Hawise turned at the door and gave me a pale smile. I lifted my hand and blew her a kiss. She smiled again and was gone.

I strode over the newly cleared courtyard and scraped at Johannes' door. He opened it quickly. He took one look at me. "I think you had better sit down," he said.

"I told you this morning that someone had gone out of the sally port last night." I sat on his joint stool.

He nodded.

"We have just found him locked in the ice of the river..it's..."

"Perkin Glazer?"

I blinked. "How in God's name did you know...?"

"I looked into his room a while ago. I searched the manor. He and I are the only able bodied men who don't belong here, so who would think to look for us? So I looked for him. Couldn't find him anywhere. No one had seen him since supper last night. Dead?"

"As week old ashes."

"How?"

"Bashed over the head, just as our peddler had been."

"Where is he now?"

"They should be bringing him in from the river. He'll be in the mortuary soon enough."

*****

It took a long while to chip the glazier from the ice and they fetched him into the manor on one of the Sylvestre's hurdles, then laid him on the bier in the mortuary, a little circular stone building at the back of the western wall. He lay and dripped onto the floor, ice still clinging to his clothing.

Johannes turned the glazier's head with difficulty but there was no rigor. "It's often the case that rigor doesn't happen when the body has been so cold, Aumary. Heat brings it on, cold delays it. I have no idea why."

I bent to look at the wound.

"It is the same as Martyn received, just above the ear, left hand side, vicious, with a blunt but very hard weapon.

"This time the man wasn't wearing his cowl."

"Why wasn't he?" I asked. "It was bitter out there in the middle of the night."

Johannes shrugged. "Perhaps we'll find it elsewhere."

He took out from his bag, the little metal probes I'd seen him use before, and prodded the head wound.

"One blow. Crushed the skull. There are bits of bone in the brain matter. Dead as soon as he hit the floor....snow."

"Might we find where he was killed? I have a feeling it was not right on the river bank."

"That's going to be difficult with the blown snow covering all over again. He wouldn't bleed much; he died almost instantly."

"Hmmm. Are there any drag marks anywhere? He must have been dragged to the river and toppled into the hole made by the fishermen. Even if it had iced over, it would have been easy to break."

"We'd need to go out of the sally and look."

"Then let us. After dinner."

It was a matter of a short while before we were standing outside the walls. We both looked round. Prints were everywhere. The children had been out - we could see their small footprints and see where they had scooped up the snow in play. Others with larger feet, including Hal and myself had trodden the snow and the men who'd gone out to recover the body had scuffed it up. We could see the shape of the hurdle laid on the bank and the footprints returning, sinking a little deeper as the men struggled with their burden.

"Worse than useless," I said. "Too much activity."

We wandered down to the river bank. "This is where he was," I said.

"Whoever put him in knew about the depth of the river here. They didn't't drop him in the shallows."

"There is nowhere to hide here. No bushes, no trees to speak of. How did our assailant manage to creep up on the glazier?"

"Maybe he didn't't. Maybe they came out together," suggested Johannes.

"Or perhaps they agreed to meet here?"

"Whichever it is, it suggests that Glazer knew his murderer."

"He told me no one in Durley was at loggerheads with him nor bore him a grudge."

"Do you think it's someone from outside Durley?"

"No sadly, I don't."

"Why not?"

"Well, it could be someone with a grudge at the glazier's camp but have you seen any of the glazier's lot creeping about the manor with a weapon ready to strike Glazer?"

"They would soon be spotted."

"And the weather doesn't help, so no, I think it's a Durley man."

"Or woman."

"Could a woman inflict that sort of damage Johannes?"

"With the right weapon," said the doctor. "Yes they could."

Johannes slapped his sides with his mittened hands, for it was cold in the open and there was no wind break. I looked back at the threshing barn.

"The horses from the middle stable were there last night as was one of the grooms, seeing to them. Bill I think. I'll go and see if he saw or heard anything. Meet you in the hall? Have the ale warming."

Bill was sitting in a hay pile with a mug of warmed ale in his hands. He was wrapped in blankets and had a heated stone by his feet. I could see the remains of his last meal on a wooden platter on the ground.

"No don't get up Bill. You look too comfortable and warm there."

"Aye ,sir, 'tis remarkably warm in hay. We brought some straw in from the hay barn for the horses to rest on and some hay for them to eat."

Horses all right?"

"Yessir. Amazing how they keep a man warm."

"Yes, indeed. Bill, did you hear anything last night, over the noise of the wind about midnight?"

"Lord save you, sir, I wouldn't know when it was midnight. I'd be long asleep before then."

"No noises woke you."

"The shutter banging you mean?"

"Aye, around about the time it started." Like me, Bill thought the banging of the sally was an unlatched shutter.

Bill pulled a face. "I'm so used to the noises the horses make in the night I kind of close me ears to them and once I heard the shutter, well, I thought, that's a shutter banging in the wind and slipped off again, sir."

"You heard no cry?" He shook his head.

"I sleeps deep, sir."

"I wouldn't have heard it I think, save for the fact I was tossing and turning." I sighed.

"You've more to worry about than me, sir" he smiled.

"Who is in tonight, Bill?"

"Cedric,sir."

"I hope he sleeps as deeply as you."

*****

Back in the warmth of the hall, a mulled wine in my hand, I reported my finding nothing, to Johannes.

"Ah but I have thought of something," said Johannes playfully.

I poised, the cup to my lip."You have?"

"Who goes out at night to look for something and doesn't take a lantern or at least some form of light with them?"

"You think, then, that he had secretly gone to search the riverbank for treasure?"

"Don't you?"

"He was certainly interested in finding out from Hawise, where the apple was found. He suggested to Hal and me, that where one item was found there would be others, the night we showed him the thing."

"It was a dangerous thing to do on a pitch black night in a snow storm. Go down to the river and trot about on ice."

"Around midnight, Hal tells me, it all calmed down for an hour or so," I said. "He probably went out then. And truthfully he probably stayed on the bank."

"So where is his lamp, his dark lantern, his flare? We didn't't find it."

"His attacker must have retrieved it and taken it away."

"It's true that you can see slightly better with the reflection of starlight on snow. Snow does light things up but he must have had a light of some kind," Johannes shrugged.

"All our lamps are made by our own Tom Potter, dark lanterns by Hubert Alder the blacksmith. They are all of a same pattern. Unless someone in the village had a special one they have bought, we wouldn't know where in the manor it came from," I added.

"We should look to see if there's a lantern or a lamp in Glazer's room still."

The clay oil lamp was still there on the floor by his bed. His chamberstick was on the table with a new candle affixed in it. The lantern, which every room of the manor guest wing had, was missing from its hook by the door.

"Now we know what we are looking for," said Johannes.

The light faded fast from winter afternoons in early January and the light was going when we despondently traipsed back to the hall after a search of the area. No lantern. Unless it had been dropped into a hole in the river ice, the murderer had taken it. We warmed ourselves yet again by the hall fire and felt decidedly dozy after our efforts and two more beakers of hot mulled wine. We were both almost nodding when Henry came in and gave me a report on the progress of the repairs to the stables.

Hal came in after him and waxed lyrical about the gravel on the manor steps.

"Why! You can almost tak'em two atta time and not slide an inch," he said. I laughed.

"You be careful old friend," I said. "At your age broken bones don't mend as well as they used to." He looked affronted but we all knew Hal was fitter than a flame and owned a body as hard as a nutshell.

"Mind me asking, sir?" he said, "Glazer. We 'as to tell the crowner about him don't we?"

"We do Hal but...."

"Aye, the weather."

"It's a lot worse underfoot than when we sent Johnathan for Glazer, or Alfred for the doctor here," I said. "I can't ask anyone to go out in these conditions."

"I'll go sir. I'll go by forest routes not main roads. They shouldn't be so congested," said John Brenthall coming up behind Hal. "I know every little path and byway."

Hal lifted his eyebrows.... "As I was goin'a say sir, John has offered to go tomorrer."

I looked long and hard at my chief woodwarden. He was a wiry little man with an intimate knowledge of the forest. If anyone could get to Marlborough and back in one piece it would be him.

"On the proviso that if there is more snow, depending on where you are, you seek shelter at the nearest forest cott, or if you are in the town at the priory. Understood?"

"I can stay in the Marsh with Agnes' stepda sir."

"Indeed you could." I caught my lip with my teeth in a gesture of worry. "If Agnes thinks it will be all right to let you go...."

John smiled. "I already asked her. She didn't't like the man, she said, but she wouldn't wish him dead like that and someone should report his death."

"Also, can you go to the castle and see Andrew Merriman? Better leave a note for the sheriff too.. At the same time, you can see if the King is still at the castle. Please."

John nodded.

"A note for him too, sir?"

"I'll pen one later."

"Yessir."

"Now if no one minds. I am for my bed for a nap till supper time. I am exhausted." I also wanted to look in on Hawise.

****

Hal accompanied me to the bottom of the steps. He knew it was Hawise who had discovered the body, of course.

"Will our brave little Belvoir be all right, sir?" he asked concern in every wrinkle of his face.

I took him by the shoulder. "You have said it Hal, she is a Belvoir. Tough as a boot sole."

He smiled at that. "But she's only a littlun, sir."

"I know Hal. I'll tell her you send your love."

He beamed at that. "Aye...you do that, sir."

"An', sir...."

"Yes, Hal?" I turned on the third step.

"We have a murderer among us, in the village. People are goin'a be lookin' at their neighbours with queer eyes, I reckon. Better be prepared fer trouble."

"Yes Hal. I know. I have thought of that.

Chapter Five

As it was, trouble came to us in another form two days later. John Brenthall made it to the town and back as he said he would. The King had gone from Marlborough into Hampshire and Dorsetshire bypassing us all together. How he and his entourage managed it I do not know. A note was sent to the sheriff and the coroner was informed though he did not think it was needful that he come out in such awful conditions to view the body of a glazier. He would wait for better weather. After all the body would keep in this cold. John also went on his return journey, by pathways and byways to the permanent camp in the West Baily, where some of the glass blowers had their homes and kilns. He informed them of the death of their master glazier. Once the women who laid out the bodies had dealt with the earthly remains of Perkin Glazer, we left him in our little mortuary, in the parish coffin, and then moved him to the altar of our church for a while. We would return his cart, with his body to the glass makers as soon as we were able. His widow could dispose of it at her will.

"I took it upon myself sir, to call at the glazier's house when I was in the town. The mistress of the house was out. I left a message with the maid. 'Twas all I could do. And since sir, his house is so close to the glazier's, I also told Little Agnes that the doctor was fine and still here with us."

"John, you are a marvel."

Johannes looked up from his game of chess with Lydia.

"She is all right, John?"

"She's fine, sir. She spent Christmas at the Barbflet house - has friends there, so she was not alone in the house."

"I must think about going home soon Aumary. John....maybe you can guide me along the byways though the trees that you used to reach the town?"

"Gladly, sir," said John.

"Give yourself time to recover from this journey and then we'll go. Can I lead a horse?"

John thought carefully. "Lots of climbing over obstacles sir...maybe not."

"All right then... he'll have to follow. Can you feed him in your stable, Aumary, till I can fetch him home?"

"Need you ask," I said.

*****

Next day I went to the church to talk to Crispin, our priest. It might be that, if this weather continued we might not be able to dig the ground for quite a while to bury our folk. I knew that one of our oldest inhabitants had died just after Christmas and we needed to have contingency plans for the keeping of the body until the ground was free of ice. I found Crispin in the priest's room, polishing the silver candlesticks which usually adorned our altar. I stood in the doorway. He had heard my boots clipping up the flagstone floor.

"Ah...I thought it was you," he said.

"Do you not leave that job to the church reeves? Surely they will do jobs like that."

"I like to do it. I find it very satisfying. Yes, they will do it but, well, there is little to do at the moment. I feel as if we are all locked in a whitened room!"

I leaned on the door jamb. "What are we to do with our unburied, Crispin?"

He put down his rags. "I can't imagine God will worry about when we bury them. He already knows where Old Tom is and has taken him to his bosom. Tom's had all the appropriate rites, as has your glazier. He will keep till the ground is freed of frost."

I nodded. "So we leave Tom in his cott untill we can bury him with all due rites."

"He lived alone. He's not inconveniencing anyone else. The neighbours don't seem to mind."

"He would hurt none in life, he will do none harm in death," I said. "He was very well liked."

"He played the symphonie didn't't he... I remember him from....?" No sooner was this sentence out of his mouth than there was a pounding of feet, a slipping and a sliding and what sounded like someone sore out of breath and at the end of their energies, gasping for air. The church door banged hard shut. I turned and peered round the door jamb into the body of the church.

Into my view at last, between the columns, came a young man, wet through, muddied from sliding in snowy puddles, staggering, wheezing, falling to his knees and then crawling a few paces at last to the altar.

I strode into the nave. "What is the..."

The young man turned his anguished face to me. He grimaced in pain and fell fully onto the floor, propped on one elbow in front of the altar. Crispin came up behind me. The young man's chest was heaving in great gulps of air. He had been running; running for what must have been, I suppose, hours, in filthy conditions, through the forest in deep snow.

"I... claim... sanctuary here... for the love of God, sanctuary...." He grasped for the altar cloth to take it in his hand but failed, before he fell again, flat on the floor and lay still.

Crispin looked at me.

"Must I grant it?"

"I think you must, for this is Harry Glazer, Perkin's son, Gilbert Cordwainer's apprentice. I know him well."

*****

I leaned over Harry and touched him. He flinched but did not speak. I hunkered down. "Harry, it's Aumary Belvoir, this is my priest Crispin Darrell of Chilton. You are amongst friends. There is nothing to fear." At that he lifted his head. He was far spent and it was an effort to speak.

"I c c c claim sanc...."

"You have it, Harry," said Crispin, falling to his knees. "I grant it. By the power invested in me, no one shall remove you from here nor harm you, whilst you are here, at the peril of losing their immortal soul. You may stay forty days and forty nights. After this time you must decide to give yourself up to justice or abjure the realm. You must make confession of your sin...."

"I didn't't do it..." he cried desperately.

"Do what, Harry?" I asked.

Harry wetted his lips; they were cracked and chapped. "I didn't't kill my father. That's God's truth. I didn't't kill him. They say I killed him. I didn't't kill him!" and he began to weep.

Crispin looked up at me and continued reciting whilst raking my face with a perplexed expression. "And you will walk barefoot and in a shirt, carrying a wooden cross, to the nearest port should you choose to abjure the realm. None may aid you. If you fail to find passage the first day, you must wade into the water up to your waist and show your intention to sail; and every subsequent day you fail to find a ship you will wade in to show your willingness to leave the realm. You may never return excepting by a pardon from the King. You will be executed else. May God have mercy on you." And he made the sign of the cross over the young man.

Harry had begun to shiver. He was wet through and now he had stopped running he had begun to cool.

"We must get him clean and dry clothes or he won't last your forty days and nights," I said quietly.

We lifted the young man between us and manhandled him into the robing room, a small space to the side of the nave where the priest kept the holy vessels and altar cloths. He tried to protest but Crispin said that the whole church was sanctuary and his best chance of staying warm and dry was in the priest's room. He collapsed then.

I went to the church door and called Hal who was at that moment running up the slight incline to the door.

"I saw what looked like...."

"You did. Get me a brazier of charcoals. Some clean clothing and blankets. Some of your hot ale wouldn't go amiss, and maybe some meat and bread, Hal."

"Right you are, sir," and he turned tail and jogged back through the manor gates. Not long after that Agnes, Lydia and he came back with handfuls of supplies.

"Hal... stand watch on the door. I doubt if anyone is pursuing this far in this weather but you never know." Hal closed the church door gently and stood like a sentry outside. It was snowing again.

The hot ale was very welcome and some colour began to come back into Harry's cheeks.

"Harry...who was pursuing you?"

"Townsmen... men from the castle. They came up the High Street yelling for me. They were shouting that my father had been murdered in Durley and that I was to be taken up for it. I had but a minute to decide to flee or not."

"You were at home, at the cordwainer's?"

"I was, sir, where I have been all Christmas."

"Would Gilbert vouch for you?"

"Aye sir he would. I'm sure."

"Here," said Lydia sweetly "have this...it will make you feel better." She gave him a plate of meat and bread.

"Thank you madam but...I can't eat...I feel sick."

She stroked his wet hair. "Later maybe."

John delivered the notice to the castle that your father is dead Harry. How did news get out so quickly?"

"I don't know. The first I knew was when they were coming down the street chanting."

Crispin who was arranging the brazier in the priest's room and lighting it asked, "Who is in charge when the sheriff and Hugh the constable are away?"

I coughed. "I am, Crispin."

"Ah."

Agnes piped up. "John says it was that idiot Picot in charge this week. Andrew has gone to see his mother in Calne for Christmas. It's just like Picot to allow something like this. John says he's an idiot."

"I see." I'd had first-hand knowledge of the workings of Picot's mind in the autumn of 1204.

Harry was now lying propped up on his elbow on the robing room's floor. "My master told me to flee through the back door. He would stall them all, he said. We could see the mood they were in. I wasn't going to be allowed a word of defense. It was obvious."

"Why ever did you run here Harry? It's three miles. Surely the church in Marlborough was easier."

Harry smiled up at me. "They were shouting that Da had been murdered in Durley. The master told me to get to you at Durley if I could. You would know what to do. He got it in my head that I had to come here to be close to where he'd died. He thought it was good to... to put as much distance between me and the pursuers as possible. And I knew m'lord, that you are a fair man...that you would listen to me."

"Your master is a good man. I have known him all my life, and I have known you a long time too, Harry."

"Aye sir that you have." Harry coughed as the hot liquid trickled down his throat. "Master Gilbert shoved me out the back door. I went through the priory grounds and out of their sally port by the river."

"I know it."

"Then I went round the walls and past the town mill. I crossed over at the tanneries at Culvermead and went at the back of the cotts on Newbury Street so none would see me from the road. Then I came up the hill and into the forest."

"You know the forest well?" asked Lydia

"I do, madam," he inclined his head. "All the back paths and byways."

"As John does," said Agnes.

"It must have been hard going through the snow though, Harry," I said.

"I'm a good runner. I won all the town prizes as a youngster for the running races."

"Come," said Agnes. "You must get into dry clothes. You will catch your death if you sit in those any longer."

Harry blushed... "I..."

"Out then ladies," I chivvied.

They both smiled, turned and closed the door behind them.

As Harry was struggling into new clothes and towelling his hair, I asked him, "Harry, you swear to me that you did not wield the knife which killed your father?"

"No sir, I swear it." His face was open and guileless.

I saw Crispin look up. "But..."

"You did not surprise him in his room here in Durley manor and plunge a knife into his back?"

"No, m'lord. He was my father, for all I disliked him. I would not kill him."

I nodded, satisfied.

"We shall see what we can do about getting the cordwainer to speak for you. Meanwhile, you are safe here. Sleep if you can. See Agnes has brought you a palliasse from the hall. You have two blankets. I think you'll be snug enough." I made for the door. "Oh, Harry?"

"Yes, sir?"

"Why is it that you think the castle guard and townsmen thought you were the culprit? I know it was well known you were not friends, but shouting at each other is, well...it's a far cry from murder."

Harry squirmed a little at that. "I...a little while ago, he came into the shop and was bad mouthing Master Gilbert. You know what a good man he is. They had argued. I intervened and…well, I struck him…my father. No more than that. To get him away from my master."

"Struck him?"

"Yes."

"What with?"

"Nothing sir… just my fist. I blacked his eye for him. 'Twas all around the town in no time!"

"Ah..now I see why they think you might have killed him. 'Twas not well done, Harry."

"No sir…I know but you do not know what he is…was like. He was a monster and make no bones."

I looked down at him.

"I have not seen that side of him, but I take your word for it."

Harry looked down at his hands.

"They could hit him…these hands…but they could not kill him."

"We shall have further words on it, I assure you. Now rest. You are safe for the nonce."

No one immediately followed Harry into the forest. The spleen which the townsmen and the castle guard had stirred up soon dissipated when they realised they would have to track their malefactor into the trees and through the deep snow. A sort of hue and cry had been called; that was enough for them. They had complied with the law. Now they went back, no doubt to their duties, jobs and businesses, tutting and shaking their heads in horror at the wickedness of Harry's crime. Murder one's father! No one would be safe if children could get away with murder. They were, naturally, blissfully unaware that it was now my job to gather information, search out the perpetrator of the crime and apprehend him, as the constable of Marlborough and environs.

"No, Paul, I did not believe that Harry Glazer had murdered his father. Not even in hot blood. I knew that he held his father responsible for the death of his

mother, that he had little respect for him, and that he hated the reputation Perkin had as a cold hearted womaniser, but kill him for it? No."

So where should I begin? Hal was the fount of all knowledge in the village. Let us quiz him and see what he thought about a motive for the murder. He had spent quite a bit of time with the glazier over Christmas. Let us see what he thought of him.

When asked, and reminded that there had been three attempts on the glazier's life, Hal of Potterne pulled on his long forked grey beard. "Why would someone want to do away with him? Hmm." He sat himself slowly on a bench in the corner of the hall and put down his whittling. He chuckled low, "Well, he were one for the ladies, we know that. He were a makin' eyes at Agnes till she told him to pi…, er potter off. Then he 'ad a go at Maud the kitchen girl but Matthew watches 'er like an 'awk, so it was no going there, besides she's a walkin' out with Phil. Sweet little lovebirds they are. On me rounds one night, I found Glazer standing outside 'is room, erm adjustin'…yes that's the word, adjustin' 'is tunic, an out pops - the new poultry girl, wassername agin?"

"Annot."

"Thass'er. She was all pink and flustered an' looked a mite tousled I'd say. He patted 'er on 'er hind quarters an' off she giggled."

"Annot is barely thirteen Hal…. Glazer was nearly fifty!"

"She was willin', I reckon."

"So John, Matthew and Annot's father, Bardol, would all have a reason to be angry…but not enough to murder. Besides, all but Annot can take care of themselves. Agnes certainly can, as you say."

"Aye. They might wanna rough 'im up a bit but, nah, I can't see any of 'em as proper plannin' murderers, sir."

"Anything else?"

"He were awful interested in that apple of ours sir. Kept asking me questions. 'Zactly where was it found? Was it in the river? 'Corse….."

Hal scratched his grey pate,

"I couldn't tell 'im what I di'nt know, now could I?" He winked at me.

I put my foot up on the end of the bench and leaned on my knee, smiling.

"Was he talking to anyone else here, particularly?"

"Only 'Enery but that was a 'cause of the mumming, sir. I don't think they had much besides that to say to each other."

"Hmmm. He talked to Martyn the peddlar, didn't't he?"

"He did, a whiles. But the peddlar knows nowt, sir. Not about the apple, not about himself for that matter."

"Who else knows about the apple besides, you, me, Lady Lydia, Hawise, Johannes, Agnes and Henry?"

Hal sucked his teeth. "Aw well. Things like this are 'ard to keep secret but I reckon we have managed it…." He looked up at me quickly.

"A corse there's one we 'ave forgotten."

We both said the name of the person in the next instant. "Dysig."

I scoured the hall. There was Agnes talking to her husband in the corner by the kitchen door.

"Agnes, can we borrow you again to talk to Dysig for us?"

Agnes curtsied as she saw me approach. "Aye, sir. What do you want to know this time?"

As we searched for the lad, I told Agnes more about the wonderful glass apple and Glazer's interest in it.

We found Dysig in the warmth of the smithy, handing tools to Hubert the blacksmith. I asked him to wait outside for a moment.

"Dysig. The lord would like to know if you spoke to the glass-man at all."

"He's dead, he got dead in the play. There was blood. He were a pagan. Pagan's are bad. They get dead."

"Yes, Dysig. But when he was brought to life again….did you speak to him?"

"I di'nt like him."

"So because you didn't't like him, you didn't't speak to him?" I asked.

"He was asking me."

"What did he ask, Dysig?" questioned Agnes.

"He said that Hawise was pretty."

"Well, she is, isn't she, Dysig?" Agnes replied, smiling. "You think so. I know you do. I do too."

Dysig showed a gap toothed and yellow smile, "I love Hawisy."

"We know you do," we said together and looked at each other.

Dysig looked from one to the other.

Agnes took up the questioning again.

"Dysig, what else did the glassman say to you."

"Nuffin."

"Was he with you a long time, Dysig?"

Dysig scuffed his boots in the rubbish of the smithy floor.

"We was in the woodbarn." Dysig roamed all over the village and folk just humoured him and got on with their jobs.

"Were you there a long time?"

"Marty made us go. He said we was getting in the way."

"While you were in the woodbarn, did the glazier ask you questions?" asked Agnes with infinite patience.

"I said I were good at snowballs."

"Did you... what made you say that?" said Agnes smiling.

"Well I am!" he pouted.

"We know you are good at them."

"He said he saw me with Hawisy the other day doing snowballs."

I turned to Agnes,

"But the glazier wasn't within the village when Dysig threw the apple into the window."

"No, but on a different day. The children have been out since," said Agnes.

I groaned.

"Of course! I told him that Dysig had thrown the original snowball which had broken the window. That is why he sought him out."

"Did he ask you about the snowball you threw through the window?"

The young man's face turned away.

"Dysig, we know it was you. I've told you I will not punish you. It was an accident. Couldn't be helped. And the glassman came to mend it, didn't' he?" I said.

The eyes swivelled but the face didn't't. "It were a 'eavy snowball."

"It was indeed, my lad," said Agnes. "Did the glassman want to know where you made the snowball?"

"He wanted to make one just as big."

"Did he? Do you think he could?"

We were shown the toothy smile again. "Nah!"

We all laughed. It was a ridiculous conversation but then so was every interaction with Dysig, it seemed.

"It was somewhere by the river wasn't it?"

"I said ...over there..." and he pointed out of the closed smithy door.

"By the two trees?"

Dysig nodded.

He said. " 'I'll go out an 'ave a look an' see if I can find some heavy snow.' "

"Did he indeed," I murmured.

"I di'nt like him."

"Why not?"

"He's a pagan. Is he dead?"

"Yes, he is dead. Really dead this time and he won't be coming back to life," I replied.

"Good."

"Dysig, that isn't kind," said Agnes horrified, crossing herself.

"So you told him where the snowball was found?" I asked.

Dysig nodded again.

"Then Marty come and told us to go. He di'n't like the glassman neither."

"Why didn't't you like him, Dysig?" asked Agnes again.

"He were unkind to Hawisy" and then he dropped suddenly to his knees and started to make patterns in the detritus of the smithy floor.

"Well, now we know for certain why he was out in the middle of the night. He was prodding the riverbank for some more buried treasure," I said to Agnes, as we made our way back to the hall.

"Oh sir. Do you really think there's more beautiful things locked up in that river bank?"

"I would not be at all surprised, Agnes," I said. "But hush about it all until I reveal what we find. I'll have a proper look when the snow has gone and we can dig. It's our secret now. Not a word to John..." I put up my hand. "No, not even John. The fewer people know, the better. Knowing might be the difference between life and death, Agnes."

*****

The work on the stables went on. I went every day to check on progress and watch the skilled work of my carpenters. There were it seemed, three kinds. Carpenters who did the large skilled work, joiners who did the rough work, and woodsmiths who did the smaller skilled jobs. Alfred was our most skilled man and it was he who made the furniture for the manor. I particularly loved to watch Alfred Woodsmith in his workshop making the pegs which would hold many of the beams together. The precision and speed with which these little items were made, by hand and eye, was nothing short of marvellous and I took a boxfull over to the stable to watch the carpenters knock them into the pre-drilled holes. Each fitted perfectly and was knocked into two pieces of wood, joining them so adeptly that it was not possible to get a breath of air between them.

The ground remained locked up. The seeds we had planted in the autumn did indeed die in the earth. It was far too cold for them to sprout.

We celebrated Plough Monday. This was traditionally the first Monday after Twelfth Night when the plough was taken from its shed and manhandled to the church at Durley village to receive the priest Crispin's blessing. The next day the lads of the demesne dragged it slowly, because of the snow, round the manor and all the houses of the village, cracking their whips and singing loudly to drive away the evil spirits. The plough was then returned to the barn and the oxen to their stalls in the end stable. We didn't't know when we might begin to plough the land for spring sowing.

My next task, I thought, was to talk to the villagers and try to find out if any of them had an idea why Glazer might have been murdered; if any might have had a reason to wish him ill. I called Walter Reeve to me early and asked him to accompany me around the village. Hal followed on behind. Peter Brenthall acted as my scribe for I was sure that I would not remember all that was said and I would want to compare notes later.

We began with the nearer buildings and moved out further into the village following the well-trodden paths which had been cleared of snow. The piled snow made it seem as if we had entered a land of white walls and I could see why Crispin had described it as living in a white room. In some places the piled snow was eight feet high.

I asked my questions. They were the same for each person, to begin with.

Did they speak to or know the glazier?

Did they know of any quarrel between a villager and Perkin Glazer?

When, if they did see him, did they last see him?

Where was this and to whom was he speaking?

I adjusted my questions according to the answers given but none had really interacted with the glazier. He had done his original job, firstly in the manor solar, my office and chapel and then the church. He had stayed within his own community camped on our village green and had used the room, we had given him again at Christmas, as his own office and he had slept there of a night. He had, perforce, spoken often to Henry my manor steward, Walter the reeve and he had exchanged some conversation with Swithun the priest last year, who, it was said, spoke rarely with him. Swithun had died in the autumn and Crispin was now custodian of the church of St. Mary.

Margaret Manton, Piers of Manton's wife (my long deceased steward and Henry's father), had spoken to the glazier often in the autumn of 1204, for her youngest son was to be apprenticed to be a glassman. She did not know of any reason why Perkin should be so singled out for violence. He was a quiet man; yes it was said he was fond of the ladies but she had heard of no opposition to him, save that which everyone knew about: his approach to the buxom Agnes and his slighting by Phillipa Woodsman.

I spoke to John. Did he feel aggrieved that Perkin Glazer had tried to entangle his wife in an affair?

He laughed. "Agnes made a fool of him and it's true sir: she can take care of herself can Agnes."

"Oh I know she can John, but still....it isn't pleasant to be so....handled..."

"Groped you mean, sir? A married woman."

"Humiliated."

John shook his head fiercely.

"The only one humiliated was the glazier, sir. Agnes dealt fairly with him, you can be sure."

"And you do not feel at all...."

"She did not cause me to be a cuckold, sir," he said sternly. "I'm proud of my Agnes for the way she dealt with him."

"I'm sure you are." And I left it there.

Johnathan Reeve reacted in much the same way.

His Phillipa had actually struck the glazier and as far as he was concerned, there was no need for him to do the same.

"You must know, sir, had he gone too far and forced Philly into...well you know what, sir, I might have called him out. But it would have been in the open, man to man and not a blow from behind on a dark night with a blunt weapon.

I would also have informed you, as my lord."

"Aye Johnathan I think you would. You have always been the most open of men... as is your father. God bless him."

I then tackled the poultry girl's father.

Our previous girl and her mother had both died in the autumn and I had had to quickly find someone willing to look to the manor's chickens, geese and ducks in their place.

Annot had come forward and had willingly taken on the role. Her father was a tied peasant on my land, who worked the manor fields three days a week and his own, three. Bardol was a simple man with few sophistications, and it was known he was over ready with his fists, when in his cups. His wife could attest to this and more than once I had fined him at the manor court, for his striking of her and their children. Walter kept an eye on the family. There had been no 'accidents' in a long while.

I approached their house and watched as Walter struck the door with his staff of office.

Bardol Wedgemoor came to the door with a blanket wrapped around his shoulders.

He stepped back.

"Wife," he said, "'Tis the lord."

His mousey wife who was called Winfled, scuttled into the room and curtsied to the floor.

"I'd like your daughter to be present please Bardol."

I waved my hand. "Please, Winfled, do get up."

"Which one?" said Bardol. Walter banged his staff on the earthen floor.

"Which one - m'lord?" he corrected.

I smiled at Walter. He really did not like this man.

"The eldest, Annot, please."

Bardol filled his lungs and yelled "Annot, get 'ere, now!" Walter and I grimaced.

From the upper loft came a rustling of straw and Annot's bare leg came down and felt for the rungs of the ladder.

"What you bin doing gel, that the lord has to come and speak to you?"

She did not answer but descended carefully with bare feet and then pulled down her skirt and curtsied.

"Annot I would like to speak to you privately a while. Will you just come outside with Walter, Hal and Peter a moment please?"

Bardol's jaw dropped. Hal stayed where he was in the doorway and Annot felt for a shawl lying on the table.

I gestured to her feet.

"Would you like to find some shoes?"

"Save you, m'lord… no, I'll be all right."

Hal waved her outside and he shut the door. We walked a little way out into the lane, away from flapping ears.

"Hal here tells me he saw you with the murdered glazier. Is this true, Annot?" The poor girl blanched as white as the snow surrounding her.

"I din't kill him sir...he was alive when…"

"I know. We are quite sure you didn't't kill him so have no worries on that score." She tucked the shawl around her in a tighter knot.

"Annot ,does your father know that you slept with the glazier?"

Her eyes grew round as plates.

"How did you know sir?"

"I saw you gel," said Hal.

"No sir...I mean..." She licked her lips. "How did you know that my father knew?"

"I didn't't. I have just asked you."

She looked puzzled but then answered

"Yes, sir….he knows. He sent me there."

I must have stared at her with incredulity written all over my face for the girl burst out, "It was all right, m'lord. He made sure I was all right and that the glazier paid me well. He was nice to me. No beating or... or... Dad made sure o' that."

I put up my hand to stop her.

"Are you telling me, Annot, that your father sent you to the glazier to sleep with him, for money? That it was his idea?"

"Yessir... he thinks..."

"I do not *care* what he thinks."

The girl shut up immediately and looked at her bare feet. I could see Hal just behind her, flexing his fists as if he would like to use them on such an uncaring father.

"He would not be angry that you had slept with a man... a man who was not your husband, for money?"

"No, sir."

"Was that the first time?"

"No, sir."

"I don't suppose you ever see any of this money?"

She smiled up at me at that. "Oh yes, sir, I get to keep some for myself. I am saving for...."

"WALTER!" I shouted,

My reeve came forward.

"Tell Henry to make sure the man appears at my next court. We shall fine the man. I will leave the amount to you both once you have ascertained how much has been made by this... pandering and questioned the man Bardol."

I took a deep breath. "It will stop, Annot. There will be no more sleeping with men for money." I looked behind me.

Peter was staring at the girl open mouthed. He cleared his throat and poised his chalk to write on the slate.

"No Peter. No record. Rub out what you have written here."

He nodded and spit on his hand to erase the words he had begun.

"No one... all of you are forbidden to speak about this. Ever, do you hear?"

They all nodded.

I sighed, "And Annot, if your father lifts a finger to you because you are defying him, tell him it is the lord's wish. That if he disobeys me, I will have him flogged. You are all, all of you, my property, and I will have you obey me. Is that clear?"

The girl nodded.

"Do you want to keep me for yourself sir...is that it?"

I closed my eyes. "Certainly not."

Hal took off his cap and ruffled his hair. I took off down the slope at a furious pace, back to the manor.

"Well," I heard him say. "Here's a squirmy pile 'o eels."

Walter Reeve opened the door and went in, dragging the girl with him.

I heard a slap and a cry.

Walter, Henry and I would fine Bardol further for that.

*****

I was still smarting from the conversation with Annot as I entered the hall.

Lydia was on her knees in front of the peddler, Martyn, who was still wrapped in his blanket and sitting on his chair. His pack was open on the floor and she was searching through the many good things stowed away in it.

"Ah my lord Aumary," she said rising and brushing the rushes from her knees. "Martyn says he is feeling a little better today and so he has allowed us to open his pack. I have a need for some new needles and some pins for my hair and I promised Hawise a new ribbon for her hair, though there is a lovely comb here which would hold back her copper locks beautifully."

I smiled at them both. I was beginning to cool down after my anger at the Wedgemoor family. I sat on the end of the bench by the peddler.

"I'm glad to find you are feeling better. We all of us feared for your life, but we have a very good physic in Johannes and are lucky he could come so quickly."

"I owe him my life," said Martyn, still with a slight drawl. "Please, you must take anything you desire from my pack to pay for my stay here. It's the least I can do."

"Nonsense," I said. "We need nothing in return. Lydia will pay you fully for those things she needs and takes...won't you Lydia?"

"Indeed I will." She looked past me. "Is that one of your men trying to catch your attention, Aumary?"

I swivelled on my seat. Martyn Carpenter had come into the hall and was hovering around in the doorway.

"Martyn..come up...what can I do for you?"

The shy wood worker came into the hall gripping his coif and grinding it to his chest with restless hands. He nodded to Lydia.

"M'Lady Belvoir. M'lord." Then he stood stock still and stared at the peddler.

Martyn peddler smiled up at the man with his lop sided smile. The bandage over his ear pushed up his hair into a loop and he smoothed it down with a shaky hand. I must say he looked a little odd.

"What can I do for you, Martyn?" I asked.

Before Martyn Carpenter could open his mouth the peddler had scooped up his hand, hat and all and shaken it.

"Martyn, Martyn...we share a name, Martyn, and I must thank you for jogging my memory for I am sure if you hadn't been here, I would not have recalled my name. Thank you..."

The woodworker snatched back his hand as if bitten and looked horrified. "I...I..I'm glad you are mending and that you have remembered. I did nothing.... it's a common enough name." He backed away a little. "Sir, you told us to tell you when we had reached the stage where the thatch can go on. We've reached that point now, sir."

"Thank you, Martyn. I'll be along to look shortly."

Martyn backed away and was out of the door in a trice.

Lydia shook her head. "There's a man who feels out of place in the hall."

"Martyn has always worried about coming up here. He's a very shy man. He is a few months older than I am. I've known him all my life. He has always been a person of few words, one who hangs at the back. We were all very surprised when he married Maggie. We didn't't think he'd have the bone to woo her, he was so tongue tied," I chuckled.

"Maybe she wooed him?" said Lydia mischievously.

I chuckled again. "Aye...she was quite a woman was Maggie. Martyn was devastated when she died."

There was a little silence as we all thought, no doubt, about our mortality, and then Lydia knelt once more to look at the peddler's wares.

I turned my attention to Martyn Summersete again. "Now that you are feeling a little more like talking, Martyn..." I said, "I want to ask you a few more questions about your life. Have you recalled anything further? I know Hal has been talking to you to try to encourage the memories to return."

Martyn shrugged one shoulder.

"I know that I was born in Dunster."

"Ah yes.... I know the place."

"I know that I wander the south of England going from town to town, farm to farm, village to village but beyond that there are only little glimpses of things."

"Lydia looked up. "Do you think you have a family, Martyn?"

"I can't recall it, my lady."

"Perhaps we should do the same as my lord Belvoir did, and see if a girl's name means anything to you. Go through them I mean."

The peddler suppressed a laugh. "Well, we might be on dangerous ground there, m'lady, for we might come up with a string of names...why, I might have a girl in every town."

Lydia chortled. "Ah yes...that's what they say about peddlers, isn't it?"

"You shouldn't believe everything you hear, my lady" said Martyn, putting his hand to his heart and showing us, at last, a sense of humour. Yes, I thought, he is recovering. Good.

"No, I don't think you are at all like the glazier....." She stopped and quickly looked up at me, afraid she had let out a secret.

" 'Tis no secret Lydia, that Glazer was a little too fond of the fair sex; almost to the point of obsession, I'd say," I confirmed.

Martyn's face creased up.

"I heard he was found dead. Is this right?"

"Aye, hit over the head in exactly the same way as you were."

Martyn crossed himself. "God take him to his bosom. I was obviously lucky."

"Have you any idea why you should have been singled out for the same sort of attack Martyn?"

"No indeed, sir. I have quarrelled with no man, as far as I can remember. I do think, now I can reflect on it, that I have never been here before, to Durley."

"Aye... we would remember you," I said. "Hal most certainly would."

"So, there is none here I have offended," he smiled. "If I was ever the offending sort, which I don't *think* I am."

I patted him on the shoulder. "It does not strike me that it would be one of your major faults, peddler," I said.

"Pardon Paul? Oh no. Peddler's have to be jovial and accommodating don't they? They must encounter all sorts of folk as they rove around. I can't see them being very good at their job if they are miserable and offensive. They wouldn't, as you say, make any money!"

I leaned forward, an earnest expression forming on my face. "Martyn, I have a feeling that you were not the intended target at all."

"Not the target, sir?"

"No. I think you were mistaken for the glazier." I saw the peddler shrink into his chair as my words registered. He was rendered speechless for a moment.

"Someone hit you from behind after watching you crossing the road. You were found just where the Durley Road branches off from the main road to

Salisbury."

"So Hal told me."

Lydia looked up quickly. "Am I right my lord...? Both Martyn and the glazier were wearing a brown cloak with a green hood. They both have dark blond hair."

"Aye... in a snow flurry one could easily be mistaken for the other. Glazer decided to bring his cart. He told me he might have had his horse. He might even have come on foot for it it's not a mile to the glass-maker's camp from here. You were on foot. Our malefactor took you, I think, for our glazier on foot and struck out."

"So later on he realised his mistake and began to plot again to murder the glassman?" asked Lydia.

"Three attempts. The fourth succeeded."

"God save me," said the Peddler, shock registering on his face.

"He most certainly did, Martyn," I said.

*****

Moments later, I was in the stables looking at the newly completed roof timbers.

"Are we sure that the two outer ends are sturdy, Martyn?" I asked my master carpenter "After all there's no point in rebuilding this part to have another collapse in the same way."

Martyn walked to the far end of the newly built room and leapt up, catching hold of the cross beam. He swung himself up in one lithe movement to balance on the beam.

"Steady as a rock, sir. You remember we did some repairs to the end bits when we tied the walls in to the new gatehouse at that end and the store room at the other."

"The middle bit was the oldest, wasn't it? The two end buildings have stone walls."

"That's right, sir." He jumped down, as supple as a cat, and dusted off his hands.

" 'Twas no wonder the middle bit gave us trouble." I looked up at the leaden sky through the rib-work of rafters. "I shall need to call the thatcher from Marlborough to come and do the work. We have no one within the nearer forest, do we, who can thatch it for us?"

"Well...I've no doubt I could do it, if we could get the right straw, sir."

"Do we have some laid by?"

"No sir, but I can find out where I can get some."

I thought for a moment. "How long would that take, Martyn?"

"Depends on the weather, sir."

"Perhaps we'll ask Master Thatcher anyway."

I saw Martyn's face fall.

"Marlborough it is then. I'll go with John and Johannes to the town and put our name on Master Thatcher's list. It may be some time, even if this weather breaks, before he can come and work on it. Can we cover it all in the meantime?"

"Aye sir. We can."

In truth I wanted to go to Marlborough to speak to Gilbert Cordwainer and to tell him his apprentice was safe and well. I needed to confirm that Harry had indeed been at home when his father had been killed. I needed too, to speak to the Widow Glazer. It was only right and proper.

John, Johannes and I set off next day in bright sunshine. It was however, bitterly cold and the sun did little to warm us or the woods through which we trudged.

We saw no one as we struggled through snowdrifts and climbed snow covered fallen trees. Once, we startled a deer and it bounded off with a wagging white tail and a frightened eye. We passed a badger's sett with its tell tale pile of new earth mixed with snow. Well, at least they had been able to dig through the drifts. We reached the path known as Long Harry and struggled down the incline, crossing over the now frozen little brook which usually trickled through the bottom. The three of us, slipping and sliding, trudged up the other side. Eventually we made the open field at the top of Forest Hill and at about midday we descended into the town.

The townsfolk had cleared the bridge and we slipped across the river and onto Barn Street.

Few people were about just here but as we entered the High Street, more folk began to cluster; talking to their neighbours, exchanging foodstuffs, buying what they could from the shops. Some were still clearing the snow from paths, those not so frequently walked. The main parts of the town had been cleared and shovelled snow was piled high everywhere as it was in Durley. Johannes headed for home; we would meet him there later.

John and I walked on through the town. At the entry to the priory we stopped and I scratched on the cordwainer's door shouting that it was Aumary Belvoir.

The door bolt was drawn and the jovial face of Gilbert the Cordwainer came into view through the crack. He had a chain across the opening and I heard it draw through the bar as it clanked to the floor.

"Come in... come in... Wife! Grace! It's the Lord Belvoir... we shall need some sustenance here." We entered the warm fug of the shop. Gilbert had a small fire lit and had been sitting alone by it, working at his last. I could see it through the open workshop door. He drew us in and asked us to ascend the stairs. We went before him and found ourselves in the warm and comfortable parlour above the shop.

Grace curtsied and took one each of their girls under her arms, pushing them into the back room: Cassie who was seven and Gytha who was about fourteen. "Come, let's heat some ale for your father's guests," she said.

Gilbert bid us sit at the table. He nodded to John, who nodded back.

"Christ's Bones..."

"Don't swear Gilbert!" came Grace's words from the back room, through the open door.

I smiled. Gilbert lowered his voice,

"God's teeth, sir, I'm right glad to see you. What a journey you must have had."

"Good John here brought me by the back roads which, whilst not easy, were less congested with snow."

"I'm glad you came, sir."

"Firstly, Gilbert, Harry made it to Durley and is now in sanctuary in the church safe and sound and watched over by Hal and Father Crispin."

"Praise be to God!" said Gilbert and drew a small pewter cross on a chain from the top of his shirt and kissed it.

"I told him to flee to you. I knew you'd take him in. Thank you, m'lord. 'Twas such a worry... why, I haven't been able to sleep a wink since the poor boy left."

Grace returned with a tray of steaming mugs.

"Gilbert Cordwainer, you snored all night last night," she said as she placed the mugs in front of us. " 'Twas me that didn't't sleep what with worrying about Harry and listening to your snores!"

"Humph."

"Gilbert, we need to know....Harry. Is it possible he may have made his way to Durley to kill his father? He tells me he was here with you and your family, all the twelve days of Christmas."

Gilbert swelled his massive chest. His wife and he exchanged glances.

"My Lord Belvoir. If the lad had as much as been a hearbeat out of the house the wife and I would've known. He could not have done the deed. No sir. Besides, he is a good lad. He's not the murdering kind."

"He did go out," said Grace. Gilbert turned and glared at his wife.

"Aye...he went out for an hour or so, to help dig the snow from the road here in front of us. He was in view the whole time. The neighbours will vouch for him."

"The same neighbours who pursued him out of town baying for his blood?"

I asked.

"Aye well....'twas a misunderstanding."

"He went out," said Grace again with emphasis, "out the back...a couple of times with the girls to play in the snow. But that is all. We swear it. Oh, and he went to fetch bread for us on that first day when we had so much snow and I couldn't get to the baker's to fetch the loaves we had there to bake, but that is really all."

Gilbert nodded once and sternly. " 'Tis God's own truth. Harry would stay with us all the time of Christmas m'lord. He's no where else to go. My other apprentice was off with his father but Harry...Harry is family," and he glared at me as if I was going to argue with him about it.

"Right," I said. "So we need all this in writing and for you to sign it. It will help greatly in his case. Can you do that Gil?"

Gilbert nodded.

"I need also to ask about the time that his father, came to the shop."

Again there was a glance between husband and wife.

"What happened?"

Grace got up from her seat and went to shut the door to the back room.

"The man was an insufferable debaucher," she said.

"Aye we have had experience of his ways at Durley. Did he try his luck with you, Grace?"

"No, not me. He tried it with the girl who comes to help me with the linen - she lives up at Chantry Lane. She has no father and so Gilbert here took it upon himself to act as a father to her and tell him to back off."

"I'm a church reeve at the new church of St. Peter now m'lord and I take my duties very seriously. The girl was at church and the glazier was pestering her. It was clear she didn't't welcome his advances," said Gilbert proudly.

"How old is this girl Gilbert?"

"Eleven or so I s'pose."

"So the glazier took umbrage at this and came bad mouthing you? These are Harry's words."

"No, not as such. You know there had never been much love lost between me and the glassman. 'Twouldn't take much for him to swear at me. You remember we were at odds over Harry's indenture..."

"Yes, I know about that."

"Perkin Glazer was angry that Harry chose to come and work here for me and not stay and learn the trade of a glazier with him. After all, he said, that was what sons are got for."

I shook my head. "Harry's been with you how long now, Gilbert?"

"Four years."

"You can know a man well in four years of living with him."

"Cheek by jowl, sir...cheek by jowl."

"He is a fine young man and no mistake.The Almighty knows how such a damaged man has managed to breed such a good son," said Grace.

"I wonder it too, Grace," I said.

"I took the lad without the usual monies changing hands," said Gilbert. "I wouldn't ask that..."

"So Glazer came to the shop and...."

"Well, Harry was here a working in the workroom. You know that adjoins the shop sir. Just a flimsy door between."

"I do, Gilbert."

"In comes Glazer as bright as brass. Now, I weren't here. I was out the back in the yard and Grace had taken Gytha to her grandma's on Elcot Lane. 'Twas just Harry and little Cassie."

I nodded. I could picture the scene.

"Cassie was in the shop a playin' on the floor with some scraps. She often does that. Fancies herself a cordwainer she does," Gilbert chuckled. "Makes little shoes for her dolls. She's quite clever really..."

"Gilbert."

Gilbert cleared his throat. "Yes, my sweet." He shifted uncomfortably on his seat.

"Now I only have Harry's word for this.....but the lad's not a liar."

"No, I've always found him honest."

"He said that Perkin Glazer picked up little Cass and sat her on his knee."

"I've seen him...at the village. He seems to like children. He's a bit like Hal. Hal loves children, especially Hawise....."

The look on Gilbert's face made me stop. "No sir...'t'aint nothing like ol' Hal of Potterne No, sir. Hal loves children like a father loves his chits."

I smiled but there was an uncomfortable feeling settling in my guts.

"Go on Gilbert."

He licked his lips and once more there was an exchange of glances between the cordwainer and his wife.

Grace looked to the closed door.

Voices were lowered even further.

"Harry said that, he put down the work he was attending to and looked through a hole in the door. Well, it's true there is a hole in that door. I've been meaning to get it fixed but well... time and...."

"And what happened Gilbert?" I asked. Gilbert passed his hand over his forehead.

"Harry said his father was a sitting on the stool a cooing at little Cassie and he had his hand up her skirts a fondling her...well...you know what's sir."

There was a small silence.

"Then Cassie started to wail that she wanted her father and that he was to let her go and she didn't't like it....and Harry came barging out the door, snatched up my little chit and pushed his father from the stool."

I swallowed. "Harry said he blacked his eye for him."

"Aye, that were just when I arrived."

"You were here when that happened?"

"Aye. Glazer got up and started to call his son names. It's what he usually does."

"Yes, I've heard them arguing," I nodded.

" 'Corse I didn't't know then what he'd been doing. 'Twas only later that Harry told me."

"Did you get anything from Cassie?"

"God's Teeth no, sir, I wouldn't be mentioning the deed to my littl'un. No, I couldn't."

"She has probably forgotten the whole thing by now sir," said Grace. "And by Harry's tale it was over and done with quickly. Best let sleeping dogs lie."

"I told the glazier to leave the shop. He carried on and on and started to push me. I'm a big man as you know, m'lord, but it takes a while to get my dander up. Had I known then what this was all about, I think I might have taken one of my awls and stuck the man in the cods with it."

"I wouldn't have blamed you, Gilbert."

"Harry hit him, blacking his eye and then he picked him up by his collar and threw him in the street. He's a big powerful lad, is Harry."

"Don't tell me....several of the neighbours saw it happen?"

"Well, yes sir. Couldn't be helped. A corse, Glazer goes amongst them telling them what a foul son his Harry is. How he attacked his father with no provocation. No word about me being there as a witness, naturally."

I nodded. "The story hangs together, Gilbert."

"Aye, sir."

I scrubbed my face with my hand. I looked over to John. He had said not a word through the whole conversation but now he said, "Did you go, Gilbert, to the authorities and report this..... this....affront to your wee lass?"

Gilbert looked to his wife again. "We don't have any proof, John. Harry won't be believed because he is in bad odour with his father already. They'll just think that he is being wicked and telling tales. Besides, she's just a young lass, as I say. She has no rights over something like this. The age of consent is twelve, yes, but.... It's not a crime sir. It's not nice but it isn't a crime is it?"

"It's a crime in my books," I murmured.

"And anyway," added the cordwainer, "who do we report it to, eh?"

*****

John and I were silent as we threaded our way between the piles of snow on the High Street, to Johannes' house.

"You go on in John. I'm going to the glazier's house to present my condolences to the widow. I know I shouldn't say it but really, I am silently full of respect for the man who brained him!"

John smiled. "Yes, sir....you aren't alone there. Where there was one young lass, there will be others."

"No one wants to talk about things like this though. It would be very hard to find evidence that sticks."

"Like the cordwainer says...it's not a crime. Murder is a crime."

"Yes, indeed but, if what Harry saw was a true account, I am suddenly much less interested in finding out who rid the world of this monster."

I realised I had used the word with which Harry had described his father. I vowed to talk to the glazier's son as soon as I returned to Durley.

*****

I found the glass-man's house easily enough. Two adjoining houses had been knocked together to make one. The place where the door for the second house should have been, was built over and plastered. You could see the outline and the beams above and below.

It was a large three storeyed town house opposite the High Cross, with a slate roof and naturally, glass in every window. I rapped on the front door, so I could be heard. It was a large house.

I waited while footsteps approached and then disappeared into the house again. I looked around behind me. Johannes and the glazier had been near neighbours. I could see the front of the doctor's house from here and the passage way at the side which led to Johannes' stable and to the church yard.

When I turned around again, the door was open and a small woman, nay more of a girl, looked at me curiously.

"Might I have words with your mistress please? My name is Sir Aumary Belvoir. My man has already been to speak to her."

She nodded and turned and I followed.

The parlour we entered was on the first floor. A huge glass window made up of several panes in many wooden frames, with stone between, fitted together perfectly, practically filled the wall which overlooked the High Street. I marvelled at it and was drawn to look out.

The door closed behind me and I turned. The small woman was still in the room and none other.

"Your mistress if you please?" I said. I had expected the glazier's widow to be a mature woman.

"I am Mistress Glazer. Juliana Glazer."

I could see now that the dress of this girl in front of me was not that of a servant. She wore a dark blue bliaut that would not have disgraced my own wife and which was fit for mourning, and the white embroidery around her chemise, just visible under her tunic, was worked on the finest white linen.

I nodded a bow, "Forgive me, madam. I had expected..."

"An older woman. Yes, I know." She gestured for me to sit and reached for a little bell. Its tinkling sound echoed around the wooden floored room.

"I had expected a servant to answer the door." I smiled, not allowing her the satisfaction of being right.

"I was downstairs. It was no hardship to answer it," she said.

"Madam," I nodded again, "I am Aumary Belvoir. Lord of Durley and Warden of Savernake Forest. My woodsman came the other day to give you our condolences and to inform you of the death of your husband. Sadly the message had to be given to a servant for you were from home."

"I received the message." Her face was stony. Juliana Glazer sat and arranged her skirts around her and nodded to a bench for me to be seated.

"I am very sorry to have to inform you that he was murdered whilst staying on my manor."

"Your servant told me he was dead. He didn't't tell me the manner of it."

"No. It was not John's place to inform you of the details. That is why I am here. I am also here in my capacity as the new constable of north Wiltshire. It has become my role to look into all suspicious deaths in and around Marlborough." I took my warrant from my scrip and handed it to her.

She did not take it but smiled, "It will mean nothing to me, my Lord Belvoir, for I cannot read."

A servant scratched on the door and brought in a tray with two finely made pottery cups and a matching flagon of wine.

The door was closing on her when Juliana said,

"So he was murdered? Now why does that not surprise me?"

I raised my eyebrow.

"Come, come, my lord Belvoir, you must know of his reputation. Surely even in Durley you must have heard of his exploits?"

"Sadly madam we have."

"Some poor husband has at last got the better of him, then?"

"This may be the case, Mistress Glazer, though we are still looking into all the circumstances surrounding his death."

She took up a cup and then put it down as if deciding speech was better than drink.

"How was his death accomplished?"

"He was struck over the head with a heavy and blunt weapon. The wound cracked his skull and he died instantly. The town surgeon, your near neighbour I believe, and my good friend Johannes of Salerno, who was with us for the Christmas festivities, looked into his wound and pronounced him dead." No need to tell her he had been found frozen in the river.

I took up my cup and sipped. The wine was awful, which was often the case with the wealthy. The Glazers were newly risen in the social strata of the town and had not yet quite learned the finer points of gracious living. I scrutinised her face as she looked out of her huge window.

"He felt no pain," I said.

There was not a morsel of grief in the widow's face, not an ounce of regret for a husband cruelly cut down. She was completely blank.

"Perhaps you can help me gather information about Perkin's life? It will aid me to build up a picture of him and it might lead us to a clue to why he was murdered."

"I am sure you know as much as I do, sir," she said. "He was born in Kent where the glass kilns are a large industry. He achieved his mastership and came to this part of the world."

"This was nigh on twenty years ago?"

"It was."

"He married a girl from Marlborough and settled in her house - this house. He travelled far and wide, leaving my dear neighbour Margery to run the house and bring up Harold, their only son."

"I know Harry well."

She looked at me then with a slightly different emphasis, "Then you will know he is away from home and apprenticed to Gilbert the cordwainer in the town. He has been there for..."

"Four years. Gilbert is one of my oldest friends," I said.

Juliana blinked as if this could not be the truth. I was a landed knight and Gilbert a shoemaker But she recovered quickly.

"I was married young, to the elderly pewterer who lived in the house next door. It was only a matter of months before, sadly, he died and I was left alone. Margery was good to me. Very good. She was the best friend anyone could wish for."

"Then she too died."

"Yes, m'lord. I nursed her a whole year and then she was taken to God and lies in the churchyard yonder. Perkin was often away in other counties."

"Two large houses, adjoining. Two neighbours recently widowed. I can see the sense in a union between you at last."

"Indeed m'lord. Many could not. Sadly."

"Harry for one."

"Harry could not settle here with me as his mother."

"No, so he told me."

I could see that she was itching to ask me what Harry had told me but etiquette did not allow it.

"I can see that it would be difficult for him. You were, after all, scarcely much older than he."

She ignored such an impudent statement and ploughed on.

"Perkin wished to set up some kilns locally and petitioned the King to allow him access to the trees in West Baily and the river here in the town, but you will know all this, my lord Belvoir. It is your forest."

"I am also deputy warden of the castle, madam. Our paths crossed when Perkin was working there on the chapel."

She inclined her head.

"Forgive me madam. You do not seem at all perturbed that your husband of four years lies dead in my manor, murdered by an unknown assailant."

Juliana gave a little, rather nervous laugh.

"My Lord Belvoir, Perkin and I married because we had adjoining buildings, as you say, and were conscious of the business possibilities which might be achieved if we joined together. Oh yes, at first I was flattered by the attentions of such a handsome and urbane man. My marriage to my first husband had been unconsummated. I was nothing but a trophy wife to Master Pewterer, to be paraded on his arm around town. This naturally was before I realised the true nature of my second husband's....shall we call it.....obsession."

A cry from the street outside the window penetrated our conversation and the solemnity of the moment was lost. I felt the instant when I might ask what form this obsession took had dissipated. However, Juliana was not willing to let it go so easily.

"You must understand my lord, Perkin was, for some inexplicable reason, irresistible to women as much as they were to him. He could no more give them up than he could cease breathing. Not even for marriage." She realised what she had said and looked down at the floor. "Our marriage has been an arrangement of distance for a long while now. He leaves me alone mostly, in the house and stays with his men and his work. And his women. I have my freedoms here in the town. He would be coming back for Christmas and such holidays but..... we met fewer and fewer times. The house is big enough for the two of us to live separately. No, there is no grief at his passing, sir."

"He was a wealthy man here in the town," I said, casting my eye around the room with its painted cloths and floor rugs, silver and pewter displayed on a potboard, oaken furniture of the latest design.

She inclined her head.

"I have married two wealthy men sir. I live well."

"Who inherits the house and the glass business?"

"I do sir. Be assured, I will continue to run it as my husband did, though I cannot be the master glazier he was. I will have another master glazier at my beck and call."

She is already bedding the second in command at the kilns, perhaps, I said to myself. Priming him as husband number three.

I stood. "Then, I will take up no more of your valuable time madam."

She nodded and rang the bell again.

"I'll have his body brought to you as soon as the roads are passable by cart, Mistress Glazer." I strode to the door. A manservant opened it for me. I recall thinking, a man servant. Hmm. More than the cost of a girl. He was a good looking lad too and well made, as my father always said.

I turned back to Juliana.

"Forgive me lady," I said, though frankly I didn't't care whether she would or no.

"How old were you when you married the glazier?"

Her chin jutted at that, "I was thirteen.....almost fourteen, sir."

"Thank you. Good day."

*****

"Ah... I see you have met our grieving widow. Mistress Frosty Face," said Johannes as I erupted through his kitchen door a moment later.

"Warmth... give me warmth. I'm frozen through. Not only was it bloody cold in her parlour but, as you say, she herself is as cold as a church stone."

"Haha, come on, stand in front of the fire and warm yourself. Little Agnes will fetch you some warmed wine."

"As long as it's better than the swill I was offered there. Christ's Bones, Johannes, it's as barren as a death house there and the wine was - well, it was as bad as one of your worst potions."

John Brenthall who was leaning on the wall by the fire-place and warming himself on the stones, laughed out loud.

"*That* bad eh?"

Little Agnes, the mute dwarf who looked after Johannes and was his housekeeper spluttered on her own pot and laughed silently till we had to slap her back, to fetch her to breathe again.

Eventually she handed me a cup of warmed wine. I sipped. "AH...nectar!"

"So, what did you find out, sir?" asked John.

I considered the question carefully. "I would say that the Widow Glazer has just thrown her cap in the ring."

Johannes looked at Agnes, Agnes looked at John. John looked at me.

"I would say that an aggrieved husband or an outraged father are not the only people wanting the glazier dead."

"Aw sir..." said John, "you can't believe that Mistress Glazer murdered her own husband?"

"Not with her own fair paw, John. No, she won't have struck the blow herself, but she has some big lads working for her, both at the glazier's camp and in the house."

"The business is hers now?" asked Johannes.

"Aye, it is."

"And she has the money to pay for silence?"

"She does, lots of it. And if I am not much mistaken she is lining up husband number three. This time, this one will be of her own choosing and will be as biddable as a lamb and as pliant as...as...."

"Molten glass?" hazarded John.

"How very apt, John," I said.

*****

Johannes and Agnes gave us dinner. There was just one more thing to do in town.

"Do you want to stay here in the warm, John? I'm off to Master Thatcher's on the Ropery, to ask him if he might come and thatch the stables."

John drained his cup. "No sir...we can be straightways off home after that. No need to return to the main town."

This made sense, for afternoons were short in January and it would be wise to be at home before it became too dark. I shrugged on my outer clothing again and we tramped down the hill, through the Marsh and made for the end building on the Ropery, close to Wagon Yard, where Master Thatcher had his works.

He was away but his wife took my instruction and said that Master Thatcher would consider my request and do the work as soon as he could get to Durley.

As we left the yard, Master Thatcher came in, his arm around his son's shoulders.

"Ah! M'lord Belvoir...it's a pleasure to see you, sir" He nodded to John.

"And you too Giles. How goes it?"

"Bloody snow! Pardon m'lord."

"Aye....our stable roof collapsed with the weight of it on the old thatch. I came to avail myself of your services. Might you come and redo it for us?"

"Aye I will. As soon as I can get a cart to Durley and as soon as I finish with the Widow Partridge's brand new barn out on the London Road. Oh and Wat Flowers' outhouse. Then of course, I have the new houses out on the Manton Road to do....six of them."

"Martyn Carpenter has finished the spars," I said. "He and his men have made a good job. They are very skilled. Of course they could thatch it too....so, if you are too busy, I'll get Martyn to get some straw and..."

"Martyn's a fine master carpenter m'lord. None better, but a master thatcher he ain't...."

"No, I suppose he isn't but he does know how to thatch a stable. After all... it isn't as if it has to be....."

Giles Thatcher disengaged his arm from the shoulder of his son.

"No, no sir...we'll come just as soon as the snow lets us. No need to get another to do the job"

"Good man!"

"Did you know that Martyn's father was a thatcher then?"

"It was in the back of my mind."

"Aye....out Pewsey way. Corse that were thirty odd years ago."

"Martyn was born in Durley. I've known him nearly all my life," I said.

"Aye he was. His Da married a Durley girl."

"I think I just remember her," I said, looking up at the sky and thinking, we must be off or we shall be walking in the dark. "Nice woman. Plump with reddish hair and a bosom to sink into...as a child you understand. I remember her at the manor. When I was very small I think she was my nurse for a while."

"Aye I think she mighta' bin. Pity about her."

"Oh?"

I had walked on past the thatcher and his son and was already exiting the yard.

"She were found dead at the foot of the manor stairs. Broke her neck she did. In your father's time. So sad. Missed her footing. Slippery stairs. Weather like this as I recall, m'lord."

I was very glad I had managed to make the hall steps safer.

"Corse there was a lot of talk and the like."

"About what?"

"Well," the thatcher scratched his bald pate. I got the impression he had been drinking a little. "They didn't get on. You could often hear 'em shoutin' at each other. If they weren't shoutin' it was dead silence and long faces."

"Oh dear. It must be awful to be tied for life to someone you loathe."

Well...she fell down the steps and a 'corse there was talk as there always is when one like that goes in a way like that."

"Gossip?"

"Didn't help when Martyn's Da married again within a three month."

"Nothing could be proven?"

"Nah," said the thatcher.

I called a thank you and goodbye to the thatcher and John and I made off up the Salisbury Road.

Chapter Six

"Hal... do you remember Martyn Carpenter's mother?" I asked when we had divested ourselves of our outer clothing and had gone to warm by the hall fire.

Hal looked up. "Aye I do...she were a lovely woman."

"What happened to her?"

"Well... no one really knows, see, 'cos no one saw it 'appen."

"Well... what do people *say* happened?"

"She fell down the 'all steps and broke 'er neck. It were yer father found 'er. You were about two or three I think."

"That's very sad" I said "I met Giles Thatcher today and he told me about it. I just about remember her. She was my nurse for a while when I was very small wasn't she, before and after my mother died?"

"She was. She divided her time between Pewsey and 'ere. Walked all the way here and all the way back."

"Hmmm."

"Seven miles away it were. Corse... sometimes Martyn's father would give 'er a lift in 'is cart to the Durley turn, if 'e were thatching a round about and 'e'd pick her up on the return journey."

"A good arrangement."

"You'd 'ear them arguin' fer miles around. Sitting in the cart. Either that or it'd be awful quiet and you just knew they'd bin at logger'eds."

"Oh dear."

"Nope... they didn't't get on... at all. Reckon as that's why Martyn is an only boy."

"No further children after him then?"

"Nope... they couldn't stand the sight of each other let alone a cohabitin'. By all accounts they jus' managed to stay sane in the same 'ouse together."

"Till death do them part eh?"

"Aye..that's a why I aint never bin married, sir."

"Ah but Hal...if you had, you could have had children. You would I'm sure, have loved that."

"Well..yes I suppose I woulda' but I can be a father to loads of 'em an giv'em back when I've 'ad enough," he said.

I laughed at that.

Then, his words set me thinking.

I called in on Harry in the church and told him the good news. As far as I was concerned he was no longer a suspect for murder, if he ever really had been. The Cordwainer family had vouched for him. Crispin clapped him on the back and pronounced him free.

The worry fell away from his face in a trice.

"Come, come up to the hall and warm yourself. You no longer have to stay in sanctuary, you have an alibi."

The warm ale was being heated as we entered the hall. I heard the sizzle of the hot poker, Hal was thrusting into the jug. Several people, who knew about the fugitive in the church, listened as I explained that Harry was no longer in danger. They cheered as Harry walked to the table and clapped the young man on the back.

Hal handed him the first hot mug.

"Welcome back, m'lad."

Harry tucked into a large bowl of stew and some bread. Hawise came down from the solar and shared a pink marchpane pig with him though, I don't really think it was to his taste. He ate it out of gratitude, I think.

With Hawise whisked off to bed, the hall began to grow quiet as folk bedded down after supper. I saw Martyn peddler walking with the aid of a stick, cut for him by Hal, lower himself onto his palliasse, in the corner under the chapel stairs.

He was beginning to totter around the hall of a day now and was not so immobile.

"I called Hal to me as a witness and we sat by the fire talking quietly.

"I called today at your old home, Harry."

His head came up.

"To inform your stepmother of the fact that your father had been murdered."

"What did she say...I suppose she blamed me?"

"Not at all. Not a word was said against you. The only thing she said was that you could not accept her as your mother."

"Well, that's true and no word of a lie."

"She seemed not at all concerned that your father had been killed. In fact I would say she was relieved."

"She's a cold fish and no mistake but yes...no doubt. Latterly they didn't't get on. Oh it was all lovey-dovey at first when she was catching him and he was wooing her. When they were first married, they couldn't keep their hands from each other. It cooled as soon as my father grew bored and went off to pastures new."

"You know she inherits the house and the glass business. Your father made it over to her and not you."

"Good riddance. I don't want any of it," he spat

"Harry you are young. You may regret that you didn't't contest the will and..."

"No! I want nothing from that man. Gilbert Cordwainer is my father now and I am more happy with him than with any wealthy father with a large house and a chest full of gold."

I nodded.

"So be it."

"I wanted to ask you about Juliana, Harry."

His eyes narrowed but he said, "Ask away. I will do my best to answer."

"She told me today, much as you did a while ago, when we spoke, that your father was an adulterer."

"Pah! That's rich! Coming from her."

"You told me last autumn that they had been 'carrying on' even before your mother died?"

"That's right. At first they pretended not to like each other and then when the old pewterer, her first husband died, they started to be a couple, if you see what I mean, sir. I can't be honestly sure they weren't 'carrying on' as you say, before he died."

"Right... and you told me too, that you had seen them..."

"Kissing and cuddling and groping each other...yes."

"And your mother too, saw this?"

"She did for she came in white faced and ready to cry and said to me, 'Harry, I don't know what I have done to deserve such pain.' I thought she meant the pain of her illness, sir. Then she pointed to the house next door and told me she had seen her friend, one who had been looking after her in her illness, in bed with my father. I have never seen her look so ill. Except on the day she died."

"Harry...think carefully, Juliana Pewtersmith, as was... could she have planned to marry your father for his wealth and then, after a while, when all the furore had died down and your father started his antics again, could she have planned to kill him?"

Harry's hands fell from the table top as he sat back on the bench, shocked.

"God's Cods... beggin' your pardon, sir."

I saw Hal smile as this was one of his favourite oaths and with the Lady Lydia now in the manor, it was one he must use carefully and sparingly.

Harry blinked a few times as he replayed, I think, the question I had asked him, and the perfidy of the two of them, Glazer and Juliana in his mind's eye.

"Well...?"

"It simply had not occurred to me, sir."

"No. Nor me until I met the cold hearted woman today."

"I'm not saying I like the woman...no I don't."

"Well, there, you're in good company I think," said Hal looking at me and grinning.

"But kill my father? Why should she? She had the will and when I left, she got him to sign away everything to her."

"He made no other will?"

"Not as far as I know. He was determined to be rid of me, as a son."

"You ask why? So that she could be rid of him and marry another. One perhaps who was more to her liking. Younger, fitter, more compliant, more loyal?"

Harry stared at the floor. "I 'spect she had plenty of time to get rid of him at home, if she wished...."

"Ah but would you, if you were going to kill someone, do it on your own doorstep?"

Harry was shaking and shaking his head. "No sir.... I don't think she would. Like I say, I detest the woman, but murder? No, m'lord, I don't think she would."

"Could she, do you think engage another to do it for her?"

Harry's eyes widened further. "There's talk in the town that she is ..erm.. rather over fond of one of her servants sir....but it's just gossip. I haven't any evidence of it."

"Tall, tanned, small beard, fair hair, nose like a beak, blue eyes?"

" Aye....that's Arnaud...why?"

"I met him today that's all," I said.

Harry stared into space. "No sir, I can't say as she would. I think she was fairly comfortable as she was. The house, the freedom, no, I don't think she's a murderess."

I sighed and sat back. "It was just something we had to explore Harry."

"Aye sir.... I understand why."

"Now we must come to why your father was so at odds with you?"

"That's easy to answer, because I hold him responsible for the death of my mother and make no mistake. I told him so. You heard me, when I was at Durley Manor, delivering your shoes. When da and I met last autumn."

"That and you knew about his womanising?"

"I despised the man, sir. He'd chase anything in a skirt, he would."

"Anything.....at all?"

Harry shifted on his bench.

"You know how old your stepmother was when she first bedded your father don't you Harry?"

"Aye I do."

"She was a widow at thirteen."

"She's the same age as I am now."

"How old was your mother Harry when she died?"

"About forty we think" he said reluctantly.

"And her neighbour and friend was....?"

"Fourteen nearly fifteen."

"More like a daughter to your mother wasn't she really. Such a large age gap. Your mother could have been her mother couldn't she?" Harry nodded.

"Do we think this was why your mother was so upset? That she thought of Juliana as a daughter and it was the fact that she was so young and your father bedded her with Juliana's consent?"

"Aye."

"So...now tell me Harry. Who else did your father bed? Who else did he molest?"

"You'll have to ask the goodwives of the town....I don't know all the women he tupped."

"No Harry...I'm not talking about *women*. Women over twelve."

Hal's face grew red with anger and he preened his forked beard.

"Well... I'll be.... Here's another disgustin' squirmy pile 'o eels."

Harry's face took on a determined look.

"I don't know. I disliked the man but I'll not speak any more ill of him than I have spoken already."

I sat back and stared at the defiant young man. "He's dead Harry. It can do him no harm...save his reputation and that is well tarnished as it is."

Harry shook his head.

"It might help us to find his murderer."

Harry caught his lip with his teeth and I could see him pressing his nails into his hand, making a fist. Hal saw it too and took his hand and opened it out, "Lad....answer the lord. If you know, tell it."

Harry remained silent.

"Gilbert Cordwainer has told us Harry," I said at last.

Harry's eyes bored into mine.

He let out an enormous sigh.

"He molested little Cassie till she cried and I saw him. That's why I blacked his eye. I've seen him before. Little Lady Petronilla....The Lord Snap's litt'un, Nilla, the Lady Hawise's friend. He molested her too."

"That's the real reason isn't it...why you were at odds with him? You knew that he was over fond of little girls. Really little girls. Not fourteen year olds, though they would do wouldn't they...for a while?"

"Aye...Yes...." and he burst into tears.

*****

A week went by with no more snow though the cold seeped into us and the ground remained iron hard. The river refused to thaw but our well, in the centre of the village became useable once more.

The roads became more passable with each day, as folk trod them or rutted them with their carts. On the seventh day, we took the glazier's cart back to Marlborough with the body of the glassman stowed away in the back, wrapped in a tarred sheet.

I mounted Harry on one of my docile horses and we rode together into town, following the cart. At first he was worried that he would not be well received but I said that I was going to the castle to issue a strong warning to anyone who approached him with ill intent. This would be sent around the whole town. He was utterly exonerated.

I would stay with Johannes for a while and Harry and I together would go to the glassman's funeral. This would show everyone that the local law and the accused but innocent were as one, on the issue.

The River Kennet, as we crossed it on the London Road bridge, was frozen solid, like our own little river and some children were skating up and down on it, their gleeful cries rising up the banks to echo around the piled snow all along the edge of the main road and up the river bank. I wondered what would happen to the lower reaches of the town, once the thaw came. Many of the houses had just been rebuilt or mended from the storm of autumn 1203. I looked back over my shoulder. Some of them had been built in exactly the same place of course; they might be at risk, come the thaw.

I thought about our little stream. Would it too burst its banks? Only one or two homes would be at risk in Durley village.

We rode slowly down the High. No one raised their eyes to see that it was Harry Glazer atop a horse. They were not used to seeing him thus, so they simply did not see him. We stopped at the cordwainer's shop and fastened our horses to the pegs set in the priory wall. John would deliver the cart to the back of the glazier's house and would meet us here when he had finished. He would ride Harry's horse home. Harry entered the shoemaker's first.

There was a squeal as Gytha, the elder child, threw herself at the young man and hugged him close.

"Oh Harry we have been so worried about you."

I saw as Gilbert turned to the doorway and a huge grin split his face.

"Welcome back my lad... welcome home." He too embraced him.

Grace came through from the back room and she too joined in and little Cassie, not to be denied, wrapped herself around Harry's legs jumping up and down and jiggling everyone, till they all fell about laughing.

I too was smiling. This was a very much loved young man. If not by his own flesh and blood then by his adopted family. We were all ushered up stairs and wine and honey cakes were brought out. Gilbert was all for locking the front door but I said that John was following and there was no real need now.

"I have written you your declaration and signed it, sir" said Gilbert, as he rose to fetch a piece of parchment from a table in the corner of the room. "Will this do?"

I read it through.

"Aye it will. Do you think any of the neighbours would affix their mark? You say that they too saw Harry when he went to scrape the snow and surely the baker will attest to Harry being in the town to fetch the bread baked by him?"

"I'll go now sir....and see if I can get them to do it. I know that Mistress Philbert will get her husband to do it too. She is very grateful to the lad for the help he gave her that day."

He was gone and Grace and I were left alone to talk about town matters and the consecrating of the newly finished church at the western end of the High Street, St. Peter's.

Harry whispered in a corner with the girls. It's like a boy with his two sisters, I said to myself.

Grace saw me looking at them and smiled.

"Aye, they are very close. Gytha and Harry are... well, inseparable."

" 'Tis young love is it?"

"Early days, but if my Gytha, when the time comes for her to marry, chooses - and yes she will choose, her father and I did and we are happy together, if she chooses Harry, I for one will not be unhappy. At all." She grinned. "Then there will be a son to follow in his father's footsteps and inherit the business after all." Her face glowed.

I smiled broadly. I could think of no better event. We heard voices and John and Gilbert returned to the house together. Their boots clomped up the wooden stairs.

"All done, sir." I managed to get three signatures. One Master Philbert. Master Fletschier was there and I asked him. We got him too... and Master Baker."

Now all I needed to do was take this, have it read out in the castle bailey and at the town cross and deposit it in the castle records. I would make sure it was cried through the town too. We stood to leave and Harry came and grasped my hand.

"How sir can I ever repay you for your kindness?"

"By being a good son to Gilbert and as fine a cordwainer as you can manage my lad." I said. He smiled a wide smile.

"Aye sir... that I shall."

"I will see you at the funeral tomorrow. It will be good that we are seen together. Call for me at Dr. Johannes'."

*****

Master Glazer had paid in advance to go into the floor of the church. Not for him the cold and frozen churchyard outside St. Mary's. He did not have to wait for the thaw to be interred.

The priest, father Torold, intoned the rites for the dead and the coffin of the glazier was lifted by ropes and lowered into the hole made in the flagstoned church floor. The flagstone was replaced. We all then stayed for a mass to be said for the man's soul. Mistress Glazer, her head completely covered by a dark veil, turned quickly and was out of the door with unseemly haste. Only a few were invited back to the house; we certainly did not merit that amount of hospitality. Harry returned with Gilbert, to his home and John and I went to Johannes' to fortify ourselves for the journey home.

Johannes had not been at the glazier's funeral. Though they were almost neighbours, he had not felt the need to say a farewell to the man. We came in by the back door and met Johannes grinding something powerful smelling in the kitchen, with a pestle and mortar.

I sniffed. "Can I smell anise?"

"Ginger root, sovereign against chilblains. Amongst other herbs. Ash bark..." he held some up to me "and hawthorn berries."

"Ah. You have become your own 'pothecary now have you?"

"Only simple things. Master Gallipot still does the difficult stuff."

"Chilblains must be the bane of folk this weather," I said

"Aye ... that and chapped and cracked skin."

"What do you recommend for that?"

Johannes put down his grinding equipment.

"Beeswax, calendula and bergamot." He leaned back on two legs of his stool reached behind him and fetched a small grey pot from the pot board surface. He took out the little wax stopper and gave the pot to me.

I sniffed tentatively but a pleasant aroma wafted up to my nostrils.

"Oh that's quite nice." I gave it back and Johannes replaced the stopper. He heated it quickly over the flame of the candle burning on the table top and it sealed in the mixture.

" ...and a bit of ginger just to get the circulation going. Can you give this to Martyn Carpenter for his poor working hands when you get back. " 'Tis paid for...." I was reaching for my purse.

"He has it every year. He swears it is the only thing which helps his hands to heal when he is working in the cold."

"Aye I will."

*****

I was tired that night but I couldn't sleep.

Lydia slept deeply beside me on our soft feather mattress but I tossed and turned, semi awake, dreaming, if dreaming is the right word for it, of overflowing rivers with little enamel apples bobbing along on the surface. At one point, the glazier appeared and sailed along on the current, trying to pick them up. I tried to follow but he disappeared and in his place, Johannes rose from the river bed holding his pot of salve and said to me "Give this to Harry, it's sovereign against chilblains." I reached to take the pot but toppled into the river. I came to spluttering and coughing and realised at last, that I was not drowning. Lydia grumbled and turned over beside me.

It was then I heard the terrible scream.

I sat bolt upright and listened again. Lydia stirred. "What?" she said.

There was a mumbling in the far room and I realised the noise had come from there.

I threw on my shirt and padded to the door calling before entering.

Felice was sitting on the bed with Hawise with her arms around her crooning, petting her and stroking her hair.

Hawise saw me, disengaged herself and scrambled to the end of the bed. "Dada!"

I took her up in my grip and she wound her little arms around my neck.

"Thank you Felice. Go back to your own bed."

Hawise's nurse pulled a voluminous blanket tighter around her and nodded.

I went back into our room and closed the door with my bare foot.

"What was the matter sweeting?"

"The man... the man...."

"Which man. There was no man there."

I heard Hal scratching at the solar door asking, quietly if we were all right.

"Aye, only Hawise riding the night mare. Thank you Hal. Go back to your rest."

Hawise was shaking and beginning to be chilled. Lydia sleepily held out her hands for the child and took her from me settling her between us."

" 'Twas just a dream Hawise."

Hawise burrowed against Lydia's chest. I lay down, pulled the covers over us and snuggled next to my daughter.

I began to feel quite uncomfortable and turned my head to ask,

"Hawise...which man was this, in your room? Did you know him?"

On the verge of sleep Hawise gurgled and then said clearly.

"Twas the dead one. The horrible one."

I shivered. Lydia turned to look at me.

"'Twas nothing but a dream as you said, Aumary. She will be all right in the morning."

There was silence as Hawise snuggled further into our bed and her breathing steadied.

"Here," I stroked her copper curls, "you sleep tight next to your ma and me and forget all about nasty men."

I saw Lydia smile by the light of our night candle.

"What's that for?"

"I am not Hawise's true mother. I am no one's mother."

"No...not yet," I said, "But we are trying to remedy that, are we not?"

Lydia smiled again.

"But it is very nice to hear you say, that I am her mama for I do feel like it," and she too closed her eyes again.

*****

Four days later the thatcher's cart rumbled under the gatehouse and stopped in the courtyard. Master Giles clambered down and one of his journeymen, went to the back to begin taking out the tools of their trade. Another cart laden with straw drew up beside it and his son jumped down into the ice of the cleared yard. He landed heavily and slipped grabbing hold of his father, nearly toppling them both.

"IDIOT BOY!" shouted the thatcher. "Have a care. You might have broken a leg. What use would you be to me then?"

He was still grumbling as he met me on the steps of the manor; his coif in his hand he tugged his sparse forelock. "M'lord. Bloody boy is as clumsy as a clerk!"

"You have a poor opinion of clerks then, Master Giles?" I said descending.

"I have when they lose your money, my Lord Belvoir!"

I chuckled.

"Had a bad experience have we?"

"So bad...I have decided to learn to carve tally sticks meself. Add up and take away and do me own accounts!"

He patted his jerkin and looked around at the newly rebuilt stables.

"Well, we'd better be at it. Can we stow our goods, sir?"

"Certainly." I called for Henry and he came running, picking his way carefully over the ice.

"Show Master Thatcher where he can put his things, Henry." The two youngsters followed Henry to the store shed on the east wall.

"Let me show you what we have." Giles and I went into the skeletal stable and we looked up.

"Well built. Yes. Just the right amount of woodwork. Course, we don't need too much woodwork for thatch. Lighter than yer slates and stones there..." and he pointed back over his shoulder to the hall roof. "Yep... just the right amount."

"Much as you would expect of Martyn, Giles. A job well done," I said. "How long do you think it will take?"

"Tssoooooo. It takes as long as it takes, m'lord. But it shouldn't be too long a job. After all, it's not a fancy roof is it?"

"No indeed. You'll stay? No need to go back and forth to Marlborough every day is there?"

The thatcher beamed at me. "Young Fred will take the big cart home but.... Oh aye..we'll stay."

I heard his son say under his breath as he passed me, meant I am sure for my ears only.

"Come here instead of Widow Partridge, din't we? Why? Cause he likes yer ale, m'lord. Finest in the area, he says. As long as he can drink your ale, he'll come."

We fixed on a price and on how much ale the Thatchers would receive per day. I would feed them too, from the common pot.

I turned away just as Crispin came in through the main gate. He hailed me.

"Aumary, Johannes told me that you are to do some research into your little apple, maybe at the priory. Might I come with you when you do and be a reader for you?"

"Naturally, Crispin. I would have asked you but I have had a lot on my plate these past days."

"Aye, how is the boy?"

"Returned to the bosom of his adoptive family, a job he loves, a master he respects and a town who will soon forget."

"And Master Glazer returned to God."

"Either that Crispin, or lowered into Hell."

Crispin's face grew grave. "Why should you say that?"

"Come up to the hall and I will tell you."

Crispin was as white as one of our linen sheets when I had finished telling him my tale.

"And so, there may be several young girls in the town, who have had experience of Perkin Glazer. Experience they should not have had at their tender age," I said.

Crispin looked down at his feet. "Maybe not just in the town either Aumary."

He looked at me sadly. "Lydia had cause to talk to me earlier."

"Oh?"

"You know how children often play at confession. They watch the adults coming to me and copy."

"I have seen them laughing with each other and making things up, getting more and more ridiculous by the moment," I said.

"Hawise was apparently worried that she 'hated' the glazier. She wanted to confess that 'sin' as she saw it. She hated him, he died. In a child's mind, especially the mind of one who had found the body, which she did, the two are connected. She loathed him. He died."

"She feels responsible?"

"In a way perhaps."

"Last night she had a bad dream in which he featured. I thought it was perhaps because she had found him."

"Lydia told me about it and in the light of what you have just told me, we must examine the real reason why Hawise might have disliked him so much."

My cheeks grew hot as I searched my memory for words which came back to me clearly.

Dysig telling me that the glass man had told him that Hawise was pretty. He had said that he didn't't like the glazier and when quizzed had given us the reason. "He was unkind to Hawise." I saw the glassman, in my mind's eye, watching her carefully at Twelfth Night. I saw him pursuing my daughter around the outer wall of the manor when she was out walking her pony; dismissing Cedric, to be alone with her. I remember Glazer coming into the courtyard his arm draped over her shoulder. I had taken little notice of how she had angrily shrugged him off. I was too pleased to see her alive in one piece and not crushed by the falling stable roof, to see her expression. I saw the look she gave a him a little while later when he came into the hall, though. I remembered the glares and the whispered words, "I don't like him." And last night she described him as 'horrible. Had Hawise too fallen prey to the glazier's lusts?

Crispin obviously thought so.

"Thank you Crispin. I will have a word with Lydia and then I shall speak to Hawise."

I trembled with suppressed anger. If the man were not already dead and buried, at that moment, had he been before me, I might have killed him with my bare hands.

I took the solar steps two at a time. Lydia was sitting by the fire with a pile of flattened wheat stalks in her lap. She was cleverly plaiting them into shapes. People, animals, crosses. I had seen her at this occupation before and smiled as I came up to touch her gently on the shoulder.

"Hawise?"

"Is sleeping." She nodded to the open door where Hawise, her copper hair thrown out around her on the pillow, was snoring gently.

"I'll leave her be."

However, I hunkered down beside my wife, poked the fire with a stick and told her what Crispin and I had suspected. I felt nauseous.

Lydia took my hand. There were tears in her eyes.

"Yes... it's as we suspected. And now you tell us there are other wee lassies he may have been assaulting...."

"Why didn't't you tell me."

"The word of a five year old girl child Aumary, who is a bright and intelligent girl, who has an imagination as fierce as a unicorn... we had no proof; now you tell me that Harry knew his father's ways and that he actually caught him. And it isn't a crime is it?"

"We begin to take it all much more seriously don't we?"

"I think we must," said my wife.

"Harry said that Glazer also assaulted Petronilla Snap."

"Richard, the Lord of Snap's little girl?"

"The same."

"He is in town for the season, I think, at his town house," said Lydia. "Perhaps a word with him?"

"I'll go tomorrow," I said. " I'll take Crispin."

*****

Sir Richard was a wealthy wool man who had been granted the Lordship of Snap some years earlier by Richard Plantagenet. He had a fine house just outside Ogbourne on the downs and another in the town just off the High Street. We scratched on the door and was let in by a servant who led us deep into the house; one which had been extended and built up in the past few years. Richard was in his office. He shook our shoulders warmly, dismissed his staff and bid us sit. Whilst pouring wine for us he said,

"Aumary it is good to see you. It's been far too long. Had the snow not prevented it, we should have seen you at our Twelfth Night celebrations."

"Joy come to you and yours Richard, though Father Crispin and I are here to talk over a delicate matter, I'm sorry to say, which may not bring you much joy."

Richard's handsome brow creased. He was a man of moderate height, well made, with tight curly brown hair worn short and a small mustache and beard clipped close as was mine. He had been the catch of the town when a bachelor and like me, had come into his estate as a very young man scarce twenty. He and his wife, Edgissa had been childhood sweethearts, much as my Cecily and I had been. In the last thirteen years they had produced four boys and one girl all living. Petronilla, known to us all as Nilla, was the youngest at 6 years of age.

I sipped my wine.

"How is Edgissa... thriving I hope?" I knew that they were expecting another child in March.

"Aye she is. The Lady Lydia?"

"As happy as an otter in water."

Richard laughed.

"Happy indeed. What is this delicate matter then?"

Between us Crispin and I sensitively questioned Richard about Petronilla. I told him what Harry Glazer had seen and that he was willing to swear an oath that his father was the sort of man who obtained sexual pleasure from fondling young girls.

"I knew that he was a womaniser of course, but didn't't realise that it wasn't just women, young women he preyed on."

"He travelled around a great deal, who knows where else his victims lie," said Crispin

"We had him here for a very short while glazing the solar windows. You started a trend hereabouts, did you know Aumary?"

I smiled. "Nilla hasn't said anything to Edgissa or her nurse?"

"Nothing I have heard. Don't tell me that poor Hawise fell foul of the bastard too?"

"Like you I'm unsure as yet. Sadly, it was Hawise found his body in the river. Hal and I were close on the event, mind you. Still, she is in shock and dreams about it. I can't be sure what has happened to her just yet."

I explained to Richard that I had been given the power of investigation into all serious criminal acts in this area, by the King.

"As much as my inclination is to let the glazier burn in Hell, as he is no doubt doing and forget all about the murder, I cannot. I am duty bound to investigate and find the one who sent him there." I told the story of the attempts on the glassman's life and finally, I laid bare the facts about his death. I did not mention the little apple though."

"I will give you any aid I can. You have only to ask."

Suddenly he looked up, his eyes wide.

"You do not suspect that I knew about his predilection and slew him in revenge for an affront on my little Nilla? I will swear, Father Crispin, on our family bible should it be necessary...."

"No, Richard. We have no such suspicions," I interjected.

"I did not do it, though I cannot say I might not have been sorely tempted."

"I think there is many a father who would say the same," said Crispin.

"He did not meet his end at my hand. I swear, I did not kill him Aumary."

"No. But someone did Richard and were determined enough to try four times before they succeeded."

*****

It was a stone's throw from the Snap household to the priory so Crispin and I took the little enamel apple to the library, a very small room off the main passageway into the religious house of canons. Rolls of parchment littered the walls on shelves. Piles of parchment were strewn all over the tables dotted about. Books were piled haphazardly on tables. This religious house had no confirmed librarian. The monks took it in turns to look after the place. As a result it was chaotic.

However Johannes managed to find anything useful here I could not fathom. Crispin and I looked at each other, daunted by the task ahead.

A small monk looked in through the door, he nodded at us and then left. We decided to wade through the parchment on the tables first.

An long while later, there was nothing at all remotely like the symbols which we had discovered around our apple.

However we had learned quite a good deal about animal husbandry, the diseases of root vegetables and how to cure canker of the ear in lop eared dogs.

"This is useless," said Crispin. "It will take us all week."

"Do you think it might help if we could find what looks like the earliest roll on the shelf. It might be the one written in the oldest language."

"I don't think that would be the most useful one, my son," came a voice.

I had met Brother Petrus before. Once twenty years ago when he had boxed my ears for scrumping apples from the priory orchard and again, last year when Johannes and I had been researching into the use of poison, in the priory.

"It is all about marvels and miracles which are attested to, in the year 844 A.D. here in Wiltshire, or Wessex as it was then. It would not help you. Unless you wish to learn about pigs with two heads and rains of stones, in Bradford. In Latin."

Brother Petrus, who was the priory infirmarian, was calm and unruffled. He came into the room, freed his arms from the confines of his habit and reached up to a shelf a little above eye level.

Both Crispin and I were surprised into silence.

"Forgive me...nosiness is my overweening sin, I will confess. I shall pay penance for listening at the door to your conversation, later no doubt.

"You know what we have here and what we seek brother?" asked Crispin, the first to recover.

"I could not help it. I did hear you. I heard you speak of a glass apple? Do you have it? May I look at it?"

I took the apple, which I had wrapped in a piece of linen, from my scrip."

"Oh, I can see why it would excite the imagination. It is a beautiful thing."

Like us, he turned the apple round and round to follow the inscription. "Now I understand. You are looking for a way to translate the words written here."

"Are they words Brother Petrus?" I asked

"Hmm I think they must be. I have seen this one before....the one that looks like a little cross." He pointed with a yellowing nail.

We both drew our heads closer to the apple to look.

"I think it is called Geofu... the gift. It's a symbol of love and goodness."

I drew back. "How do you know this brother?" I said. "Do you read these words?"

Brother Petrus smiled and shook his head. "No, but, up in the North of England, where I was born, this symbol, with others, is often to be found on stones which are set near graves. The land was overrun by the Danes, hundreds of years ago and this was their language, my lord."

"Not our southern Saxons then?"

"The languages are related, they have the same roots."

"So, where do you suggest we begin?"

He had a little calfskin bound book in his hand. He proffered it to me.

"This is the only book we have which contains some runes."

I took it gently.

"It's a book of poems...well...we think they are poems, for there are some we can read, in Latin and the writer has set them out in lines."

"We, brother Petrus?"

He tucked his hands into his sleeves once more. "Brother Paul, he is our porter and myself. I think between us we have read every book in our little library."

"My brother Robert told me that the Saxons were fond of riddles, is this truly so?"

Brother Petrus chuckled. "They were obsessed with them! With that and rhyming and repetition of the same sounds."

"Each of these symbols..." I said pointing to the apple now in Crispin's hand, "is a word?"

"No... no not a word, a symbol for something but they are also sounds. For example Geofu would be a 'g' I believe, though this is a guess you understand. I think it has other names too but that they are all beginning with a 'g'."

"Thank you Brother you have been most helpful," said Crispin.

"Might I borrow the book Brother Petrus? This is going to take us far longer than we have time for here."

The little monk looked sternly at me. "In the absence of our prior, who is in London and has been delayed by the snow...it would of course, be his permission we would seek for you to remove it, I am the next in command and I will say, yes."

"Thank y...."

"But my Lord Belvoir guard it well. It is one of a kind. We cannot replace it."

"We will take great care of it, sir," I said.

"Wait!"

Brother Petrus scrabbled under the table and came up with a small cloth bag made of some thick material. At the top was a drawstring.

"Take this to protect it. We always carry our books in book bags. Much safer."

He opened the drawstring and I dropped it in. The top was tied and he handed it back. "I must make a note that you have taken it. No doubt I will forget in time." He smiled to himself, "a remarkably short time."

*****

We returned to Durley with our treasure and our find. I took the book bag from my saddlebag, vowing to lock it in my safe chest in the office.

Richard Marshall hobbled out of the nearer stable on a crutch, which had been fashioned from a piece of wood. Hal had made it for him, as a T shape, he said and Agnes had padded it so that it might fit snugly and comfortably under his arm pit. He could get around by raising his foot from the ground and hopping.

"No, Rich....get one of the younger men to deal with Bayard, you cannot do it all one handed."

"It's amazing, m'lord, what one can do, if one is pressed," he said but he handed Bayard's reins to Cedric who had come out from the side of the gate-house.

"How is the foot?"

"Sore sir, but mending. Thank you for asking, though I wondered what I bothered to get this for, saving the glazier, if it was just for him to be struck down again and shoved into the river."

I smiled. "Your effort will not go unrecorded Rich," I said. "It was a selfless act. Your reward will be in Heaven."

" 'Twas the act of a moment without thought," said Richard. "One which we just do and then wonder about afterwards."

"Aye we have all done that, at some time," I answered.

I stowed the little book in its bag in my cotte.

I was turning to walk to the hall, when there was an almighty shout, a flurry of thatch and a body came tumbling from the roof of the middle stable. It flew off the edge of the eaves and landed with an 'oomph' of expelled air, almost in front of me."

"Arghhh!"

Master Thatcher's head appeared above the roof ridge.

I looked down at my feet.

There, writhing on the flagstones, clutching his elbow and screeching profanities was Giles' son, Brice.

"God's bloody wounds lad...what da ya wanna go and do that for?" shouted his father, from his ladder at the eaves."

Brice grimaced, "Jesus in Hell! I didn't't - he pushed me," was the answer.

I knelt beside the boy and looked up again. Martyn Carpenter was clinging to one of the roof beams of the stable. He too had missed his footing it seems and had toppled backwards from the thatch which had already been laid. Luck was with him for he had managed to grasp the purlin as he descended. He'd smashed through the lathes laid horizontally between the rafters and was dangling. He had a gash on his head and was obviously dizzy for his grip had begun to slip.

"Boys!" I cried, "Get underneath him." Two of the stable lads ran into the bay and stood under him and Cedric thrust Bayard's reins at me and bolted to join them. The three of them caught Martyn just as he fell.

Chapter Seven

"Let me look, Brice," I said. Brice was reluctant to let go. He gripped his left elbow as if it would fall off if he took away his hand.

His father came bustling up. "Brice, lad... speak to me. You daft plonkett. You clumsy clotpole! "

"Argh... Chr... bloody... grrrr." Sweat was standing out on Brice's forehead despite the cold and his breaths were taken in short, sharp snaps, exhaling in puffs of white freezing fog.

"Elbow....bloody hurts. Gonna - be - sick."

"Deep breaths," I said then shouted, "Ben, fetch John."

Brice was trying to take deep breaths but in between was moaning in pain.

"What 'appened?" asked the master thatcher, all bluster gone.

"That we shall find out later, Giles," I answered.

Brice's eyes rolled in his head and he fainted. Naturally he let go of the elbow.

I lifted it and carefully pushed up the sleeve. It was broken, of that there was no doubt. A small bone was protruding from the skin.

"Bill, run to the Lady Lydia and tell her what has happened. Ask her to prepare to receive us in the hall and tell her it's an elbow wound where the skin and bone is broken."

"Yessir!"

Brice spluttered awake. I reached for some clean snow which was piled up against the stable wall and packed the wound with it holding it there until the warmth of my hand melted it.

Again I reached for a snowball. Johannes had told me that extreme cold prevented wounds such as this from hurting too much and from swelling and bruising beyond all help.

"God's wounds sir...it hurts."

"Aye it will lad, but we shall have it fixed... never fear."

"Gonna...be ...sick...sir..."

"No, you're not" I said with authority.

Brice leaned forward and was sick on my knee.

Eventually John came and the two of us carried Brice up the steps and into the hall. His father followed silently. Lydia was there with a couple of the kitchen women and we laid the lad out flat on the hall table. My wife looked at the elbow and shook her head.

"It's broken beyond my power to mend, Aumary," she said. "Best I leave it."

Behind us, Martyn was being helped into the hall by Hal and Bill. Lydia turned.

"This one I may be able to help." Hal laid Martyn on the largest and widest bench and Lydia went to him. I called for Bill.

"Go to the town and fetch the doctor. Explain what has happened. A fracture of the elbow - broken and a bone sticking through the skin. And a head wound, banged on a beam. Got that?"

"Aye, sir."

"Take the fastest horse Bill. Speed is essential."

"Aye sir...you mean... Fitzroy sir?"

"Aye Bill...I do."

The lad beamed.

Fitzroy was a racing stallion. He had been given to me by a grateful father, ostensibly as a bribe to keep quiet, in the autumn of the previous year. Johannes and I had solved the mystery of the murder of his only son in a locked room in Marlborough castle and this was my reward. Fitzroy had once belonged to his dead son, Guy de Saye. Fitz was a temperamental beast but he was very swift over short distances and Bill was used to riding him out on the downs.

"Ride him carefully Bill, but swiftly. Stick to the road and to the rutted paths. No risks taken, all right?"

"Yes, m'lord."

"I am as concerned for your safety as I am my horse, lad," I said. "We have enough injuries on the manor as it is!"

Bill hopped off, glee oozing from every pore. It was one thing to ride Fitzroy on the lonely downs with only your fellow grooms for company, another to ride into town and deliver a message with many townsfolk possibly looking on.

I saw Martyn Summersete looking askance from his bed in the corner by the stairs. He smiled at me, but I could tell the scene before him was one he would rather not see. His own injury was too raw. I saw him finger his head wound, no bandage now but a pink scar in a new fuzz of hair where Johannes had shaved the curls away to get at the wound.

Lydia came up to me and took my elbow. "Martyn is all right Aumary, he is just stunned. He'll have an egg on his head soon enough. I'm off to get some arnica from the still room."

I nodded.

"I've sent Bill for Johannes, for..." and I nodded at Brice who was tossing his head in pain on the table.

"Some burntwine perhaps?" she asked.

"Aye....quite a bit of it," I said.

"I'll fetch a jug."

I went to the solar to strip off my soiled tunic and hose and was back in a trice and I headed for Martyn who was sitting up now.

"Martyn. How is it?"

He looked up groggily. "All right now sir, thank you." He pointed his nose at Brice, lying on the table, "Will the young lad be all right, sir?"

I turned to look at Brice. Hal was dribbling water into his mouth and Janet was pressing a cold cloth to his head. Someone had had the foresight to put a pile of rags under the broken elbow. Giles was at his other side, holding onto his good hand.

"I don't know. I've sent for Dr. Johannes. We'll see what he says." I sat down beside him and handed him a pot of ale.

"Tell me what happened."

Martyn took a swig. "Difficult to say, sir. I was up there helping. You know that I can thatch and that I learned from my father, m'lord?"

"So I heard."

"Well, we were both, me and Brice, by the wall, the western wall, when the lad lost his balance as he stood up. He slid down. I tried to grab him but he just knocked me backwards and I fell through the open roof, between the timbers and lathes, grazing my head on a purlin, I suppose. I managed to hang on. The lad didn't't."

I nodded. "Go home and get some rest. It's nearly supper time. There'll be no more thatching today."

"Aye, sir."

"If you feel ill, get Janet next door to come for us. Dr. Johannes will be here soon."

"Thank you, sir."

*****

Johannes, it seemed, had flown through the forest, keeping pace with my racehorse Fitz and his groom. We had plied poor Brice with burntwine and he was in and out of consciousness or rather a drunken stupor all that late afternoon.

When Johannes arrived, Brice was sleeping the sleep of a drunkard, which, I thought, was a very good thing considering what Johannes had to do to him to save his arm. By the evening hours, the bone had been pushed back into place; luckily it did not seem to be shattered; and a splint had been fixed to the lad's arm. Pain killing remedies had been shoved down his throat. We fetched a hurdle from the hay barn and he was manhandled into one of the guest rooms, where his father and Johannes would watch him by turns overnight.

I took Giles aside before the shaking man went down with his son. I handed him half a jug of burntwine. "Here, you will need it. It's very good for shock."

He smiled weakly looking down at the jug. " 'T'aint yer good ale then, sir?"

"Did you see what happened, Giles?" I asked.

"No. I had my back to them. I was just packing the coatwork with me legget when I heard Brice cry. I was a little further along than them, see, but at the edge on me ladder at the other side."

"Did they have a ladder too?"

"Martyn was yealming... that's the bundles of straw sir, yealming the straw for Brice to lay...well, that's what I think they were doin'. That's done on the ground and Martyn had come up on the roof to hand him the next lot... I think. There was a ladder but neither of 'em, were on it."

"Hmmm" I touched his arm. "Off you go. And don't worry. There's no hurry to the roof, is there? Take whatever time you need."

It was a long while before Brice surfaced. I was up late in my office with the door open, reading, or trying to read, by the light of a candle, the little book we had borrowed from the priory. The outer door had not yet been locked as Hal was in the hall talking quietly to Martyn Summersete and hadn't yet been out on his rounds.

Johannes scratched on the doorpost. I looked up, stretched and rubbed my eyes.

"What news, Johannes?"

"It's too early to tell if there is serious damage but he is young and the bone was not difficult to re-set. He may not quite have the complete use of his elbow again but enough to manage, I think."

"...and Giles?"

"Weary now, but talking about going off to Marlborough tomorrow to bring back the lad's mother."

"Well, he may heal at a quicker rate if nursed by his own kin."

"Aye...it often happens that way."

"Has he spoken about what happened?" I asked.

"A little. I think you should come and hear what he has to say. He's very groggy, you understand, and his mind may not be as clear as it could be."

I reached for my winter cloak from its peg behind the door, blew out the candle and put the little book in my scrip.

Johannes went before me as I paused to lock the office door, then by the light of a flare I had taken from the wall sconce by the buttery, I descended the steps and crossed the courtyard. Wyot the gatekeeper, conscientious as ever, poked his head from the gatehouse and nodded.

"All right Wyot. I don't think that Hal will be long now. Good night."

"Good night, m'lord."

The night was very crisp and the stars were as bright as candle flames, thousands upon thousands of them; all was silent save the barking of a dog somewhere beyond the walls in the village. My feet crunched on the frozen courtyard.

I entered the warmth of one of the little rooms built up against the eastern wall. I had asked for a brazier to be wheeled into it, for Johannes said that warmth was one thing the patient needed.

Giles tried to rise but I waved him down, "No, stay put, Giles," I said.

I threw my cloak on the only available stool and hunkered down by the bed.

"Brice, it's the Lord Belvoir. Do you hear me?"

It was as Johannes had said. Brice was awake but very sleepy and groggy.

"Do I still have me arm, sir?" was the first thing he said, weakly. I patted his good hand.

"That you do and are likely to be able to keep it. Thank Dr. Johannes for that."

The candles placed around the room flickered in a draught and I saw a smile creep over his mouth.

"I do," he said in almost a whisper.

"Can you tell me what happened before you fell off the roof Brice?" I asked.

" 'Tis all a bit hazy." His voice was very slurred.

"Do your best then. We shall speak further when you feel better but I would like to know what you think now, for memory can play tricks on us the further away from the event we get."

Brice licked his lips. "I was just about to put the last yealm onto the roof by the stone wall, where it abuts the next stable - you know, the first one. I was kneeling down on the straw. I saw Martyn come up beside me to hand me the next bundle. He had been doing the making up of the bundles, to save time, see..."

I nodded.

"Next I knew, he had thrown himself in front of me. I couldn't see what I was doing and so I goes to stand up...and...."

"You lost your balance."

"Oh no, sir. I could'ave leaned against the stone gable and been quite safe."

"So...?"

I saw Brice's eyes flick to his father on his other side. They closed a moment and then he said, "He pushed me backwards."

I noticed a shadow flickering. It was Giles, shaking his head. "Why would he do that, eh lad?"

"I dunno, dad."

"You are quite sure?" I asked.

"Oh yes. As I was falling I thought, now why would he want to do that to me? We aint quarrelled. We haven't had a cross word. I don't dislike him nor he me. Nothin'. I managed to twist as I went down. I knew I had to because if I didn't't, well I would'a landed flat on my back and I would'a broke me head. Then there you were sir."

I nodded.

"I'm sorry for being sick on you, sir," said Brice and closed his eyes.

"Think nothing of it, young man," I said. Then there was silence.

I looked up at Johannes who mouthed the word, 'sleeping'.

I walked away from the bed and turned away. Before I did, I saw his father lovingly tuck the blanket up under the lad's chin.

The doctor joined me in the corner.

"Is this a likely product of the drugs you have given him Johannes, this story?" I whispered.

"I cannot say, though I hear he said it before he had any drugs. Or any brandywine, for that matter."

"Aye... in my hearing," I replied. "He said... 'he pushed me.'"

Johannes took two hands to his face and scrubbed away the weariness. He looked back at Brice.

"His father said he's a clumsy boy. Always throwing himself around. He's had no major accidents, even so."

"And you think he seeks to blame Martyn for his own lack of care?"

"His father says that Brice can be a clown hasn't always taken the care one should when atop a roof. He can be a little bit, what's the word...?"

"Slapdash...I think I've heard Giles call him that before."

"Aye. Slapdash. A mite careless."

I smiled. "He's young, we were all slapdash at twenty."

"Aye but we weren't all on top of a slippery roof twenty feet off the ground."

"No, indeed."

I yawned. "I'm for my bed. I'll speak to both Martyn and Brice again tomorrow."

"Good night my friend. Giles and I will take it in turns to sleep and keep an eye on the lad."

"And I no doubt, will toss and turn in my bed, even though I am dog tired. There is so much going round and round in my head."

Johannes smiled. "Crispin tells me you have a book from the priory. I'll come tomorrow and look. It's one I wasn't aware they had."

I threw on my cloak again. "It's a tiny thing." I took it from my scrip. "Here... read it tonight, when you are watching your patient. Some of the poems are...ha, ha, well let's say, they are spicy enough to warm a man on a cold night."

Johannes laughed quietly. "Not the sort of thing you would expect a priory of monks to have then?"

"No indeed! God keep you Johannes."

*****

I slept, despite the little symbols dancing around in my head. Into the little book, now with Johannes, had been copied line after line of little symbols exactly like the ones which ringed our apple. Some of the same symbols; the little gift rune, the cross, the one that looked like shears. New ones too which I had never seen. One that looked like a person rooted on one leg with his hands thrown up to the sky, one like a wriggling snake and another like a house with a pent roof and only a door.

Despite my rest, I came down in the morning feeling worn out and lacklustre, to find Johannes already breaking his fast in the hall.

He chuckled. "You were not wrong about the little poems, Aumary. Most interesting. I had heard of this Catullus fellow before and of his muse Lesbia, but never the one called Sappho. I must see if I can look him up."

"Then you will never find him," said Crispin, coming in through the door and doffing his cloak, "as long as you are looking for a 'him.'"

"A woman?"

"Indeed she was."

We both looked at him with a new respect and raised eyebrows.

"Time spent in Rome on church business does not mean that church business is all that can be accomplished," he said, breaking off a piece of bread and popping it into his mouth.

"So firstly, how is our patient?"

Johannes cleared his throat. "Pained but comfortable. 'Tis early yet to know if the arm will respond but the fingers work, albeit painfully, so I am hopeful."

"Good," said Crispin, "I'll look in on him later and give him God's blessing.

That will make him feel better." He sat at the bench. "And... what have you found, besides this erotic poetry, in the little book?"

He poured himself some ale.

Johannes shrugged, "Lines and lines of little drawn symbols. None of which I can understand."

"Some of them look familiar... have you the book with you, Johannes?" I asked.

The doctor took the book from his scrip and emptied it from the little bag. I took it.

"See here... this one... does it not look like a wriggling snake? Like our 'S'?" I turned a page, "and here... this to my eye looks a little like a 'B', though more pointed. Do you suppose that is what they actually are?"

"And this looks like an 'F' but then so does this one...and this..." said Crispin, grinning at me.

"Humph."

I sat down defeated by the seeming enormity of our task. To translate something from these squiggles to a language in our own script, then translate it yet again, from that language into words we could understand.

I took from my scrip, the piece of birch bark paper onto which I had, the first day I had seen the little apple, copied the runes from the gold band.

What made me think it was poetry, or a riddle? I had no idea. It was just a feeling.

I smoothed out the paper and sat staring at it. Wait! Lines. The little book which we had borrowed from the priory had runes in lines, in exactly the same way our words had letters which we organised into lines, for poetry, or songs.

Might I be able to organise these into lines?

I fetched a piece of graphite and a further piece of birch bark paper from my office, and sat at the table. I began to carefully follow the symbols as they marched in a long line around the apple, which I had scribbled on my first paper.

Johannes and Crispin were engaged in a desultory conversation about

Oxford, a place they both knew well. Johannes had been born there and Crispin was educated there.

Their chatter fell away into the background and I ceased to listen. There in front of me hovered a repetition of symbols.

A long stalk, a symbol which looked like a pointed 'c', the rune which we now knew was called Geofu, a cross shape, another familiar shape like a capital 'M'. This was followed by a pointed P, another long stalk and two stalks bent over at the top which resembled the letter 'r'.

This was repeated three times - did not Brother Petrus say that the English loved repetition? There were other symbols following these and I wrote them down after each repetition. I now had four short lines; each one beginning with the same symbols. The final words were very different, no repetition here. Except this line was the same as the last of the first piece.

I brandished my piece of paper, now covered with little squiggles.

"Well, I may not know what in Hades it says, but I think I have just organised the symbols so that they make sense."

Crispin and Johannes looked up. They came to sit one either side of me.

"Correct me if I'm wrong, Crispin, but Brother Petrus said that the English loved repetition of words."

He nodded. "He did, and repeated sounds too."

"I looked for repeated patterns in the symbols and found them. Here they are."

I pointed to the beginnings of my first three lines. "It may not be much, but it's a start," I said.

*****

Estate business claimed me much of the morning. I felt quite cross with myself that I hadn't been up to the downs to see how my sheep and shepherds were faring. My wool factor, who now lived in Marlborough, struggled to Durley to see me and we were closeted together till the early afternoon, when he must leave or be travelling in the dark. John said that he would accompany him part of the way and then branch off and brave the snow covered hills, to check on my shepherds and their charges. I accepted his offer gladly.

Winter life on the manor went on, despite the bitter chill and the fact that no agricultural work could be done, for the ground was too frozen. Folk managed to find jobs to do indoors. The forest too, lay covered in snow and ice and no one could go out to work there. People, who were used to physical activity began to be irritable without an outlet for their energies.

Walter Reeve reported that there were more domestic arguments in the village though none had yet boiled over into violence.

Giles and Martyn were continuing to thatch the middle stable. They worked together but one could see that Giles did not trust the carpenter and a few cross words were had, though Martyn mainly took the insults on the chin.

We had had a partial thaw and the manor eaves had dripped into sharp icicles and then refrozen as the extreme cold revisited us. It snowed yet again in the night.

Out in the courtyard a day or so later, I was indicating where these sharp points lay so that they could be knocked off. John was standing on the manor steps and with a long pole in his hands, stretched to crack the icy fingers so that they fell to the ground, shattering into a thousand pieces. Young Cedric was doing the same standing on a small cart a little further along. We moved to other buildings. Now if there was the beginnings of a thaw, the icicles could not fall and injure anyone. Abruptly, from the furthest stable by the gatehouse, a furious shouting erupted.

We all turned. Voices raised in anger could be heard clearly coming from the roof space where the brothers Ben and Bill had been billeted with Tostig and Edward, two more of my grooms.

John put down his pole and with a determined face, marched across the yard. He had not quite reached the steps when down at a pace came Tostig, his face red as an autumn sunset, followed by his brother Wilfrid, who was a forester. Wilfrid slipped down a few steps but continued to yell and scream abuse, and catching himself on the wooden handrail, rose to yell after his retreating brother.

"Come back... you can't get away so easily. This village isn't big enough for you to hide from me, you cockered coxcomb."

Tostig turned.

"Hide... from you? I've never hidden from you in my life! Why should I start now?"

"Well, if you weren't hiding at the back of my cott just now... what were you doing?"

"Taking a piss if you must know," yelled Tostig, "that's all the place is fit for!"

Wilfrid came down a few more steps. They both seemed oblivious to the audience they had attracted.

"I won Hilda fair and square brother," he spat, "and if you have a problem with that...."

Walter Reeve came out from the undercroft. "Wilfrid." His voice echoed around the courtyard. "Go home, go home now!" He stared at the young man. "If you are so concerned what is happening with Hilda, go home and look after her."

John had now drawn level with Tostig.

"Tostig" he said in a quiet but firm voice. "Come away - now."

Neither young man listened to their elders and betters.

"She chose me... ME! " shouted Wilfrid. "Remember?"

"Aye and we all know what a mistake that was!" countered Tostig.

It was well known that these two brothers had been courting the same girl. Many an argument over her had been settled with fists. At last she made a decision and married Wilfrid. Tostig had withdrawn to the manor, out of the way of the married pair who took over the family home in Durley village. He now lived over the stables with the other grooms.

The wound had obviously festered.

"Leave her alone, do you hear me?" said Wilfrid

"So that you can abuse her like you have been doing?"

"She is my wife and my business and you have no right to tell me what to do."

I looked to Walter, whose infinitesimal shake of the head said there was no truth in the rumour that Wilfrid had been abusing his wife Hilda.

"No!" I shouted. "But I have and I say leave it...both of you!" Wilfrid reached the ground by the stairs. Both brothers ignored me.

"Leave her alone or I swear, you will regret it."

"What you going to do? Breathe on me....your breath is as foul as rotten eggs, you drunkard! Go home and get yourself sober."

"I'm good with a stave.... I'm good with a cudgel. Maybe you'd like to see your brains, what brains you have, before you die. Splattered on the snow!"

John reached for Wilfrid and he swung round and gave John a buffet.

Luckily John was quick and stepped back before any damage was done.

"That's enough!" I yelled at the top of my voice.

Cedric had come up now and was trying to reason with Tostig, who was the more controlled brother.

"Oh you mean like you did the glazier. Yes... didn't' think I knew about that did you, you murdering bastard?"

Wilfrid launched himself at his brother and went for the throat. Tostig caught him a blow to the head with his brow before they both went down in a welter of legs and arms. They slipped and slid on the courtyard cobbles, each trying to get a purchase on the other to punch or bang a head on the stones. Tostig was sober and managed the first blow, grabbing his sibling's hair and banging it several times on the hard ice packed ground.

"Enough, I say." I threw myself at them and grabbed Tostig, who was on the top, by the collar and the seat of his hose. He was no match for me for he came up only to my nose and was a very slight man.

John and Cedric hauled Wilfrid from the ground to stand him up against the gatehouse wall, away from his brother. He was still trying to land blows when

John slapped him hard across the face. His brow was bleeding and his lip was cut. What damage there was to the back of his head, I couldn't see.

I looked at Tostig. His nose was bleeding and he wiped it on his sleeve. I let go of him.

"John, Walter, I want these two in hall NOW! John, Cedric, Hal, Walter. No one else. Fetch the doctor please Bill. I think he is with young Brice."

I looked up, Johannes was standing in the doorway of Brice's room, his arms folded over his chest.

"No need Bill... he's seen."

*****

Everyone who had been in the courtyard had stopped to see the action. The grooms had come from the stables. The thatchers had poked their heads over the roof ridge. The woodsmith had come out of his workroom with a length of wood firmly clamped in his hand. Tom Potter had poked his chestnut head round his door. The farrier was staring out his doorway. He kicked it shut and went on with his work once he saw order restored.

Lydia had come out onto the hall steps, Agnes had emerged from the undercroft, where she had been talking to Walter.

Matthew Cook was having a break from his labours, a beaker of ale in his hand and had come to the kitchen door. He shook his head and then went back inside.

I saw, as I made for the hall steps, a face at the window of the chapel. Crispin too had been aroused by the noise.

Henry was hovering in the passageway. "M'lord?" He looked anguished. Lydia took his arm and moved him into the buttery. "No bones broken this time, Henry," she said.

The brothers were marched up the steps and into the hall by John, Cedric and Walter. Hal, who had been out in the village field when the fracas began, followed with a face like a thunderous sky.

"What the 'ell 'as bin goin' on sir?"

"You'll see."

I jumped up onto the dais, spread my feet wide and planted them firmly on the wooden surface. I put both my hands to my waist.

"Disobedience to one's lord is a flogging offence!"

Tostig shook off Cedric's restraining hand and opened his mouth to speak. Hal bounded forward and put himself between me and the offender.

"Now me lad...jus' you watch what yer doin'- you's in a deal of trouble already."

Tostig's chin jutted but he fell silent and didn't't move.

John kept a hand on Wilfrid.

I looked at him. "And striking a senior forester warrants an even tougher punishment."

Wilfrid sagged and fell to his knees.

I turned to Walter who was at the back of the group. He had his fingers on the pulse of village life; he would know the history of this disagreement, though I did know a little about it.

"Reeve, give me an account as you see it, of today's unfortunate fighting."

Walter sighed. "It goes back two years m'lord. Tostig courted Hilda Fabricant, the daughter of the sewing master in Marlborough, off Cock Lane?"

"Aye, I know him,"

"Wilfrid, his younger brother by two years, came to court her too."

"He stole her!" said Tostig under his breath.

"Quiet! you will 'ave a chance to speak when m'lord says so..." growled Hal. He pushed Tostig to his knees and kept hold of him.

"By all accounts, the girl's father favoured the one who was, as he saw it, going to make the most money and he advised his daughter to marry the forester. Grooms were going nowhere, he said. Am I right so far, Cedric?"

Cedric suddenly woke and pulled himself up to his full height.

"Aye sir reeve, though I can't agree with him."

"No, you wouldn't." Walter transferred his staff to his other hand. I saw Johannes enter the hall and hang back, his medical pack over his shoulder.

"Well, Hilda marries Wilfrid, and comes to live in the village. Tostig moves out and lives above the stables. There has been bad blood between them ever since."

"Has the girl encouraged the groom to pay her attention, do you know?"

Tostig's head came up and he looked furiously at me. "No, m'lord, she would never do that. She's true to her vows."

"So you have tried eh, Tostig?"

Tostig hung his head. "I've spoken to her. She is unhappy with that clod!"

Wilfrid glared and tried to rise. John pushed him down.

"Liar!" was all Wilfrid managed to say.

"But I would never encourage her to break her vows, sir, never. I love her. I can't help it."

"Perhaps we should get the girl here now and see what she has to say?" I said.

"No sir... don't ..." pleaded Tostig, "It would be very hard for her. He," he spat, "is her husband and you won't get the truth from her as long as he is here. She will be loyal, see... do her duty. He would be angry with her else."

"As she should!" piped up Wilfrid. "Yes, let's have the hussy here and she can tell me what she was doing with my brother this morning, behind the cottage?"

"I took her some of my rations... that's what. My manor bread and meat. Food so that she might not starve. No doubt food you'll put down your gullet, you selfish bastard!"

They broke free and fell to fighting again and it was a while before the restrainers were able to part them.

"ENOUGH!" I yelled and my voice echoed to the rafters.

"The more you prolong this the longer you will endure punishment."

John coughed. "M'lord, may I speak?"

"Certainly, John."

"I can say that Wilfrid is a jealous man and becomes more so when he has had a little too much to drink."

Wilfrid looked up at John and blinked as if John had just said he was a man with two heads.

"He has been at loggerheads with several of the village men over his wife. I don't think there was anything in it. Agnes will bear me out, sir. It's just he likes to control her beyond what is necessary for a husband to do. The reeve, I'm sure, will tell you what he knows."

"Any violence, reeve?"

"Not to my knowledge sir. Just words."

"What was all this about the glazier?"

There was silence.

"Tostig... speak."

Tostig passed his hand over his mouth. He spat blood into the rushes. "The last one to pay attention to Hilda, sir, ended up dead."

"Perkin Glazer?"

"Aye sir... Hilda is a good looking woman. We all know what the glazier was like."

"It seems we all do...now," I said quietly.

"Walter, can you fetch Hilda here please? Ask her to come and speak with me." Walter turned about and as he passed Johannes in the door, I heard him say "Now we shall have some fun." He disappeared.

Crispin came slowly down the chapel steps. I waved him over.

I sat down and beckoned for Johannes to come up. "While we wait can you see to these two idiots please, Johannes?"

It was a short while before Hilda came up, her apron flying as she randown the hall. She took in the sight before her and curtsied to me.

"Sir...?" She looked at the state of her husband and her brother-in-law and her face paled.

I jumped down from the dais and took her elbow.

"Come with me, Hilda...."

I guided her to the long bench by the fire and bade her sit.

"Have they been fighting over me, sir?" she asked.

"I'm afraid so."

"Oh, they are such fools."

"Aye... many men are." I smiled.

"I want the truth, Hilda, does Wilfrid mistreat you?"

Her eyes became guarded but then her face cleared. "No sir...not in that, does he beat me? No, he doesn't beat me, though he has every right. He is my husband and my master and has that right."

"So what does he do?"

She looked away. "He is rough when he has been in his cups, sir... but I can manage that. He's a good man, a fine forester and provides well... when we haven't...."

"Yes. What else?"

"He is very jealous. Not just of his brother."

"Tostig loves you, you know that...?"

"Aye, sir... I know... and not as a brother should love a sister, but there isn't anything be done about it now."

"I shall ask this question once and I want a true answer. I shall not repeat it. Neither shall I repeat your answer to any man. Have you at any point lain with your brother-in-law Tostig, since your marriage to Wilfrid?"

There was no hesitation.

"No sir, never."

I nodded. "The glazier, Perkin Glazer....did he pay you unwanted attention, Hilda?"

"That old man?" she spat. "Aye... he was one who couldn't keep his hands from anything in skirts."

"Did Wilfrid see him?"

She took her lip between her teeth. "Wilfrid never said anything to me... but I'm sure he saw the old man once, when I was up at the church - I'm one of them as does the cleaning, m'lord. I was bending over with me brush and the old lecher comes up behind me. I thought at first it was Wilfrid. Well...he does do daft things like that," she smiled

"Then when the hands came round me I saw the arms were all scarred and I knew it was that old man, the glass-man."

"What did you do?"

"I stuck my elbow in his ribs, sir", she chuckled. "Made him fair wheeze and when I turned round Wilfrid and Henry the steward were coming through the church door."

"You think he saw the attempt?"

"Oh aye, sir... he saw."

"You are very definite about that."

"Oh yes, sir."

"Why?"

Hilda shuffled her feet a little in the rushes and shifted on her seat. "He went up to the glass-man and took his hand as if to shake it, sir."

"Odd thing to do."

"Then he squeezed and squeezed real hard and the glas-man, his face was all screwed up. Wilfrid is a worker sir, he has strong hands."

"No words spoken?" Hilda looked away and said in the quietest whisper you could imagine... "If I as much as catch you within feet of my wife again I swear...."

"Yes?"

"I swear I will kill you."

*****

I sent Hilda off and with one backward look she disappeared through the hall door. Interesting, I said to myself... it was Tostig who got the look, not Wilfrid.

I marched back up to our fighting pair.

Johannes was just finishing...no major damage, he said. A split lip, a bruised nose and head, a broken tooth and probably a black eye which was yet to materialise. There would be no further concussion or injury. I nodded my thanks.

"Hal, can you go and ask Henry to step in here a moment?"

"Right you are, sir."

"Henry, can you fetch the keys to the lockup. And two sets of irons."

"You aren't going to put them both in there at the same time…" said Cedric staring at the miscreants. "They'll kill each other, m'lord," he finished.

"And can you and Hal and John go down with our prisoners and shackle them to the walls so that they cannot reach one another, please."

" Aye... one at one end... near the privy and the other at the mortuary end," smiled Hal.

"A night in the cold and no food or water should do them a world of good," I said.

When they had gone, I asked Cedric to go down and ask Wyot, the gatekeeper, who would be on duty that evening and night, to look in on them often to make sure they were not dying of cold. One blanket each would be provided but nothing else. It was exceedingly cold at night.

I saw Johannes smile. "A flogging offence eh?... or worse?"

I shrugged. "I am too soft... I know."

Crispin laughed. "Aye, too soft by half. There's many a lord in the past would've had their hands off for this."

"And then what, eh Crispin? No good to me without hands... and they are both good workers. Besides you well know I am a stickler for the process of the law. "

Crispin put up his own hand.

"I'm not disagreeing...just saying."

Henry came back with his key and told me all had been done as I requested.

"Tomorrow they will be let out - leave them till midday, Henry. Then let Tostig out first and then Wilfrid."

"Yessir."

"Then Hal, follow Tostig to see where he goes. Make sure we have enough time elapsing between the two being freed for Tostig to go where he will."

"Aye, sir..."

Johannes was cackling in the background. "You crafty old hound..." he said, "I see your plan."

"We shall see what they do."

I called Henry back.

"Tell me, Henry, did you go in to the church with Wilfird one day church, when we were having the windows put in and the glassman was there?"

Henry thought for a while..."Aye I did...'twas before my brother... died."

"Yes... indeed." I put my hand on his shoulder.

"And did you see the glazier accost Hilda? Put his arms around her?"

Henry smiled. "Aye I did... and I laughed when she walloped him with the sharp end of her elbow."

"Did you hear what Wilfrid said to the glazier?"

Henry's smile set on his face. He looked away and then back at me. "Aye... I did... though I paid it scant attention... for many say things..."

"What did he say, Henry?"

"He threatened him... m'lord. He said he would kill him."

Henry looked down and he blushed.

*****

Elbows. Elbows. That reminded me. I hadn't spoken to young Brice in a while. Time for me to do so, I think. Off I went to the corner room on the east wall. Brice was sitting propped up in his bed with his splinted arm resting along his blanket covered leg.

He was dozing, for he still had pain killing syrups given by Johannes; less of them now, but the lines of his face were not so stressed and his eyes snapped open as soon as I entered. They were clear and bright.

"Hello lad," I said. "How are you today?"

"I still have pain, sir but at least I got my arm." He brought his injured arm up with his good one and wriggled his fingers, which were poking from the end of the bandaged splint close to his face. "And see, my fingers all work fine." He laughed.

"Well, that is a wonderment." I laughed too. This was the sort of fellow who would ride the adversities of life with a smile. I'm sure people like that do better generally and mend much more quickly.

I told him so. He smiled sweetly at me.

"I can't help it...I have always been a happy sod sir, glad to be alive. I love a good joke and a laugh."

"Your father calls you a clown."

"Well, yes he does. But me mam says I took after him when he was young so he can't complain really. Maybe I'll get old and miserable one day, just like him."

"Your father is a good man, Brice, and he loves you greatly, for all you try him dearly."

"Oh Lord!" said Brice, sitting up straighter. "What's he bin sayin' now?"

I sat on the joint stool. "I was watching him and Martyn out on the stable roof earlier. Your father seems to have become a little more, shall we call it... distant... from the carpenter since you fell from the roof? More guarded."

Brice sniffed. "Well, at first he didn't't believe me. Said I'd imagined it. Then he started thinking and watching, he said. He's known Martyn a good few years, knew him before his wife and littl'un went. Knew *his* father before him, he did."

"And...?"

"Dad says that Martyn is wary. He's tense. He's never been a whole person somehow but he's a whole lot worse now. Jumpy, quiet."

"I've known Martyn all my life, he's always been quiet, a man of few words."

"Well,... ask dad. He thinks something's up."

"And he thinks that something is that Martyn is living with the fact that for some reason, he pushed you from the roof and caused your injury?"

Brice nodded. "He could'a killed me."

"You, I take it, are still saying he pushed you?"

"If I could demonstrate to you, m'lord, I'd be off this bed and a showing' you what happened. He pushed me...of that there's no doubt. That's why I've taken to keeping this under me pillow." He felt behind him with his good arm and grimaced at the pain it caused his broken elbow.

He brought out a knife.

" T'is dad's. Says I gotta have it when I'm on me own. Just in case."

I smiled. "I don't think you need to worry, Brice."

"Dad worries. He worries too that Martyn will have another mad fit and try to throw him off the roof..."

"Aye...I think he does," I said. "Like I say, I've been watching. Martyn isn't the only one that's jumpy," and I patted him on the good arm and left.

Now for Martyn. It was dinner time and everyone had gone up to the hall or were in their own homes, eating whatever meagre supplies they could eke out. The winter was biting now.

All except Martyn that is, who was sitting alone on a pile of straw in the stable. He had an onion and a piece of cheese wrapped round with two small pieces of black bread.

An ale flagon was sitting steady in the straw beside him.

He jumped up when he saw me and took off his coif.

"Sit, Martyn, and finish your food."

I sat beside him and made a nest for myself in the straw. He sat and replaced his coif.

"How goes it?"

"One more day and we'll be done, sir," he said.

"I meant...how goes it with you, Martyn?"

He raked my face with his cool grey eyes.

"Aw... the head is mended now and I'm back to normal."

"Good. You've mended quicker than Brice has. It'll be a good few weeks before he can use that arm, I fear. Then he'll have to build himself up slowly. It might take as long as a year, Doctor Johannes tells me, before he can be back to his climbing over the thatch like a squirrel!" Martyn did not immediately answer. He took a bite of his bread and cheese and chewed. "Is he still saying that I pushed him?"

"Aye he is."

"Why would he say that?"

"If it's not the truth, I have absolutely no idea." I leaned forward and put my elbows on my knees, presenting as nonchalant an attitude as I could. I didn't want to be, at that moment, his lord and master, I wanted to be someone who had known him from childhood, someone he could trust. A friend.

"Did you push him?"

"It might have seemed to him as if I did, I suppose."

"Ah...."

"But like I said, he stood up, lost his balance and I made a grab for him, to save him."

"He tells me that the reason he lost his balance, was because you threw yourself in front of him."

"Why would I do that? I'd have to be crazy to try that on a half made roof!"

I shrugged.

"Did you lose your balance and cling to him to...?"

"No. I didn't."

"Then we shall maybe never know what truly happened."

"No one saw us?"

"No one has come forward."

"Then it's my word against his?"

I watched in silence as Martyn sliced a piece of onion with his eating knife. His hand was shaking.

"What do you have in there Martyn?" I wondered suddenly if the man had started drinking to excess and that was why he was shaking and was careless on the roof. I picked up his ale flagon. It was almost empty.

"Be my guest, sir," he said, obviously one step ahead of me.

I upended it in my mouth. It was not good manor ale.

"Water," said Martyn. "I don't drink ale in the day; not done that for ages sir."

*****

I came into the hall shivering and chilled through and made straight for the fire.

There was Martyn Summersete, sitting on a bench. He had his back to me and he was humming to himself, whilst he poked the fire with a stick.

The hall was deserted now, for it was past dinner time and all had gone back to their work on the manor, or to their homes. Suddenly, the peddler broke into song. I stopped abruptly and listened, afraid to spoil the moment.

My, he had a good voice. A light tenor, clear and pitched to perfection. As he sang, the words unfamiliar to me, I was mesmerised by the tune and the way it dipped and fell and became so plaintive. It was the sort of song, that I'd heard could reduce grown men, hardened warriors of old, to tears. I noticed too, there was no trace of a hesitation, no slurring of the words.

When the song died away, Martyn reached for his stick and once more poked the fire in front of him.

"Martyn" I said, "that was one of the most beautiful things I have ever heard anyone sing."

He jumped up, for he had been in a world of his own. I came up to him and threw my cloak on the table. The man blushed and laughed nervously.

"A peddler must have many talents, m'lord."

"You have a very fine voice. Do you have a store of such songs then?"

"Aye, I do m'lord, and the strange thing is I can remember them now, when I cannot remember where I was going nor from whence I came."

"Strange indeed. You must sing for us of an evening after supper. Folk are becoming bored. It's just the sort of thing that will warm their hearts. You may be able to teach a few songs to Johannes and the Lady Lydia. They too have fine voices. One or two of the folks play instruments. Bill, my groom, has a small harp and I think Johnathan Reeve is quite competent on his rebec now. We could make a jolly time of it. And a few pennies might come your way too."

"I have been telling tales for the Lady Hawise too, sir.... I hope I haven't done wrong by it...?"

"Not at all. She needs cheering up."

"I have a fund of stories, you see. Like I say, a peddler needs to work for his keep of a night. A warm place by a kitchen fire can usually be secured with a fine tale or a sad song."

"I'm sure it can. We would be very pleased to have you sing for us, Martyn."

The man smiled self-deprecatingly. "I'd like that, sir... I would."

"Tell me, in which language were you singing just now? I didn't't recognise it at all."

"No sir... it was a song of fairies and elves and came from out of Cornwall. They have an odd language all their own down there."

"You range thus far Martyn, with your pack and your wares?"

Martyn's face lit up. "Aye sir... I do. And that is another thing which has just come to me... I do. I go as far down as the Land of the Sea... Cornwall is surrounded by sea. Memories are coming back to me, m'lord. They are coming back."

I sat on the bench beside him. "You collect songs wherever you go?"

"Aye, and stories too."

"Throughout the whole of southern England?"

"And some French songs too, sir. Though where I learned those I have no idea. I've never been to France." The man beamed. See sir...." He grinned again, "I know that now, just by talking to you... I know I have never left these shores."

"You must have a good memory for words, Martyn."

The peddler touched his broken head. "Aye, I must have. I think if I hadn't, I would still be floundering around trying to work out what my name was."

"So that was a Cornish song. What others do you know? You'll have to tell us the meanings of the words if we are to understand them... even though the feel of the songs will shine through from your voice."

Martyn furrowed his brow.

"I think I shall have to sing them to remember what I know. The words and the tunes just come when I sing. Then they stick again, as if I have dug them out of the mud and they lie drying on the surface once more."

"Dig away, my man," I said. "We shan't mind if you get the odd word wrong."

The peddler laughed. "Once I have them...I have them. 'Tis good that I have remembered I can sing. It's a huge part of who I am, I think."

*****

I bounded up the solar steps. In our private room, Lydia was teaching Hawise to hem a sheet. Lydia had the greater part of one on her knee and Hawise had the remainder. She was frowning in concentration.

Felice was sitting a little behind them also sewing at something. They all looked up at me as I entered.

"So are you going to tell us what happened this morning in the courtyard, Aumary?" said Lydia." "We are itching to know."

"Oh no..." I mocked. "It's far too rough for ladies' ears."

"Nonsense..." replied Lydia. "Just leave out the swearing."

I sat down and laughingly told them the story of Wilfrid and Tostig, the two brothers and their shared lady love.

"Aw dada," said Hawise, "that sounds just like a story which Martyn peddler has been telling me about a king and how he was going to chop a baby in half because two mothers were arguing over it."

"I'm not going to chop poor Hilda in half!"

Hawise giggled. "No, you wouldn't do that."

"Martyn was saying to me that he has been singing to you and telling stories."

Hawise bounced up and down on her seat.

"He is really good. He does all the funny voices and everything. He makes me laugh."

Felice tutted and looked to the rafters.

"He was telling me this morning about a monster called Grumble..."

"Grendel, Hawise," corrected Lydia.

"...and how he was eating people and things. Then a hero called Beer Wolf came and slew him."

"Beowulf Hawise," said Lydia not looking up from her sewing and biting off a thread.

"Be -o- wulf. He was very brave and chopped off his head." This was accompanied by the action. "Then Grendel's mother came looking for him. Well, she would wouldn't she?"

"Oh undoubtedly," I said.

"Well, if someone chopped off my head, you would go looking for them wouldn't you dada, and you would...."

"If they were a monster, yes, I might," I said, not sure where this was going.

Hawise went back abruptly to her sewing.

I looked at Lydia who was searching the face of her step daughter.

"And what happened then? "I asked, "Did the mother monster eat Beowulf?"

Hawise looked up slowly.

"No, he killed her too."

"These are very gory stories for a young lady to be listening to."

Hawise put her eyes down to her sewing again.

Lydia caught my eye and raised one delicate eyebrow.

I hunkered down in front of my daughter.

"We haven't really spoken about you finding the body of the glass-man, in the river, Hawise."

There was silence. "I think it would be a good thing for you to tell us now, now that you have had a time to think about it, why you said you didn't't like the man."

"I feel sorry now that he's dead," Hawise said quietly, her eyes downcast.

"Well... yes I suppose you do. But you didn't't kill him did you, so..."

"But I did wish that he would...."

"Did you wish for him to die, is that it?"

Hawise jutted her chin and looked up suddenly. "He was horrible."

"Why was he horrible? You can tell your mama and me."

Hawise shook her head.

I thought in silence a while.

"All right. You like stories. I am going to tell you a story, rather like the ones the peddler has been telling you."

Lydia's brow furrowed but she did not interrupt.

"There were once three girls. Three very pretty little girls."

Hawise's face suddenly became animated once more. "What were they called dada?"

"One was called Nilla, one Cassie and the other Hawise. They lived in a nice house with their mother and their father. One day a man came to the house. He seemed a really nice man with a smiley face. He said he liked little girls and so the little girls were happy to be with him. Then when the mother and the father had gone into the forest to collect berries one day…"

"It was autumn then?" asked Hawise.

"Yes, it was. So they were in the forest and the man said he would look after the little girls and keep them from harm."

"Were there some monsters in the forest and he had to look after them in case they came to eat them?" asked Hawise wide eyed.

"That's quite right. Monsters indeed. These were monsters which could change their shape into anything they liked. Even into nice, friendly, smiley men."

Hawise put her hand to her mouth. "Oh no!"

"Oh yes! So when the mother and father were gone, the nice, smiley man changed into a monster."

Hawise blinked. "And he ate them all up?"

"No, he didn't't. He took them on his knee and he started to kiss them and hug them. He started to take off their clothes. He put his hands all over them. They didn't't like this at all and cried out, asking him to stop. But he would not stop. He was a very strong monster."

Hawise looked stricken. "They told him that their dada would not like him to do that."

"That's right."

I rose and took her in my arms.

"And then a brave knight came along. His name was Harry. He fought the nasty monster."

"But he didn't't kill him?"

"No, the monster fled and he ran and he ran. He was wounded on the head. He ran into the river and fell and was drowned."

"The next day?"

"One of the little girls was by the river collecting....

"Duck eggs..."

"Yes, that's right, and she found the monster who had changed back into a man by then.

She felt sorry to see him because he was dead."

"No, she wouldn't because he was a monster," my daughter stated blankly.

I looked to Lydia who smiled. "Well, she did a bit, because when he wasn't a monster, he had been a nice man."

"Oh all right then."

"But she felt glad because he couldn't try to be nasty to the little girls ever again."

"No, he couldn't," said Hawise. She wound her arms around my neck and I felt her breath in my ear.

"You know, dada, don't you?" she whispered.

"Yes, Hawise, I know. I know what a nasty man Perkin the glassman was. I know what he did to you and to Nilla and poor Cassie."

"Now he's gone to God," she said

Lydia harumphed but said no more.

"God will know what he has done and will be very cross with him."

"He will?"

"He will, for God knows everything."

"Will he know that....?" Hawise squirmed in my arms and looked at Lydia. She brought her mouth up close to my ear again and whispered.

"That he tried to put, you know, his pizzle between Cassie's legs?"

My heart was pounding but I answered calmly.

"Yes, he will know."

Hawise shivered. "I don't think that is very nice," she said firmly.

"Did he ever try to do that with you, when you were alone with him?"

"No."

Felice started up then. "Sir, the only time she has been alone with the glassman was here once in the solar and on that day we thought she had been buried in the stables."

Lydia backed her up. "Once, I think, when I was called away and Hawise was sleeping in her room and Felice, you were down in the kitchen fetching some goat's milk. A matter of heartbeats."

"All it takes Lydia."

She nodded.

"What happened with him Hawise?"

Hawise climbed down. I had forgotten how big she was getting now and how my arms ached after holding her for a long time.

"I was asleep in there," she pointed to her room. "The glass-man was in here doing the window. He was the only one here. He came into the room and lay down on me and squashed me."

"What did you do?"

Hawise giggled. "I was wriggly like a worm and I fell out of the bed and ran down the steps and went into the hall."

"Good."

"Hal was there and we played backgammon."

"You played backgammon with Hal?"

Hawise looked exasperated at me, all worry gone.

"Hal doesn't play very often but he is really good. He beats me sometimes."

The nightmares ceased.

Chapter Eight

That afternoon I sent a message to Richard of Snap telling him what I knew. He could deal with the matter as he saw fit. I would speak to Gilbert Cordwainer when I next visited the town.

The night drew in. My messenger returned with a note from Richard which told me that there seemed to be no lasting damage to his daughter Petronilla, physical or emotional and since the man was now dead, we hoped this was the end of it all. He finished with the sentence, "Should I hear of any other child in the town or immediate county who has fallen prey to this beast, I will let you know."

The night came in with an icy grip and about midnight it seemed to relent and let go. All at once it warmed, only to snow again until the hours of daylight.

Once more we would have to shovel and scrape, dig and pile.

My malefactors in the lock up were released at midday and as instructed Hal of Potterne followed the groom from his incarceration. Tostig went straight to his billet in the eaves of the far stable and fell asleep on his bed. Wilfrid went home to Hilda.

I crossed the courtyard, again a hive of activity with almost every able-bodied manor person out shoveling snow.

I called out for Wyot, who in the main slept during the day, for his duties kept him awake much of the night.

"Warm enough, Wyot?"

"Aye... thanks to you, m'lord."

He was wrapped in two good woollen blankets and had straw stuffed into his boots. I saw the stalks sticking out from the top.

"I'm as snug as a miser in a mint sir, in this little room you built for me."

I laughed. "And last night?"

"Quiet. All I could hear was the chattering of their teeths, sir."

"Good."

"Mind you... afore that....in the afternoon, there was a lot of swearin' and cussin' and shouting at each other."

"As to be expected, Wyot."

He chuckled deep in his throat. "Oh my... they'd put a sailor to shame for the names they called each other."

"I'm sure."

"They exhausted themselves I suppose...or their stretch o' words maybe."

I chuckled at that. "Did they talk to each other in a sensible manner at all, Wyot?"

"Aye they did, towards the end of the night a bit o' whispering between them."

"Good, this means they may have talked over their differences."

Wyot shook his head. "Maybe... but that lad Wilfrid... he is a hothead. 'Twouldn't take much fer it to start all over again, I feels."

"We'll keep our eyes on them."

"Good idea, m'lord." Wyot gave a huge yawn.

"Thank you for your help. Sleep well, Wyot. God keep you."

I could not get what my groom Tostig, Hilda, Wilfrid's wife and Henry my steward had said out of my head. That Wilfrid had seen the scuffle in the church and had threatened to kill the glazier in a fit of jealousy. It would do no harm to revisit the moment with Tostig.

I climbed the outer stair of the gatehouse and ducked through into the entrance to the upper floor of the far stable loft.

Tostig was a hump on his palliasse covered in blankets and curled up in a ball. I called to him; there was a rustle of straw and his face came over his shoulder and he peered out of bleary eyes.

Slowly he got up, wrapped one of the blankets around him and stood watching me.

"Tostig, sit."

He did as he was bid and perched on the edge of his wooden platformed bed.

"I will ask the steward to fine you two day's pay for the disobedience to me yesterday," I said.

"Yes, sir."

"I will ask Henry to fine your brother the same when the manor court comes round."

"Yes, sir."

"Do you think that is fair?"

Tostig sighed.

"Aye, m'lord, 'tis fair."

It was very dark in the eaves of the stables and I allowed no naked flame to be taken there for fear of firing the thatch.

However, there was a lantern, which I took from its place on a hook in a beam and fetched it nearer to Tostig's bed. I fiddled in my scrip and took out a new tallow candle and lit it from the old one, now almost burned down and replaced it, pinching out the stub.

I wanted to see the results of my interrogation on Tostig's face.

"So.." I sat on a stool and put the lantern on the floor. "What is all this about? Wilfrid and the glazier?"

Tostig turned away.

"Nothing. Just words I spat at him in anger. I wanted to wound him."

"And that you did...for it was that particular insult which fired him to leap on you."

"Aye. Well. It's not every day your brother calls you a murderer, is it?"

"Do you truly think he is?"

Tostig shuffled on his bed and made himself more comfortable.

"I can't be the only one... no Master Brenthall said it, didn't't he; said he thinks that Wilf is the jealous sort? He has always been so, since a lad. I was the first born, he was envious of that - as if I could help it. Damned fool. I learned the bow first… as the elder... he was envious of that. I was the taller as boys... still am...he is envious of that too."

I shook my head. "I know all about the envy of a brother... but go on, Tostig."

"This business with Hilda. He didn't't really want to marry her but he had to because I courted her. Envy again. He had to possess what I wanted. Well, he has her now... a lot of good may it do him."

"He does not care for his wife?"

"Not as I would,"

"No… you love her dearly, don't you, and she you. I can see that."

"There has never been any... not since...."

"No, I know. I believe you."

"Wilf sees everyone as a threat to him; to his prowess and his ability as a forester, his prowess as a husband, anything. Any man as merely looks at Hild, sir, and he makes out they are about to run off with her. Keeps her on the tightest rein he can, like you do with an errant horse, sir. But she isn't a bad girl. She's loyal and she sticks to him...God knows why."

I nodded. "And so you, of course are the biggest threat, having been her previous lover and his brother to boot, and you live too close for comfort."

Tostig's eyes glazed over as he thought about the object of both the brothers' desire.

"So what happened with the glazier?"

Tostig's gaze again fixed on my face. "I wasn't there but Hild told me what happened."

"She told me too. Am I right in saying that as a result of one of Glazer's attempts at seduction, Wilfrid threatened him?"

"He did."

"Yet Wilfrid didn't't immediately act on his threat, did he?"

"Sir?"

"Well, the glazier has been gone a few months. He completed the church windows and was gone...he returned only a few weeks ago to mend the solar window. I take it he made no further attempts on Hilda's virtue?"

"But that's it, sir… when the glazier came back, Wilf caught him ogling Hilda and winking at her and making suggestive… well… remarks."

"You saw this?"

"Yessir, I did."

"When was it?"

"Twelfth Night, sir… before the dancing."

"I saw Perkin Glazer that night and he was sober and sitting on a bench close to me."

"Hilda was helping serve the food, sir. When she was going round he made a grab for her and she avoided him, spilling some hot fat on his arm."

"Well, that wouldn't be the first time the glazier had been burnt would it?"

Tostig smirked. "No, sir. I expect not."

"So what happened?"

Tostig was obviously uncomfortable telling me this tale for his face seemed agonised and he squirmed as if the words would not come from his mouth.

"As God is my witness sir. I wish I hadn't heard it… but I did. Wilfrid went up to him and sat by him really close and…."

"And what Tostig…?"

"He called him out sir. He said, "you were warned old man, and you took no notice. Leave my wife alone or I will kill you, I said. I'll meet you out there…" and he pointed to the piece of land by the threshing barn, "out there at midnight. And then I'll kill you."

I sat for some time digesting this. Tostig sat before me his face open and seemingly free from guile. I fingered my close clipped beard.

"Do you think he carried out his threat?" I asked, at last.

"I don't know… but…"

"But you are afraid he did?"

"Aye, sir…I am."

"Did anyone else hear this?"

"I dunno, sir."

"You realise I can't just take your word for it?"

"No m'lord."

Again we sat in silence.

"Why would the glazier go out?"

"Sir?"

"Why would the man go out there, unarmed and alone to meet someone who had threatened to kill him?"

"Again, sir, I dunno."

"It truly doesn't make sense."

I thought back to the day after Perkin's murder when Johannes and I had gone looking for evidence in the snow. "There was no sign of a fight having taken place, though it snowed again after midnight and maybe signs were covered."

Tostig nodded.

"I shall have to speak to Wilfrid. Perhaps we can force a confession from him."

Tostig scoffed. "That I don't think you will ever do sir, he's as stubborn as your horse Bayard."

"Even he can be brought round Tostig," I said. "Eventually."

I started with Hilda, for she was the one I found first, milking their goats in the small outhouse which they shared with a couple of neighbours.

It was surprisingly warm there and filled with the smell of goat and hay.

Hilda wore an apron of felted wool, thick and warm and a jacket of the same material. Of course, she was the daughter of a sewing master in Marlborough; she would have learned to felt wool and to sew, at her father's knee.

I came in behind her just as she was starting on her second goat.

"Hilda, I'd like to ask you a few further questions."

"About the day in the church, m'lord?"

"No, about the second time Perkin Glazer accosted you, at Twelfth Night."

"Ah... so you heard about that, sir? It was nothing much. The old lecher made a grab for me. He'd been quietly teasing me all evening, making eyes whenever I came near him, secretly trying to paw me."

"And you saw him off with some boiling fat did you not?"

She chuckled. "Yes sir, I did."

"Did you hear your husband make a threat, a second threat to the glazier?"

She turned cautiously towards me at that and ceased to pull at the udders.

"Did Tostig tell you that m'lord?

"Just answer me please, Hilda. Did you hear?"

"It was only a threat... an empty threat. All Wilf's threats are empty. He's a man of bluster. He's threatened me a few times. 'If you go near my brother, I'll beat you black and blue. If you as much as look at Hubert Alder with those cow eyes, I'll put them out...' it's all bravado. He would never touch me. It's all words."

"Why did you choose him Hilda? It seems to me you could have had a much better life with..."

"No, sir," she swallowed. "Please don't. I made my bed, now I must lie in it."

"Talking of beds, is Wilfrid in his?"

"Aye sir... in the loft. He was awake all night in the lockup. It was mortal cold. And they were thirsty and hungry."

"It was only as much as they deserved. If I catch them again going at each other like that and they disobey me, John or the reeve, I will have them at the manor court and suggest that they be flogged."

"Aye sir... thank you for being so lenient. I know you could have had them flogged for...."

"They are both free men with rights, Hilda.. They owe me a loyalty, only because I pay them and they have sworn service to me, but if they continue with this ridiculous feud, I will have no choice but to turn them both off the manor. That means...."

"I know sir, I too would have no home."

"Think on it Hilda."

*****

I rounded the corner of the little cottage in which Hilda and Wilfrid lived, close by the priest's glebe in a small stand of trees.

I could hear the snores from outside the house.

I banged hard on the door with my foot and entered shouting, "Wilfrid, up and look lively, I want a word."

There was a scrabbling in the loft and Wilfrid appeared, bleary eyed and tousled. He rubbed his eyes and yawned.

"Down here if you don't mind."

After a moment, Wilfrid shinned down the ladder and bounced onto the floor in front of me.

He knuckled his forehead. He immediately regretted it and closed his eyes in pain.

"Sorry, m'lord, I was catching up on some rest, for some reason I didn't't sleep a wink last night."

"Enough of your sarcasm."

I sat on the edge of the table which took up the greater part of the ground floor living room and locked my hands together.

Wilfrid ran his hands through his lank, straw coloured hair.

"I want to know where you were at about midnight on Twelfth Night."

The forester fingered his stubbled chin and raised his eyes to the rafters, in an exaggerated gesture of puzzlement and furrowed his brow. I noticed the bruises along his eye sockets and the huge lump on his forehead.

"Erm..."

"No thinking about it, that shouldn't be necessary. Most folk could tell me where they were without digging it out of their memory. It was only a few days ago."

"Here m'lord. Asleep."

I folded my arms.

"Right....so you were here asleep, no doubt with your wife?"

"You have the right of it, sir, the very right."

"So you did not make good your threat to go out to the land by the threshing barn and teach Perkin Glazer a lesson?"

I saw the pupils of his eyes shrink. He looked away.

Before he could answer, his wife entered the cottage. "I talked him out of it, m'lord."

I turned to look at her. She stood stock still in the doorway and her eyes never wavered.

"We talked a moment ago, Hilda, there was no mention of this."

She came into the room and put the pail of goats' milk on the table. "You didn't't ask me, m'lord," she said. "I would have told you, if you had asked."

"You can vouch for the fact that he was here asleep in the loft at midnight, lying beside you?"

"Aye m'lord. I can. All night."

"A wife's testimony is worth nothing in law, Hilda. You could swear on every Bible in the land but a justice would not take any notice of you."

"He was here, sir."

"Did he leave you at all?"

"Only to visit the pot...'twas all the drink, see," smirked a confident Wilfrid.

I stood. There would be no shaking them.

"Anyone else able to tell us where you were before midnight?"

"I were at the feast sir, anyone can tell you that. Hild was helping to serve the meats. I went along for some company."

"This was when you saw the glazier paying your wife some unwanted attention, was it not?"

Wilfrid's eyes shrank.

"Aye... he's a...he *were* a lecherous sod. I told him fair and square, to leave off."

"O, more than that surely, Wilfrid?"

There was silence.

"You were heard threatening the glazier and arranging to meet him out by the threshing barn."

I saw a look flash between husband and wife.

Wilfrid sighed. "Aye, I did... but I had had a deal of drink then, even though it were watered. Hilda... like she says, persuaded me not to go. So I didn't't. I stayed here in the warm arms of my loving wife all night."

"You don't feel that, by not going, you might be seen as cowardly then?"

"Sensible, m'lord," put in Hilda quickly.

"I'm sure a few heard you make your threat... I can ask... I can find out. You don't think that they would think you cowardly?"

"Let them think as they chooses, m'lord," said Wilfrid. "I do threaten... I know, when I have had a skin-full but I'm not a murderer, sir."

He felt the lump on his head. "I'd fight fair, in the open. You know that, sir. You saw me."

"Yes, and you might kill a man by accident. Was that how it was?"

Both of them yelled "No!" together and then startled, looked at one another.

"No sir, I never met the glazier that night. You will have to look elsewhere for his murderer," said Wilfrid.

I stared them out for a moment or two.

"Very well." I swung myself into the doorway. "No more, Wilfrid... no more nonsense, or you'll find yourself losing even more sleep, in the lockup."

I closed the door quietly behind me.

*****

I crunched my way through the snow, noisily for a few steps and then back tracked as deftly as I could and put my ear to the door. Let them think I had gone. For a moment there was silence and then I heard Wilfrid let out a huge sigh. I heard him sit down heavily on one of the stools by the table.

"Thank you wife," he said.

Hilda too sighed. "You are a fool Wilfrid Frithson", she chastised but rather gently, I thought. "This nonsense with Tostig has brought us nothing but trouble. It has to stop, like the lord says, or we shall be out on our ear."

I heard Wilfrid scratch his stubbly beard.

"Nah, he'd never do that."

"He would, he has threatened it."

Hilda must have moved to pour the milk into a jug for I heard her splashing the liquid and putting down the bucket.

"If you want to keep your job, then you must keep your temper."

"And you must keep yourself to yourself, wife."

"By all the saints Wilfrid, I do, it's only you who thinks otherwise." There was a sob in her voice.

Hilda had moved to feed the central fire with twigs, I heard them crackling and spitting on the stone hearth.

I was about to move off when the next words stopped me in my tracks.

"You sure you were not seen?"

"I saw them, but they did not see me."

"They didn't't see your lantern?"

"No, 'twas a dark one. I shielded it as I rounded the south wall."

I held my breath.

"Like I told you, I never spoke to him at all. Someone was with him. I didn't't see who - no doubt it was the man who murdered him."

Wilfrid got up and I heard him cross the floor.

"There... it can do us no harm now. If he didn't't see you, we are safe...."

"No thanks to you."

I inched the door open slowly and quietly.

The two of them were in an embrace by the fire hearth.

Hilda was leaning over her husband's shoulder. Her eyes were fast shut as if she were trying to block out an unpleasant image.

The draught from the door made the smoke from the fire billow and Hilda opened her eyes to see me, my arms folded, leaning against the door post.

The two of them sprang apart.

"So... it wasn't you after all who went out, Wilfrid, at midnight to confront the glazier." I closed the door again, "but you, Hilda?" I said.

Hilda put her hand to her mouth and tears sprang into her eyes.

"I didn't't kill him."

"So why did you go out?"

She swallowed.

"She went to tell him that I would not be coming. That I had changed my mind. This time. He would not be dying that night. Not by my hand."

"I went out," said Hilda at last "at about the midnight hour. It had stopped snowing. I rounded the wall with my lantern. I was just about to walk up the side of the south manor wall, when I saw a pinprick of light."

"Another lantern?"

"Yes, sir."

Wilfrid went on. "She was...."

I stopped him. "Let Hilda tell it, Wilfrid. Sit Hilda."

The girl sat on the stool recently vacated by her husband and put her hands between her knees. She was shaking.

"I said to myself that it must be the glazier come to meet Wilfrid."

"Where was the lantern light exactly?"

"Close by the stream where the two alder trees are. I reckoned Glazer must've come out of the sally port and I was just going to make my way towards the lantern light, when I realised there were two men there."

"Glazer was still alive then?"

"Yes. I knew it wasn't Wilf, I'd left him at home in bed waiting for me. I shrank against the manor wall and ducked back round the corner."

"And then...?"

"When I looked again...there was only one man standing. I fled home then."

"She came in quick. She had no time to find the blessed man and give him my message. That I swear," said Wilfrid. "She can'ta killed him."

"I carried my lantern sir. I could just about manage to drag myself through the snow. It were real deep there. There's no way I could have taken a weapon of any sort. My other hand was holding up my skirts. Have you ever tried walking through snow with skirts on, sir?"

I just looked at her.

"No of course you haven't but I can tell you, it's damn hard work, m'lord!"

*****

January blew itself out in blizzards so severe, we were worried to cross the courtyard. February settled bitterly cold. There was no more thawing. Eventually we emerged and once again, dug our way out to the wider world of the village.

Thatching recommenced on the stable again; luckily it was only the ridge and work was begun to put in the attic room for the grooms at the far end; to be reached by an internal wooden stair. Martyn Carpenter and his team were working as hard as they could from first light to sunset in the short daylight hours, to finish it.

Wattle hurdles were used between staves, for the walling and these were plastered with a mixture of dung and straw mixed with soil. We had to dig a long way down through the snow for this and as the ground was so frozen, it was a hard job. Hot water was mixed with the soil and it came up a sticky mess to be stirred into the dung and straw.

February marched on. Giles Thatcher tried to drive his cart back to Marlborough; his son Brice sitting in the back, with his arm now in a sling. He turned around after a while. The drifts were too huge and he could not reach the Salisbury road.

Two more village inhabitants died. The very old and the very young. Little

Johannes, the newborn son of Richard and Marian Ash was called to God, and Old Ralph, his great grandfather, who had been over seventy and the brother of Old Tom Piper, who was still awaiting burial, followed him a little while later.

Late one afternoon, as the sun was setting, Henry my steward and I met in the stable to discuss the new room at the end. The old stable had had accommodation for about ten people. I had built new rooms a few years ago from good solid stone with stone roofs, on the northern wall and so now we did not need such a large room above the horses. Four men could live comfortably in the end room, which was still standing after the snowfall, and this new accommodation was big enough for a further four.

I kept only seven grooms and stable lads. In the past I think my grandfather had employed over ten.

Richard my head groom was about to be married and was going to take over a vacant house in the village and rebuild it, so I would be housing five men here. Anson, a young lad of twelve, lived with his parents, in Durley village.

Henry looked up. "It's an improvement on the ladder that was there before, sir," he said. "A proper stair."

"Aye it is, Henry. If I am forced to rebuild, I shall build better, with more thought."

Henry smiled.

"It will be better for Tostig. He can be alone in the new part for a while before Anson comes of age and moves in. He's a miserable so and so much of the time. Best he doesn't inflict himself on another for a while."

"They have been quiet this three weeks or so, Henry, the brothers," I said holding onto the new hand rail and giving it a good tug.

"True sir. I think a spell in the lockup was just what was needed."

"That and me threatening Hilda with eviction if she could not keep them in check."

"That was clever, sir. If you want to get something like that done... get the women to do it. They always get their way."

I chuckled.

"Well, she certainly had her own way the night Wilfrid threatened to kill the glazier."

"She did?"

I ran up four steps, turned and ran down, testing the treads.

"She did. She managed to convince Wilfrid that it would be foolish to go out and challenge him."

"We all know how much of Wilf is bluster, sir," said Henry, looking up at the roof where it abutted the partition wall.

"Eventually, she went out to tell the glazier that Wilfrid was not coming."

"She did that?"

"Aye."

"Did she see him? If she did, she was the last..."

"No, Henry, she didn't't speak to him, but she did see the man who killed him, I think."

Henry spun round.

"No! Who?"

I shrugged. "Hard to say. When she first looked there were two men by the alders. When she looked again, only one."

"What did she do?"

"What do you think? She fled."

"And she cannot describe the man?"

I slapped Henry on the back..."Come, I'm getting cold. Let's go and have some nice warm watered ale."

Henry laughed. We were out of the stable door and half way across the courtyard when I answered him.

"No, she could not see. A man in a dark cloak and hood, that's all."

"Well, that's every man in the village, sir...."

"Exactly, Henry. No use to us at all." I climbed the hall steps. "Not a scrap."

The next day dawned sunny and bright. We had all been there before. We knew that it was just as cold as it had been and there was no chance of a thaw.

I stood on the manor steps and stretched till my sinews cracked. I remember thinking, I must do some sword practice. I am getting stiff. Perhaps we could clear a space in the threshing barn. The horses were being moved that day to their newly rebuilt home.

I had just turned to step up to my office door, when John appeared at the top of the steps and said.

"Sir, Wilfrid's here. Hilda has gone missing."

Wilfrid came up behind him and blurted.

"She wasn't there when I woke this morning, sir. She isn't with Tostig. She isn't with her goodwives. She wouldn't go far this weather."

"She will be somewhere in the village no doubt, Wilfrid."

"No sir... I mean yes sir, but...."

"Spit it out man."

"I found some blood, on the snow outside the cottage. I'm afraid something's happened to her."

I frowned. "Why would something have happened?" An unpleasant idea was forming in my head.

Wilfrid shrugged.

"Sir, please… can we organise a party to look for her?"

Six men from the courtyard, including John, Hal, Stephen, Peter and Alfred the Woodsmith came to our call. I knocked up Hubert the Blackmith too. He was a handy fellow, tall, broad and strong.

John and myself made the party seven. Nine with the concerned husband.

We fanned out from the door of Wilfrid's cottage.

John hunkered down and examined the blood. There were drops and some smudging, as if someone had been hit (another blunt weapon perhaps, in the same manner as our peddler and glazier,) had staggered and then fallen. He nodded. "If this is Hilda, she was hit, she staggered, fell, her head bled onto the snow. Either she got up again and went off in a daze or someone lifted her and carried her somewhere."

"No drag marks."

"No..just a mess of footprints."

We searched the village. Others joined us as we met and explained what we thought had happened.

Hilda was a popular girl in Durley. Folk came out of their warm homes, wrapping their winter cloaks around them and carrying sticks to poke and prod the drifts.

We agreed to meet on the village green, what we could see of it, in front of the reeve's house and then spread out again and search further afield.

Tostig ran up to us then, pulling on a thick felted jerkin and smoothing down his hair.

"I'll help too, sir."

"Good man," I said.

We spread out from the reeve's house. Johnathan, his youngest, and two of his other sons, Athel and Warin, joined us. Walter Reeve bid us go with God. We fanned out towards the church fields to the west and the Ramsbury road to the east. There was no sign of the girl. John, Hal, Wilfrid and I circled back via the edge of the forest. God forbid that she had struggled into the trees. We should never find her there. We met Tostig and the reeve's sons at the edge of the fishpond. They had checked all the houses to the west of the Ramsbury road. Nothing. Tostig prodded the ice and snow at the edge of the pond in a desultory manner. "We must start again, sir," he said.

There was no body in the pond or the immediate river. I was all prepared to see Hilda's freckled face staring up at me from the river bed, as I had the glazier, but no.

"All outbuildings and barns. If she went out before it was light..." though I could not see why she would, "then she may have taken refuge and fallen into a faint."

We plodded through the snow again, prodding the bigger drifts with poles, kicking the smaller ones over with our boots.

All at once there came a cry.

"Hush."

We listened. No one breathed; no white breath came from any mouth.

There it came again. Faint, weak. It was hard to distinguish what it was crying. It was almost like the bleat of the newborn.

"Here sir..." Tostig forged off towards the village green again. We followed.

We stood and waited, listening. Again no one breathed. Faint but a little louder, came the bleating.

I circled and stared at the houses here.

The reeve, Martyn's house, the widow Giffard's house, an outbuilding belonging to the butcher John Kellog, then his house and the bothy which housed the dead body of Tom Piper. Two woodsmen lived in the other two houses.

"Tostig... the outhouse. John, the widow's house, Johnny, the piper's house. I'll take the butcher's. We know the reeve's is no good."

We were just about to move off when the voice came again. I think that Hilda had heard us.

Tostig started. "Sir... the well. The voice is coming from the well!"

Chapter Nine

The well had been covered over with snow but folk had scraped it back and it sat in a depression in the middle of the village green, with snow piled up around it. It had frozen again. Hal had been lowered down on a rope last time to break the thick ice with a spike. It was so thick now, it would need a hefty blow with a pickaxe and that could not be accomplished in such a small space. The bucket lay useless on the snow beside the wall.

Tostig cried out "Hild… we're coming. Oh God!" and ran down the piled up snow to the wall of the well, which was made of undressed rough flint stone. We followed.

"She's here sir," he yelled back.

I shouted to Johnathan to find the other searchers, tell them we had found our quarry and to find Wilfrid and bring him here.

.I looked down into the well. Hilda was huddled in her cloak, her knees drawn up to her chin and she was shivering violently. Her hood was bloodied and she was using it to pad her head wound. It had stopped bleeding but she was still clutching it. The well was about twelve feet deep to the surface of the ice, upon which Hilda was sitting.

"Hilda!" I cried "Are you injured beyond your head wound?"

Her pale face stared rather vacantly at me as if she didn't't recognise me.

"No… no…."

"No bones broken in the fall?"

"No. I am so cold… so cold."

"We shall have you out in a moment."

It was a matter of a few heartbeats before her husband came up.

"Hilda… oh thank God. I'll get you out my love. Just wait."

John had run to the butcher's house and he came back with a stout rope which Wilfrid tied around his middle.

Gradually we lowered him, inch by inch, over the stone parapet.

Poor Hilda came up shivering and weeping with relief. Her husband handed her up over the stone edge and she held out her arms so we could catch hold of her. Tostig reached down and pulled her close to him. At last Wilfrid climbed out and disengaged the rope from his waist. Hilda fell back into his arms, in a dead faint; he just caught her.

We carried her to the nearest house which was the reeve's where Walter bawled for blankets, hot stones and warm ale and his wife Alice bustled off for some linen to dress poor Hilda's head wound.

She sat on the bench by the fire wrapped in Wilfrid's arms and a huge woollen blanket.

I went down on my knees in front of her.

"Hilda... tell us what happened."

A beaker of warm ale was given to her and she hugged the warmth to her before sipping it gently.

She cleared her throat. I think she had been shouting to be heard for hours but no one had been about on the green and her voice was weak.

"I went outside...."

"Why... why did you go outside?"

"It was still dark and I heard a voice calling me."

"So you got up... were you still in bed?"

"Yes, I was. Wilf was fast asleep facing the wall. I got up and threw on my kirtle and cloak."

"Who was calling you, Hilda?" asked her husband. He looked pointedly at his brother Tostig.

"Not me, brother."

"I don't know. I got to the door."

"What did the voice say?" I asked.

Hilda's eyes filled with tears and she began to weep once more. "I thought I heard someone say that Tostig was sore hurt."

We all fell silent at that.

I tipped the cup to her lips. "Drink more ale Hilda...it will make you feel better and will enable you to carry on and tell us your tale."

She drank, quite a beaker full then and colour began to come back to her face as the fire warmed her from without and the ale, from within.

Wilfrid took the beaker and then chafed her fingers, to bring back some warmth to them.

"So someone called to you to ask you to come out because Tostig was hurt?"

"Hurt and asking for me." She threw a quick glance at Wilfrid, "Sore hurt and like to die."

"Did you recognise the voice?"

Hilda shook her head and grimaced at the pain of it.

Wilfrid merely carried on with his rubbing of her fingers. I saw Tostig look away and a variety of emotions passed over his face. Anger, bewilderment and finally relief.

"But I am hale and hearty. I am fine..." he said at last.

"It was a ruse to get Hilda out of the house," I said.

She nodded and then turned to allow Alice Reeve to wipe her wound and dress it.

I stood. We all shuffled round and found places to stand so that we might not be in the way.

"You left the house?"

"Yes."

"Did you see who was waiting for you?"

"No... sir." It was dark and they were hiding by the wall. I came out further looking round for the person and the next I knew I was spinning onto the snow. There were sparks in my eyes and a huge pain on the side of my head."

Hilda closed her eyes. This was a great effort for her.

"Rest if you need to," I said. "We can hear the tale later."

"No!" she reached out for my arm. "No sir, I will tell it now and then rest."

"Very well."

Another beaker of ale was put into her hands. She cradled it like a baby in the crook of her elbow as she wrapped her arms protectively around herself.

"I was so groggy. I think the person who hit me thought I was dead. I played dead."

"You saw nothing?"

"No... I lay on the snow, keeping still. I thought he would go away."

"He didn't't?" asked Wilfrid.

"No, he picked me up and threw me over his shoulder."

Wilfrid hugged her to him once more. "My brave girl!"

"I still played dead. I thought it was my best chance of staying alive." A smile played around her mouth, "if you see what I mean sir"

"I see exactly, Hilda."

"He trudged away from the house and though I was still sore, woozy and wasn't quite sure where I was or what was happening, I thought he had gone by the poultry bothy - you know the one which...."

"Yes."

"We passed the back of this house, the reeve's house."

"My God," said Tostig. "He took a risk didn't' he? Anyone might have seen him."

"My feeling is that at any other season...or if the weather were not as bad as it is now, yes, it would have been a terrible risk. But now we are all huddled around our fires. Sleeping late, we have few jobs to do or go out to. So few folk would be out."

"But still.... "

"Oh, no doubt. Had he been caught, he would have said he found poor Hilda in this state and was taking her... somewhere for help."

"Bastard" said Wilfrid, with venom.

"I do think he thought he had killed me, sir," said Hilda. "I tried not to call out or cry or whimper."

"It saved you I think, Hilda."

"Next I knew I was tipped in the well and landed on the hard packed ice."

"Did you look up…did you see a face staring down at you?" asked Tostig.

"I kept my eyes shut, playing dead still but through my eyelashes I could see a blurry face."

"Who was it?" we all asked at once.

"I can't say, I was swooning then with the impact of hitting the ice and I banged my head again as I went down. I really *was* stunned then. And it hurt when I hit the bottom." She rubbed her side.

"So you cannot identify your attacker?"

"No, sir. Then I think I fainted."

I sighed, stood and stretched my back.

"No identification. That is a shame."

I rubbed my tired eyes. "We shall keep watch over you, Hilda. I'll set the boys Peter and Stephen to guard you. Once he knows he hasn't done the job properly, our murderer may try again."

"Oh sir…" said Hilda, looking terrified. She pushed her fist to her mouth. "That is frightening."

"Do not fear. We shall take good care of you." I addressed her husband. "For a while, I want both of you to come up and live in the hall. Just till we can uncover a little more about this attempt."

"Aye sir," said a much chastened Wilfrid. "Thank you sir."

I made for the door.

"There is one thing, sir…."

"Yes, Hilda?"

"I may not have seen the man, m'lord."

"No."

"But I did see the weapon he used to fell me."

"You did...?"

I came back to stand before her again.

"It was a large piece of wood, sir....heavy, like a stave or something. I saw it coming and I drew away. I think that saved me from... from death, sir."

"Something like a barrel is made of?"

"Aye... something like that. Er... bigger. A fence post maybe." She closed her eyes. "It was like a long piece of heavy wood, with an edge."

We helped Wilfrid support Hilda all the way to the manor hall. Folk had turned out to line the route and there was a lot of cheering and calling of good wishes. I was pleased the way my manor folk stuck together.

Lydia was waiting for me in the hall. We sat Hilda on a bench and covered her with a blanket. Suddenly she perked up..."Oh sir...who will look after Audrey and Arlotta if we are here?"

Wilfrid could see my puzzled look.

"The goats, sir."

"Ah yes...we shall deal with that. Can someone please ask the neighbours to look to the goats for a while, Walter?"

"The wife will do it, sir," he said and the moment passed.

Lydia took me aside. "Is it true someone tried to kill her?"

"Yes, in the same manner as the peddler..." I looked round for him, "Where is he, by the way?"

"In the warmth of the kitchen with Janet."

"Ah...."

Lydia smiled and raised her eyebrows.

"Do I detect a whiff of romance there?" I asked.

"I think you do," she said. "They have spent much time together. At first it was forced but then..."

"It was by choice. Yes, I have noticed, even though you probably think I haven't."

"It's nice to see Janet so happy after her horrible experience with her husband and well, the peddler is a fine fellow."

I smiled and I pecked my wife on the cheek, regardless of who might see me.

"Don't you go getting all romantic over a peddler."

"And don't you go getting all jealous like Wilfrid, over a man who won't be around much longer..."

"Ah, but I think...there you are wrong."

"Hmmm?"

"I think our Martyn might just stay with us... I have a feeling."

You think he will ask for Janet? Would you give permission?"

"If my permission was needed I would, but Janet is a free widow woman with her own plot. If anyone must be asked, it is her father, and I am sure Walter will not stand in the way of Janet's happiness. No, she is a widow, she may do as she pleases."

"Good!" said Lydia with a note of finality. I waited for her to add, "as I did."

"So, Hilda stays here until...?"

"Until I can work out what is going on," I said. "Or until I feel there is no further threat."

I sat heavily on my chair on the dais and Lydia perched on a stool close by.

"Damn this weather that keeps us cooped up like a horde of harlots in a harem."

Lydia laughed and chuckled at that and clutched her sides. "You are beginning to sound like Hal!"

I snorted, "God forbid!"

I rubbed my forehead. A headache was beginning to form there. I knew the signs. Ever since I had been clouted on the head by an angry woman, in the autumn, I had been experiencing headaches. This was especially so when I was worried or was puzzling something out, or I was very tired and not allowed to sleep.

"No, Paul, you know it was not my wife. You remember our tale of my horse

Fitzroy and the Hungry Pool? Then you will remember it was not Lydia. Fool boy."

"I must say I feel responsible for Hilda's near miss."

"Whatever for?"

"I shan't say anything to her for she has enough to worry about, but I was talking to Henry yesterday... about the glazier's trip out to the riverside at Twelfth Night."

"Why should that make a murderer want to dispose of Hilda?"

I told Lydia the tale of the midnight challenge, how Hilda had gone out to confront the glazier and how she had probably seen the murderer.

"Well, now you know she has seen him. If it were some innocent, there would have been no need to strike Hilda dead."

"But she did not recognise him. Someone overheard Henry and me and put two and two together and made ten."

"He panicked."

"Aye he did that."

"He believes she may be able to identify him?"

"Yes, and as long as that is the case, Hilda is in danger," I replied.

*****

I trudged across the courtyard to find Henry in the stables, supervising the reallocation of the horses to their new home. Fitzroy was being difficult. He had enjoyed himself in the threshing barn and was not going to be cooped up in a smaller space. He was thrashing about and snorting like a pig.

I called out. His eye turned but not his head.

"Fitzroy horse. This is setting a very bad example for the rest of the lesser beasts."

The grooms and stable lads burst out laughing. Perhaps it was my stern voice but eventually we managed to calm him and he stood in his stall, tossing and tossing his head and flicking his tail. Poor Bill, on the end of the leading rein, was nearly lifted off his feet.

I took Henry aside. "Yesterday when we were here and we were talking about Hilda and the man she saw by the river... who might have overheard us, Henry?"

Henry looked puzzled but then light dawned and he looked decidedly uncomfortable.

"You think that someone, the murderer, overheard us and imagined that he had to be rid of poor Hilda because she had seen him?"

"That is precisely what I think," I said.

"But she didn't sir... recognise him. You said so."

"No, and I feel very bad about this. Had I answered you when you asked me if she could identify the glazier's attacker, instead of walking you out of the door and out of earshot, perhaps... there would have been no need to try to kill her."

"Oh Saints preserve her."

"So...who might have heard us, Henry?"

We made a mental list of all those we felt could possibly have been listening to us.

"Two of the grooms who were moving tack and suchlike back into the stable. They were Bill and...."

"Edward. I saw him."

"Alfred was crossing the courtyard. We passed him on his way in here."

"Aye, Alfred Woodsmith."

"Hubert might have heard us from the smithy if he wasn't making noise himself."

I chortled. "Which he usually is."

Henry scratched his head, shivered and then put up his hood again.

"Wyot... maybe."

"Too far I would think. We weren't shouting."

"Richard came out of the haybarn."

"I think we can disregard him. He wouldn't be able to get through the snow quick enough."

"Ah... yes his bad foot. Even though it's getting better, he's still slow."

"Matthew was crossing to the kitchen I think. Been in the undercroft."

"Again too far away."

"Erm...there were the carpenters upstairs in the stable loft. Though again, they would be making a lot of noise, hammering and sawing."

"Hmmm. I'll think on it, Henry. Thanks." I slapped him on the back.

I raced up the pristine wooden stairs and looked around the new room above the stable. Four partitions were nearly finished. Palliasses, stools and other equipment and furniture would soon be dragged up into the space to make it habitable and homely.

The stairs debouched from a wattle wall which reached about eight feet in the air. This wall was being daubed with the sticky mixture we had begun to make a couple of days ago.

"How goes it Martyn?" I asked.

He did not look up from his work.

"It goes. Bloody cold. Daub won't set, m'lord."

"Oh... the cold?"

"I have never made a wall in such cold. I dunno. Must be."

I nodded. "Must be very frustrating."

"Aye it is. That, and you can't feel yer fingers after a while."

I smiled.

"No, I suppose not."

I looked behind me. A lad was sweeping the debris of the workings into a pile in the middle of the room.

He touched his forelock. "M'lord."

"Who was up here yesterday Martyn, working in the loft?"

"When, sir?"

He stood and put his chapped and aching hands under his arm pits to warm them.

"Oh... about sunset. Late anyway. Vespers."

Martyn gestured to the lad.

"Pick it up boy... we can re-use that. We don't waste what we can re-use."

The lad fetched a shovel and swept the leavings into it.

Martyn gestured to a pot on the floor and the lad tipped the bits into it.

"The lad and me, and I think that Alfred was here."

"No, before that."

"Ah well that was me and Ralph here. Oh yes... and Tostig came up for a while, to see where he was to live."

"And..."piped up the treble of Ralph, the carpenter's apprentice, "the fellas what brought the hurdles."

"The wattle hurdles?"

"Yep, sir."

"The Sylvestres?"

"It were them, yessir."

"They just dropped the hurdles and left," said Martyn.

I nodded. "Anyone else?"

The two of them conferred with a puzzled look.

"At dusk...? Well, Johnathan Reeve looked in, sir."

"Why...this place has little to do with him? He has no work here," I asked, puzzlement in my voice.

"Well, now," said Martyn. "He came to see, cause his da, Walter Reeve, had sent him."

"What for?"

"To see how long it were going to take us. See, much like you sir, how much work we had got through."

Now I understood why Johnathan Reeve might be there. His father was an elderly man. He was grooming his son to take over from him, those duties he could no longer easily perform. He would find the steep stairs difficult to climb, I know.

"He stood where you are now sir, and took in the rafters and the thatch and the good wooden floor and then, the hurdles and the daub."

"Was it quiet in here, Martyn?"

"Quiet sir?"

"No nailing or sawing."

"No, we'd done all that for the day, I think sir. We'd begun the daubin'. "

Martyn Carpenter blew on his hands.

"He stood there a looking and a weighing it all up. Quiet like."

I nodded.

"You'd better get some of that grease into your fingers tonight, Martyn. The stuff that Dr. Johannes makes for you. Using that daub stuff and in this cold... your hands must be very sore."

"Without it, sir, I couldn't do the job," and he went back to pressing the mixture to the wattles.

*****

That night, as is my custom, I sat in the office after supper and on a piece of parchment I scribbled the names of all the people who might have overheard Henry and myself talking about Hilda. I could not see why any of them would wish harm upon Hilda. For that matter I couldn't see why any of them would want to kill Perkin Glazer. I could hear the noise in the hall. There was much cheering and laughing. Folk were obviously finding their own amusements of a bitterly cold evening. Was there a game going on, that there was so much cheering? Were two bravos pitting their strengths against each other with arm locked into arm over a table? No, Hawise was still in the hall and I doubt that Lydia would allow such a coarseness to be witnessed by a young noble girl. There would no doubt be swearing and cursing if this was the case.

I left my parchment and wandered out into the screens passage. Through the hall door, I could see several people sitting at the long table, the one we left up all the time, not the trestles which we put away after supper each night. Many of them were bending over something.

Martyn Summersete seemed to be in the middle of all this gaiety. His face was flushed and he was laughing and fiddling with something in a bag.

Standing by his side was Janet Woodsman. She had her hand on his shoulder and she too was laughing.

Lydia was sitting close by with Hawise on her knee. Hal was standing protectively behind her, though his eyes were all over the room, rather than what was on the table.

Wilfrid and Hilda were sitting quietly chatting with each other, a little way off. Stephen and Peter were not far away.

I turned and locked my office door and quietly entered the hall. No one saw me but Hal, who nodded.

"No, no more... I can do no more. It's tiring stuff this is, for a man who only a month ago had a head as smashed as a boiled egg top!" said Martyn with a chuckle in his voice.

"Sing then Martyn," said Hawise, clapping her hands. "Sing the song you sang for me ... the really sad one about the ghost on the grave."

Some people crossed themselves and drew slightly away, others laughed and egged the peddler on.

"Oh all right... all right. I'll sing, though I won't sing that one. T'is too miserable for such a gathering as happy as this. I'll sing you a riddle."

People clapped their hands and whooped and fell still as he edged his way to the back of the seat and threw up his head, closing his eyes. Janet squeezed his shoulder lightly.

He sang.

"I was abandoned by my mother.
I did not yet breathe.
A kind woman covered me with her body,
Kept me and looked after me,
Cuddled me as close as if I had been her own child.
Under that covering I grew and grew large.
Even though I was unkind to my adopted brothers and sisters.
This lovely woman fed me
Until I was big enough to set out on my own, a long, long journey.
She had none of her own dear sons and daughters left, because she did so."

The song did not rhyme but it didn't't matter. The tune was lively and folk tapped their feet to the rhythm, if rhythm there was. Don't ask me. I am as note deaf as a croaking frog. Folk began to chatter and at last, Matthew said, loudly, "I think it's a cuckoo."

"Well, done my ample covered friend," said Martyn smiling. "And another....
"A warrior is wondrously brought into the world
For the use of lords by two dumb things;
brightly extracted, which for his hurt
foe bears against foe. Strong though he is
a woman binds him. He obeys them well,
serves them quietly, if maids and men
tend him duly, feed him fairly.
He exalts them in comfort for their joy in life,
grimly rewards one who lets him grow proud.""

"That's an easy one," cried Hubert the blacksmith, "It's fire."

"You are all too good for me," chuckled Martyn, "Let me sing to you all in a forgotten language. Then at least it can remain a mystery to you for a while. And he began to sing a plaintive song, some words of which were recognisable, others were not. Just as you thought you understood, a word, another word would confound you and you would miss the rest, for trying to fathom out the ones you had heard.

It was like trying to grasp a bush in a mist. Sometimes you managed to grab a leaf or two, and then... it was empty air.

I saw Hal edging towards me through the press and drew back to the door so that he could reach me and say what he was obviously dying to tell me. We whispered.

"M'lord."

"Hal."

"The peddler has been very entertaining tonight, sir."

"So it would seem."

"Not only does he 'ave a whole barrel load o' songs, sir..."

"And riddles."

"Aye, them too. I bet you can't guess what 'e 'as in that there bag."

I looked over the heads of the folk who were rapt in the song. Now what might a man keep in a bag like that? I asked myself. A hessian bag, small enough for a few jewels, a tiny knife, some love letters? I'd seen this bag in his pack but had not opened it. His pack was his own.

"I have no idea, Hal."

Hal fixed me with a grin as wide as the River Styx. He confidently puffed out his chest and stuck his thumbs in his belt.

"Stones, sir."

"Stones ,Hal?"

"Aye sir, stones. And on them stones?"

I raised my eyebrows.

"On them stones he has written a lot of squiggles, sir."

Light dawned.

"Ah I see, sir..you are with me now."

"Aye Hal, my good man. I think I am," I smiled. "Runes, Hal?"

"Indeed they are, m'lord."

Hal looked back at Martyn.

"What's more Sir Aumary, sir, he can read'em!"

Chapter Ten

"When there is a break in the singing Hal, can you ask Martyn Peddler to come and see me in my office please?"

Hal looked at me sidelong. "I better tell 'im that there's naught wrong then. 'E might be a bit worried bein' called in and the like."

"Tell him I just want a word and his advice. That should do it."

"Aye sir." Hal pulled down his bright blue cotte and adjusted his belt. "Right you are, sir."

Martyn came in moments later, his rune bag in his hand. Hal had obviously told him why I needed his advice.

"Martyn, please sit. How are you now? You seem to have made a remarkable recovery."

The peddler pulled up a stool and lowered himself onto it. "Aye, I am feeling almost back to normal. The head is still a bit sore and I do get a headache now and again which lays me low but if I sleep, it goes."

"I too had a similar head wound last year. We share the pain of a headache. I suppose it's to be expected really."

"Dr. Johannes said it might diminish with time."

"Well, he knows what he is talking about. What about the memory?"

"Oh that comes back daily, sir... I now know for certain that I had never been here before because I always stayed on the Roman road and never got off to come further north. East and west but never north, as far north in the county as you are here sir, in Durley. I thought, before the snow came in, that it might be good to come up here. I never been past Salisbury afore, you see."

I nodded. "And have you recalled anything about your home?"

Martyn smiled. "I have. I have no wife back in Dunster, though I did have an ancient mother, till last June when she was called to her rest, God save her.

So I have no one...no one at all to miss me."

"Friends... neighbours?"

"The life of a peddler is solitary, my lord. Not much time for friends. Yes, I had drinking companions, if you can call them friends. Neighbours? Well, it was my mother's house we lived in see, so they were her friends really."

"And the house in which you lived?"

"Belonged to the abbey at Wells, m'lord. They took it back when my old mum was taken."

"Ah." I looked him in the eye.

"Can you swear to me, upon any saint by which you care to take an oath, that you are not a married man, Martyn?"

The question made him blink but he recovered quickly.

"Yes, my lord. Upon my mother's soul, for she was a saint and make no mistake, and may St. Andrew strike me down if what I say is not the truth. He is my saint sir, for he has the cathedral at Wells and my birth day. No, I have no wife, on Andrew's bones. I've never bin married."

"Good, for I would not have Janet strung along and misled. She is a good woman and has had much pain in her life."

"You've noticed then, sir?"

"Aye, I have," I replied smiling

"I would not give her pain, sir." Martyn looked genuinely hurt, "I love the very ground on which she stands. She is priceless beyond measure is that lady, sir."

"Will she have you, do you think?"

"If I don't do too much going away to sell my wares and stay here to help with the plot, I think she will."

"You don't need my permission, she is a free woman and a widow. Might be polite to just ask her father though. I'm sure he will not make it difficult for you both."

"I will sir... I will. And, beggin' your pardon m'lord, you won't mind if I plonk meself down on your lovely manor and take root?"

"Not at all Martyn. Though if there is as much as a sniff of a rumour that you are not what you seem, you will answer to me...personally."

"Aye, sir." He stood and he held out his hand for the bargain. I took it and we shook.

"Now I have something I'd like to show you." I had previously taken the apple from my secure chest and hidden it in my scrip. I leaned back and fished it out. Martyn sat down again.

I put it on the table but did not relinquish my grip.

"I must ask you to keep this an absolute secret for the moment. I cannot let it be bruited abroad that we have found such a thing, for fear of...well, I know not what. Fear of someone trying to steal what else we might find at the same spot, when we can at last look, when the ground will give up its possible treasures." I told him the story of finding the little enamel apple.

Martyn's eyes grew as round as the apple in front of him.

"Oh, that is a wondrous thing."

He wiped his hands on his jerkin.

"May I... may I pick it up m'lord?"

I nodded and Martyn lovingly picked up the little apple.

"Hal tells me that you can read runes. I would love to know what it says here. I hear you can read and write Martyn?"

"Aye, I can a bit."

Martyn was transfixed by the little work of art. He turned it round and round as all who had handled the thing, had done.

He shook his head.

"Aye, I can read the runes... I *can* read them." He looked up, "But I cannot really read what is written here."

"Why not?"

"I read runes for folk, sir. They choose some and I can tell them the answers to the questions they ask. The runes answer those questions and I just interpret them."

"You can't read what is written here?"

"To a point I can."

Martyn pointed to the golden band in the middle.

"I could take the letters written here and write them so that they came out in English....in a version of it. But they would still be foreign words."

I pushed the paper towards him. "Here is what I have worked out." I pointed to the lines. "Four lines, three repeats and one very different."

"Aye, I see it." Martyn brought the candle closer and compared my notes with the little apple in his hand.

"Well you have it right, sir. The lines all begin 'Ic giefe."

"And that means...?

"Now luckily, I know what this means because...you remember the song I sang tonight m'lord, the one where I said it was in a forgotten language?"

"I do."

"Some words are the same. When I learn a song, I learn it by rote and I don't always know what the words mean exactly. I just have the gist of it. This one I know quite well. It's Old English see. It's - I give."

"So, this says, I give, three times." I said.

"I think it does. And see here, we have the words for 'my love'...well they crop up in songs all the time and that is why I know. This one I think says apple..... well it's a lot like our word isn't it?"

"So the first line might say. I... give... my love an apple, perhaps I will give my love an apple?"

"And the second line...well I don't know but there is the word, 'without, būton.'"

"Then it goes on "I give...my love a?"

"House, sir... same word as we use. Then we got without again and the word door. Again... same as we use. Nearly."

"I give my love a...now what is that then?"

Martyn screwed up his eyes. "I think that is..Oh 'cmon brain..you know that one...." and he began to sing a song in this strange language until he got to the word 'palendsan'.

"Aye that's it. I knew if I sang it I'd remember. It's palace sir... I will give my love a palace. I get that from the Fairy Palace song."

"Right! It sounds like one of your riddles, Martyn."

Martyn's face split in such a smile, I almost hugged him.

"I have it sir. The word is definitely 'will give'.

"I will give my love an apple, a house and a palace?"

"Yessir."

"Each second line begins with 'Without' then?"

Martyn peered again at the apple and then at the piece of paper on which I had written my 'poem'.

"I think it does. Oh I must go through all the songs I know in English sir... real Old English ,and I know a few, and see if I can come up with any other words I recognise."

"Shall we write these down then, one by one, letter by letter, and then you might be able to work out what they say?"

"Aye that would be good."

And so the rest of the evening was taken up with the two of us, our heads together, me transcribing and Martyn shouting out the letters and telling me where the words began and ended.

By the time folk were setting up their beds ready for sleep in the hall, Martyn and I had written down all the words on the apple, in the ancient language of the English.

We stretched and yawned.

"Come to me soon and I'll show you what we have managed to borrow from the priory.

It's a little book with many more runes in it. You will be fascinated Martyn."

Martyn made for the door.

"Aye sir...I'd love that."

I smiled.

"Thank you for your help."

Martyn knuckled his forehead, though he was no serf of mine and didn't't need to.

"And... Martyn."

He turned back, his eyes tired and reddened.

"Hmm?"

"Welcome to Durley village."

*****

The next day, Matthew Cook came to me and said that some of the stores were running low. We had not been able to get to Marlborough or put into the forest to replenish stocks.

Agnes Brenthall came and gave me a detailed list of what we had left and what we might be able to do to survive the next few weeks or so, should the freezing conditions continue.

I called together the village elders and those men of importance in the village, like John who was chief wood warden and Walter Reeve, Henry the steward and Hal of Potterne.

It was decided some of us would try to get to Marlborough on foot and drag home some supplies behind us on a hurdle.

"But lord," said Walter. "What if the town is also short of supplies and they will not sell us anything, for fear of losing out themselves?"

"We cannot make them help us, Walter," I said "but we shall know if they are telling us the truth if they say they too are short. Whatever they can spare we shall be pleased to buy."

"Aye, an' I know what'll 'appen," said Hal quietly, almost to himself. "They'll wring the lights outa us an' it'll cost us double to buy anythin'."

"So be it Hal. We cannot come home empty handed."

*****

Hal and I went to the carpenters' workshop to look for some stout sticks to help us walk and to prod into unknown depths of snow. The carpenters kept a store of good hazel poles which, amongst other things, made the best walking sticks.

I walked into the barn-like workshop and looked about me.

"There sir," said Hal as he gestured towards the far wall. Here seasoned planks, beams, posts and poles were lain horizontally on a framework of other woods so that they would not warp or bend.

There were fewer pieces of wood here now than the last time I had been in the store, for much of it had been used in the re-building of the stables.

"I think six poles should do it, Hal. Six of us will drag the hurdles by turns and the rest will walk and guide the load through the snow. Each will need a stick to help stay upright."

We neared the store and began to scan the shelving.

There was a stack of shorter pieces leaning up against the wall. Pieces which no doubt had been saved from past projects. Pieces that the woodmen considered good enough to keep, many of them oak and other hard wood. Offcuts too good to discard or burn.

Hal jumped up onto the nearest pile and steadied himself.

"Mind it doesn't roll. It looks none too safe, Hal."

Too late. The pile which had looked so solid a moment ago, shifted and Hal managed to jump clear.

"Well, I'll be...."

"Badly stacked, Hal," I tutted. "I shall have a word with Martyn. One of the lads must have saved himself a few moments and thrown the pile together."

"But the outside is well stacked, sir."

"Aye… it was. Ah here is the culprit. An offcut shorter than the rest. It should have been laid over there…. No wonder it…."

Hal came closer. "One short one and a lot o' longuns. Bound to roll around like a dog in a cowpat!"

I lifted the length of stout ash from the haphazard pile. Both Hal and I stared at it. Slowly his eyes rose to meet mine.

"Blood, sir?"

"Aye… it's blood and a few strands of fine hair. Blonde hair."

"Hilda's hair maybe?"

"And what's that at the base?" I gave the offcut to Hal. He peered at it.

"It's greasy. Well, no, not greasy… it's marked with grease. Looks like a hand mark. Where someone has gripped it."

I felt behind me and I sat down on a convenient saw-horse. The world had lurched unpleasantly. No, it could not be. I could not believe it.

"No word of this yet, Hal. Not to anyone. Put the wood back as we found it. I need to think… think carefully before I act."

"Right you are, sir…"

"Before you do… hand it back a moment."

Hal handed me the sharp edged offcut, his hand in the middle so as not to disturb the blood or the prints.

I brought the greasy end to my nose and sniffed.

"Bergamot and beeswax and something else though I don't remember what it is. I have smelt it before."

Hal made no further comment and we tidied the pile and fetched our hazel poles.

However, I knew that like me that Hal was shocked. Shocked at what we had found and hoping against hope there was some simple explanation for it.

On the way back to the courtyard I said to him, "Hal, can you ask Martyn to join us on our trip please?"

"Ask sir?"

"However you put it Hal, make sure he comes. The others can be volunteers."

We went off to Marlborough on our errand with my mind in turmoil.

How would I deal with this? How could I deal with it? Nine of us, dressed in our warmest clothing, gathered up cloth bags in which to put what food we could manage to find. We dragged three hurdles with us which we attached by ropes and some of the men carried shovels should we need to dig our way through impenetrable drifts. Others carried further ropes to bind our purchases safely to the hurdles.

We made quite good time until we reached the huge drift which had stopped Giles Thatcher and his cart from reaching the Salisbury Road. We dug our way around it and trudged on.

One side of the north-bound road to Marlborough was relatively light in snowfall and so we veered to the eastern side and managed to keep going. We passed the Big Bellied Oak, so called, for he was ancient and huge. The snow came up to the top of the branching trunk.

Towards Cadley we found it especially hard going for the hill was steep there and the snow had piled up with the fierce winds which had blown for days. The hill was icy and we struggled up it, often losing our footing. We staggered on, holding each other up and dragging the hurdles painfully slowly behind us, every one of us taking a turn. How much more difficult was this going to be on the return journey, when we had laden them with provisions? Eventually we dropped down into Marlborough. It had taken us seven hours to travel three miles.

We were all of us so tired that it wasn't going to be possible for us to search the town for food that day and set off back home; besides the light would be fading soon. I sent Martyn Carpenter, Johnathan Reeve, Hubert Alder, Tostig Frithson, Cedric Groomsman and Alfred Woodsmith to the priory to beg a bed for the night. John and Hal, I sent to Johannes. I knew he could bed them down in his warm kitchen. Crispin the priest had joined us at the last minute, his ecclesiastical garb exchanged for warm hose and a thick pale grey tunic. He would beg a bed at the priest of St. Peter's house, he said. He had things to discuss with him.

I called in at Nicholas Barbflet's house on the High Street and told him of our plight.

He was an up and coming man in Marlborough and had been voted by the townspeople into the position of town reeve. This role allowed him some power and meant that he was at the head of the group of men who ran the business of the town. Nicholas owned the mill on the River Kennet which ground the flour for the town and was a well respected Marlburian.

He took in my bedraggled appearance and bade me come into his parlour and sit by the fire. I noticed he had fine glass in his windows. I steamed gently as my clothes dried out; many a time I had fallen in the snow and ice and my boots and hose were sodden.

Warm wine was fetched and I spoke to him at length about the troubles at home in Durley.

"You must stay with us tonight, Aumary," he said. "Your men will be well cared for at the priory."

"That is most kind of you, Nicholas , but I must speak to my friend Johannes and I have left John and Hal there. I'll bed down with them."

"As you wish."

"I have called on you because, as the town reeve, you have your eyes and ears everywhere and will know the true state of the supplies to be had here in the town."

"It's true. We had a meeting about it only yesterday," said Nicholas. "The town elders, business men, artisans and myself."

"Do you think that some might be able to spare us a little something? We have no wish to deprive any of their fair share but..."

"Aye, I know what it must be like out in the forest."

"We are not starving yet, but by our trip here I hope to stave off the worst shortages."

He slapped me on my back. "We shall see what we can do. Many a time has the forest helped the town. Perhaps it's time to pay it back eh?"

We sat in front of the fire and chatted amicably. Meat and bread was fetched for me and I fell on it hungrily.

"There is one other thing I should like to ask you, Nicholas."

I stretched my hands to his ample fire.

"The young lass who you had here with you, one of my folk... what was her name?"

"Madalen, Madalen Carpenter."

"Aye, that's her. What can you tell me about her?"

Nicholas stretched out his legs to the fire and cradled his ale pot.

"She was a sweet thing, eight or nine as I remember. It was two years ago now. Felicity, my wife, had a fancy for a maid. Well, you know what these women are like. You will remember that the lass had lost her mother that autumn and she was all alone with her father in Durley."

"I remember. Before I was called away to Normandy, Martyn asked me if I minded if she came here to you, for he was finding it hard to manage and besides, I think he felt that it was a step up for a girl of his to be in service in the town."

"Originally, just to see how things went, she came to be a companion to my little lass Aedelind, We only had her then. Now of course we have the twins." He cast his eyes to Heaven "And don't I know it."

Nicholas' wife had given him twin boys in the autumn.

"Felicity soon realised that the girl was a quick learner, was fine and fastidious and would make a good maid and so took her on, to train her, so to speak."

"Her father was happy about this, even one so young?"

"Very. She was very happy here."

"She took to the tasks that were allotted to her?"

"Aye she did... nothing strenuous of course, she was only a wee lass. Helping to dress, brushing and plaiting hair and looking after clothes. Learning to sew and mend, helping Felicity in the still room, that sort of thing." Nicholas looked towards me in puzzlement.

"Why the questions, Aumary?"

"I cannot tell you just yet but I promise I will lay it all before you soon. So, at first, she seemed fine. What happened to change all that?"

Nicholas' face grew grave.

"I really don't know. One day she just stopped talking. Oh, she went about her duties, such as they were still, but she wasn't the happy child she had been. There was no more laughter. She shunned the company of Aedel, when she could. Aedel grew cross with her for she would not play or speak."

"You could think of nothing which had happened to bring about this change?"

Nicholas frowned. "No, nothing."

"What did you do?"

"We asked your friend Johannes to come and talk to her. To look her over to make sure she was not ill or touched in the head somehow."

"And he found?"

"Nothing."

"I will see him later, I will ask him. So then what? It's a far cry from not speaking and becoming solitary, to wasting away as they said she did."

"She ceased to eat or drink. We could not make her. Oh, the times we tried... it's painful to think on it. Then naturally, we had to call for her father."

"Was Martyn able to make some sense of it all?"

"No, she would not speak to him and turned her face away. If he tried to take her in his arms, she would scream and fight."

"Fight her own father?"

"Aye, it was as if a demon had got into her. We asked the priest of St. Mary's to come and bless her, just in case, though to be honest, I am not so sure that folk can be possessed of the Devil, but you will not repeat that."

"Nor I Nick," I said truthfully. "Every devil I have ever met has been flesh and blood and walk on ten toes and not cloven hoofs. And no. I will not repeat it."

There was the hint of a smile on Barbflet's rugged face.

"Her father tried to take her home to Durley but the fuss she made and the madness it caused…well, we abandoned that plan."

"Hmmm." I stared into the flames.

"She became very weak. I called for Johannes again for she had begun to cough. Little water had passed her lips for three days even though we had tried to force her. He tried to listen to what was going on inside her chest but she fought him, weak as she was. I think he thought that her breathing was affected and that sixth night she passed in her sleep."

"Was Martyn still here?"

"Aye, he was. He said that at the very last she whispered something to him but he would not tell us what she said."

"For a father's ears only."

"Perhaps."

I sat back and contemplated the fine room in which I sat.

"Tell me, Nick, who was here in the house and the outbuildings at the time little Madalen fell ill?"

Nicholas looked perplexed but pursed his lips and said, "Besides the usual folk you mean?"

"Yes."

"For what it's worth… um… Let me see. I had some building work going on at the back. We built a new kitchen," he laughed, "not quite as grand as yours but… and I had the tiler in to repair the roof after the gales. Oh yes, and the glazier was here with a couple of lads, though mostly on his own for he did much of the work on the front windows himself. He lives across the way… before he… um, before he… died."

"Yes, I know," I said.

I took a deep breath. "What I am about to tell you, Nick" I said, "must be kept quiet from the town at large for I do not want another harmed by the tale.

I want you to know, for you have a girl and it is young girls who have been at risk. I have a reliable witness who will attest to the truth of what I say and the testimony of some of the girls themselves, though I know in law they cannot be accepted. One of them is my own dear Hawise...."

Nicholas looked at me with wide eyes, as I told him the tale of Perkin Glazer and his helpless victims.

The fire crackled and spat in the silence that followed. Nicholas could not take in the enormity of it and, with his head in his hand, whispered. "It was rape then? Rape of a little one?"

I shrugged. "We shall never truly know but all the pointers lead to him and to rape, yes."

Nicholas Barbflet was a hard headed business man. He had dealt with many unpleasant situations both in his own business and in the wider town. He had a reputation as a fair but forceful man. He looked up at me with tears in his eyes.

"I had no idea...I was powerless to stop it. Oh Blessed Mary Mother of Jesus, my little Aedel might have gone the same way."

I stood and took his arm.

"I cannot be sure, but I think wee Madelen died of shame, shame at what Glazer had done to her."

He looked up sharply,

"Do you think her father knew....at the last?"

I turned on my way out. "Sadly, Nick, I have to say, I think he did."

*****

I made my way slowly and unhappily to Johannes' house at the top of the High Street. I called out as I entered the yard and banged my boots noisily on the doorstep, ridding them of snow and slush. Little Agnes opened the door and bobbed a curtsy at me, her face glowing with glee. John, Hal and Johannes were sitting in front of the hearth and John and Hal jumped up when they saw me and I waved them down.

"It looks as if we may be successful in our quest," I said. "We have Nicholas Barbflet on our side."

A beaker of warm ale was pressed into my hands. My face was glowing from the last ale I had drunk and from the flames in front of which I had previously toasted myself. John and Hal were similarly ruddy. Johannes made a place for me on the end of his cushioned bench and bid me welcome. I recall he congratulated me on the journey we had made and on making contact with Barbflet. Then he thoughtfully said that he had gathered together some further supplies, which Agnes and he could spare and that we were welcome to take them home. I think I thanked him.

I sat silently, my ale cup in my hands, turning over the facts in my mind. The other three carried on their conversation but it faded into the background for a while.

Agnes touched me on the shoulder and tilted her head on one side. This was her sign language for, 'What is it? What is troubling you?'

I shook my head, "Agnes, you really do not want to know. Tonight I have learned something so foul that I know not quite what to make of it."

"Hal coughed and pulled on his forked grey beard, a sure sign he was upset.

"I've said naught m'lord but the little lass sir.....was it, as you thought?"

"Aye, Hal... it was. And worse."

Agnes lowered herself to a stool and once again, I launched into my tale. This time, I added the information I had gleaned from Nick Barbflet to the end of it.

"I remember the girl," said Johannes. "God's bones, I had a hard time of it. I am sure she wanted to die, willed herself to die, though I said nothing at the time for, as you know..." he tailed off and put his hand over his eyes. "I could not consign her to a cruel burial as a self-murderer."

"She was barely nine Johannes, would the church have been so unkind as to enforce it on so fragile a flower?"

"Ask Crispin. I do not know the theologies of it. All I know is, just in case, I kept silent."

"As shall we all. Are we agreed?"

Everyone nodded.

Johannes shook his head. "I never thought to examine her for... well... interference. Never entered my head."

"Why should it?" I said. "We were all taken in."

"Not that I could get near her mind you. The dying are uncommon strong, Aumary!"

*****

My bones and muscles ached that night as I lay on a pallet under several blankets in Johannes' warm, parlour. Despite my exhaustion I could not sleep. Ghostly forms would invade my head. Little girls in bloodied shifts, their mouths screaming in agony and shame, would rise out of the ground and stagger towards me. Pieces of wood, sharp and bloodied, danced in front of me. I recalled the glazier, his face glowing with the passion of a lifelong love of glass, handling the little apple and explaining how it had been made. I saw him too, dripping and icy as they lifted him from his riverine grave and laid him on the hurdle. And then I saw Martyn Carpenter, weeping at the death of his only child, his face a mask of anguish and horror. I saw him too on the roof of the stable, handing the straw to Brice Thatcher; I saw him striking the glazier. Then I saw him, sharp against the snow, raising the offcut of wood he had used to bludgeon poor Hilda. It was that last image which stayed with me all day.

I came awake with a start and realised that it was fully light and that John was calling me from the doorway.

"Sir, the town reeve is here."

Slowly I got up from the pallet and pulled on my cotte. Everything was crumpled and soiled. Mud crusted the bottom of my clothes where I had slid in the scraped earth. I ran my hands through my hair. I took a swig of the ale left for me by Little Agnes as a night drink, should I awake thirsty.

"Good morning Nick," I said, "God granted you rest I hope?"

"Well, it doesn't look as if he was all that kind to you, Aumary," he smiled. "No, I slept poorly." I understood and I nodded.

"And do you have anything to report about the matter we discussed in private yesterday?"

Nicholas turned his head to the few men who loitered outside the doctor's back door,

"As to the first matter - we have managed to cobble together some supplies for you. It is as much as we can afford. Some wheat, a little smoked meat, some cheeses, some dried goods."

"I must pay you for it."

"No, it is a gift from the town. The town knows that the King has appointed you above us, to act as the constable and to search out and detain malefactors within the area, and we are agreed that this is to be your fee for so doing. Let us call it a thanks for your help... present and future."

I smiled and bowed as graciously as I could, in my somewhat tousled state.

"Thank the town fulsomely on our behalf, Nick. And the second matter?"

Nicholas came further into the kitchen, nodded to Johannes and took in John and Hal standing by the fire. "I have investigated that matter. My own tell me that it was as you suspected. The person we talked about was left alone with the suspected wrongdoer on several occasions. A huge oversight on our part. We shall never forgive ourselves." There was a catch in his voice. Eventually he went on, "My own told me that no such approach was made to them and that they have been safe from harm."

"God be praised," I said.

I conjured up the face of Nick's only daughter Aedelina, now eleven. She was a plain girl with a wide face, nondescript grey eyes, a pouting mouth and mousey hair. As she had grown, she had put on weight as many spoiled lasses, who own overindulging fathers, are wont to do in their late childhood.

I pictured little Madelen in my mind's eye. Small delicate, blonde, elfin faced with...no! No more. I could see why she would be singled out by the likes of Perkin Glazer.

"I am glad that I could bring this matter to the attention of the town. We who have children must be extra vigilant. I for one, naïve that I was, did not suspect such wanton wickedness was abroad in our streets. I will be much less simple in future."

I saw Johannes look quickly at the floor. This had affected my friend more than I had realised.

We loaded the supplies and stowed them away on our hurdles. I left John and Hal, with Johannes helping, to secure the ropes and trudged down the High in the direction of the priory. Firstly I had a visit to pay to my old friend the cordwainer.

I raised my fingers to scratch on the door when it was opened rapidly and a smiling Grace, his wife, beamed at me from the door hole.

"Come away in, my lord," she said. "He'll be pleased to see you. We saw you from our upstairs window, threading your way through the muck of the street."

"I am interrupting the breaking of your fast, Grace..."

"Ooh... that doesn't matter. Come and take some bread with us. We still have a jar of honey left, the ones you gave us from Peter's bees."

I smiled as I jumped up the stairs. These people were like family to me.

Little Cassie was sucking her fingers of honey, sitting on her father's knee. The elder girl, Gytha, was sitting close to Harry Glazer. They were both finishing their morning ale. The other apprentice, Felix Castleman, engaged in telling a tale to the others was, seated at the far side of the table, as I entered. He swivelled as I appeared and jumped up, as did Harry. I smiled at Gytha and she took this as her signal to stay seated.

"Do not rise Gilbert, but carry on. It looks as if you are having fun."

"Sit, sir and take bread with us," said my old friend.

"I would love to, but I must not, for I should not take food from your childrens' mouths, Gilbert in these straitened times."

"Bless you sir, we are all right here in the town. Did you get the stuffs we sent to you? We the Aldermen, as we like to call ourselves, met this morning early about it and voted to give an eighth of what we had. Those of us as had it of course."

"I am grateful for your help, Gilbert, and the people of Durley will ever be in your debt."

Gilbert preened but feigned embarrassment. "No sir... for all you have done for us... the town is grateful."

"Indeed we are," said Harry quietly.

I accepted a hunk of bread with Peter's honey, and sat on the end of the bench with Felix.

"You will know Gilbert, that the matter we spoke about is now out in the open."

"Aye sir... I know what is known."

"I have solved your father's murder, Harry, and will in due course speak to you of it in private."

Harry was about to open his mouth to ask me a question of his own when a look from his master sent him into silence.

"Down to work my bravos," shouted Gilbert. "Down to your stitching and cording, to your cutting and piecing!"

Harry smiled at that and threw his leg over the edge of the bench. He bowed.

"Till later m'lord... perhaps."

"Aye Harry my lad, till later."

Grace came to take a sticky Cassie away and Gytha followed her mother into the back room complaining that she did not want to, yet again, do her sewing. We both laughed, but the moment was soon lost.

Gilbert's face at once became grave. "Nick Barbflet told me about your visit last night."

"Aye... it was not a pleasant call. Poor Nick; he was horrified and I know he feels in part responsible for what happened."

"How did the devil get away with it? After all... there must be a young girl somewhere who complained to her da or ma about the man."

"Aye... perhaps. But do we really listen to our girls, Gilbert? We think their heads full of feathers and fluff."

"Well, some do, but you and me..."

"He was a respected artisan. Their word against his. I suspect he told them that too. I can just imagine him saying, 'You tell your mam and such and such will happen. Or I'll come and take my belt to you. Or...I'll send a devil to devour you,' something like that."

"Fear then?"

"I suspect if we dig further we shall find more wickedness comes to light."

Gilbert nodded.

"But I am loath to dig too deep for the sake of Harry."

"Aye, were it to become widely known that his da was a, was a...."

"Degenerate?"

"Aye... well... they might think..."

"That Glazer blood runs through his veins and in that blood lies the perversion just waiting to leap out."

Gilbert crossed himself.

"He's like his mam, is Harry. Thank God." Gilbert became conspiratorial, leaning over the table and whispering. "What are you going to do about... you know who?"

"Nick told you what we thought?"

"He did."

I sighed. "I could forgive him, yes, I could, the death of the monster Glazer. I cannot forgive that he tried to kill Hilda."

Gilbert sat up. "What…has he tried it again? Oh no!"

I told him, as briefly as I could, the story of Hilda and the well, for time was marching on and we must needs be off if we were to make it home before dark.

"And I also suspect he tried to kill Brice Thatcher by pushing him off the roof…I cannot be sure but I think I know why he might have done that."

"Giles' lad?"

"Aye, the same."

"Oh no sir… you cannot let it go. You must do something. It sounds as if grief has turned his brain and he's become a monster himself."

I was licking my own fingers of honey as I reached the bottom of the stairs. Harry was busy in the work-room; Felix was out the back in the store house. I secured the outside door from the inside, passing the bar into its socket. I would have no interruptions. I called to Harry and entered the workroom and closed the door. He was bending over a last, nailing down a sole.

"Stay lad, I can talk to you whilst you work."

And I told him everything I knew and some of those things I suspected.

His face grew grave.

"Oh the poor bairn…. he used the old word for the girl. "He drove her to her death. Oh, it's at a time like this, that I wish I *had* killed him, sir."

"Aye I know… and I think, to be truthful, I would have held him down for you… but no one must hear you say this Harry. It's between us."

He smiled, a very winning smile. "So what are you going to do, sir? You are the law I hear?"

I ran my hands through my mess of hair. "I don't know yet… something. But as yet. I don't exactly know."

Chapter Eleven

I knew I had to do something. Here was a man I had known all my life. A good man, for all that he had killed and had tried to kill two other innocents. The problem went up and down in my head.

I rounded the corner of the priory gatehouse and knocked on the door. Brother porter let me in. In the large hall my men were lounging, talking quietly. To a man, they all jumped up as I was spotted.

"We are away, boys. The supplies are at Doctor Johannes' house stowed and ready to drag. I hope you are feeling strong today."

I feigned a levity I did not feel. Hubert the Blacksmith, ever the joker, flexed his considerable muscle. The others laughed.

"Nah…" said Cedric "I think I'll stay here, the food is better than at home."

"Don't you let Matthew hear you say that, or he will be baking you in a pie, Cedric," I replied.

Again there was laughter.

"The food will be worse still if we don't get this pile to Durley, so let's be going. We shall collect Father Crispin en route."

The seven of us reached the doctor's yard. He was dressed in his outdoor gear and was giving Agnes some last minute instructions.

"Change the dressing every day. And for Margaret Baker, I have left her medicine on the table - the one in the green pot."

Agnes nodded.

"I am coming with you to help, Aumary," said the doctor. "The more hands on the tiller, the faster the boat weathers the storm… or something like that. I am not a sailing man, you understand."

"What? You who have been half way round the world, not a sailing man.

How did you get there then? Fly?"

Everyone guffawed at that. We all knew that Johannes had been at the crusade with King Richard.

"You may scoff," said Johannes in jest. "But some people think that us doctors are angels. And angels can fly!"

"So they can my friend," said Crispin as he rounded the corner of the yard, coming from the priests house close by the church of St Mary.

"Time we flew back to Durley I think."

Everyone shuffled their feet.

"We shall draw lots to decide who shall haul the heaviest hoard up the hill first."

I held out a bunch of straws which I had filched from Johannes' stable.

Cedric pulled out the second shortest.

And yes, I was left with the smallest one.

*****

Cedric and I struggled up the hill with our burden. Martyn and Hubert came next with the second hurdle. Crispin and Alfred brought up the third; a much lighter load. It took us hours, it seemed. We changed over at the top of the hill and Johannes and John led the way towards Cadley with the heaviest load. No surprise that the lightest hurdle, now drawn by Hal and Tostig, soon overtook them. Martyn and I hung at the back of the line, which was strung out over just less than a quarter of a mile. I made sure we could not be overheard. Once I had caught my breath and we were on the flat, I engaged Martyn Carpenter in conversation.

"As you know, Martyn, I went to see Nick Barbflet yesterday."

"Aye sir, he's a good man."

"It's mostly thanks to him, I think, we are going home with such a good haul."

"I think the town is the better for having him at the helm m'lord."

"Aye, so do I." I paused.

"I talked to him at length about your little one, Martyn. Madalen."

I felt the man's body stiffen beside me as we walked. His face was grim and he stared straight ahead.

"It was kind of him to look after her as he did, I thought. Many a man would call for the father and want to be rid of such a vexing problem." There was no answer except the same stern face.

"Yet he called for the doctor. He treated her like family, didn't he?"

"Aye, Sir Aumary, he did," was the reply at last. Martyn rarely used my name nowadays, though as boys we had been on first name terms.

"He is very, very sad about Madelen's death. Almost as if she were a daughter of his own."

He turned about to look at me then and those grey eyes flickered.

"Maybe he could have taken better care of her, then."

"Maybe he could."

"He still has his own daughter."

"Yes, God be praised," I chuckled. "And two lusty lads in tow, now."

Martyn looked down at his boots, forging ahead in the snow. We took nine or ten paces, matching our steps before I said, "It's always so sad when a young one is taken to God."

"You would know the pain of it m'lord, the way your young'un was taken."

Martyn was referring to my son Geoffrey, who at five years old, had been crushed by a large stone falling from the newly built gatehouse. There had been little left of his head. My only consolation was that he died swiftly.

"Yes, there isn't a day when I don't think of him at some point, see his face full of mischief grinning at me, hear his piping voice laughing. He was always laughing."

"But you still have the Lady Hawise."

"Aye and I thank God for her every day. Though it could have been so very different. It might have been a further tragedy."

I could see him from the corner of my eye, weighing this statement carefully. "How so, sir?"

"Well… like your unfortunate Madalen, she could have taken her encounter with Perkin Glazer to heart so much that she too, starved herself to death."

We had walked on fifteen paces, our boots crunching on the icy frosting, when he said,

"Hawise too?"

"Hawise, Cassie Cordwainer, Petronilla Snap and no doubt a dozen others."

I could see him flexing his hands and making a fist by turns and was instantly on my guard, though I could see that he was not working himself up to strike me, merely deep in his own thoughts and perhaps re-running the killing of Glazer in his head.

"There is no doubt he was a beast of a man," I said. "Not only a menace to grown women, but a wicked threat to small girls."

"Many's the man wouldn't think that a problem, sir. It goes on….everywhere, even in families. Only girls see. There's no redress in the law."

"Aye, but to you and I and to Gilbert, and Richard too, they are, were our girls, Martyn."

"Aye, we cared about them."

"Did you care about Madalen enough to put a piece of wood through Glazer's brain, Martyn?"

I had not meant to ask such a question. I had wanted to lead him to his own confession slowly but somehow the question popped out of my mouth and I was instantly annoyed with myself.

He did not speak but trudged on a while. I did not press for him for an answer.

Crispin joined us for a moment and the subject faded away.

We came at last to Cadley. The hill here was steeper going down than it had been coming up, it seemed. Our efforts at dragging the hurdles down the slippery incline only resulted in us overturning one of them.

"Wait there," I shouted to Johannes and John, who were standing sideways on, one leg shorter than the other in order to maintain a grip on the snow and ice.

Together, the men righted the hurdle, pushed the foodstuffs back into safety and, taking one of the ropes from the next sledge, we fixed it to the back so that it would act as a brake. Hubert's brawny hands grasped the end, Johannes and John pulled gently and slowly they inched their way to the bottom of the incline without further spillage. We came back for the next sledge and did the same. Then Crispin and Martyn, with me acting as the brake, attempted the last of the food-stuffs. Again there was a heaving of the heavy loads up the other side and onto the flat. Only small hillocks to negotiate now. I looked up at the sky. I could not see the sun. A grey-brown pall hung over us. We stopped to take a breath.

"What do we think the time is, John?" I asked, concerned that we must be home before it grew too late.

"Coming up to mid-afternoon I'd say, sir. Our pace has been very slow."

"Please God, it doesn't snow." The words were barely out of my mouth when a few flakes began to fall and we all raised our heads skywards.

"Fulla' the bloody stuff," said Cedric.

"Aye c'mon. Pull away."

By the time we reached the Big Bellied Oak it was snowing heavily.

*****

We tried to keep together, but it was a white mass of whirling snow and we were drawing apart in the fog of it. The wind had risen and puffs of snow rose from that which had been fallen to the ground already and it stung our noses and eyes. We gritted our teeth and screwed up our faces.

"Stay together...do not wander off the track." What track there was.

I caught glimpses of Hal in his bright blue jerkin and followed as best I could. The rest of us wore dun colours and greys, hard to pick out against the background of muddy coloured trees, speckled with white.

"Stop a while and regroup," I hollered.

Now Crispin and Cedric were at the front and they stopped for us to catch up. I counted. There were still three hurdles and eleven bodies. I half thought that Martyn would be missing but no. He was still with us, his hands on his knees, taking deep breaths after a spell pulling the heaviest load with Johnathan Reeve.

Hal's beard was white with snow and he shook it out as a housewife might shake a mat.

Some laughed at that and it lightened the moment. On we went. We approached the Durley road and slowly we cornered and guided the laden hurdles one by one towards the gap we had made on our outward journey in the huge drift. The hurdles would not pass.

"We shall have to dig, boys" I said.

Hubert downed his staff, grabbed one of the shovels which had been pushed under the bags of flour and started to dig. On our outward journey we had only made a path big enough for a man to pass. Now we should have to dig it out over three feet wide. We had handed our hurdles over the first time. This time we could not.

I grabbed the second shovel from my sledge. I gestured to Hal to take his from the hurdle by which he stood.

I did not want Martyn to have a weapon. My wily man at arms winked at me and began to dig. Those that had mittens, helped by scraping the snow with their hands.

Johnathan Reeve took the first sledge through; it slipped and slid but got safely to the roadway. Johannes came through the gap and pulled the next.

The third was pushed and pulled by Alfred and Cedric. The snow piled up around us. It settled on our eyebrows. It flew into our hoods and melted down our necks. It softened with the heat of our bodies and wet the hems of our sleeves.

"Right...only a short distance now," I said encouragingly. "Pull, my pack mules, pull. Put yer backs into it!"

We had gone on a few yards when Hubert, who had been the last in the line, cried, "My stick's gone. I can't find it. Musta' got covered over."

I gave my rope to John and motioned for Hal to come back with me.

As I passed down the line, I grabbed a stick from a startled Cedric and counted my men.

Hubert was the tenth and last.

"We have lost Martyn," I cried.

As if there had been an echo of my words, I heard a scream followed by a pitiful cry.

"In God's name!" I yelled.

Crispin came forging back along the line.

"Cedric," I yelled, "get Johannes back here. The rest of you wait."

Hal came up.

We four ran back through the gap we had created in the drift and looked around.

"Martyn...?" we called.

Crispin ran on a little and shielding his eyes from the snow, pointed. "There by the holly trees."

We struggled on. Johannes joined us. He was soon on his knees down in the snow. Martyn was curled in a ball on his side, half on the track, half in the snow covered brush at the side of what passed for the road.

The hazel twig he had taken from Hubert lay by his side, broken in two. I picked up the piece which lay behind him. It was a wicked and jagged sharp point. Johannes attempted to turn Martyn on his back. The resultant scream, turned my blood to water and pierced through the snowfall hissing around us. Blood had pooled in the snow and was spreading out as an ominous stain. It steamed around him.

Martyn turned on his side again and brought his knees up to his chest. He grasped the piece of hazel protruding from his groin.

I yelled at the top of my voice. "Cedric... here to me."

Cedric came slipping and sliding in haste, through the gap in the drift.

"Empty the biggest hurdle. Stack the foodstuffs at the side of the roadway as best you can. Get it back here. Quick!"

Crispin too was now on his knees by the stricken carpenter.

"What on earth were you doing here, Martyn?"

He could not answer. His teeth were gritted in pain.

"Stopped for a piss maybe," said Johannes.

"We shall drag him back to the village on the hurdle and recover the food later," I said.

Only Hal and I knew what had actually happened: that Martyn had possibly tried to flee.

I cursed myself for the idiot I had been in letting him know that I had guessed his secret and handed the hazel stick to my man at arms. He stared at it for a while, then at Martyn on the ground.

"Bloody thing broke. Sharp edge that. Musta stumbled on it and it and... it..."

"Pierced him, I know."

Crispin had now begun the rites for the dying for we had no idea what was happening to Martyn and it was safer to do it now whilst he could still answer, albeit with gentle nods.

Hal, Johannes and I moved away.

I saw Crispin draw back on his heels. No, Martyn had not died. Crispin had just heard something he did not like but like a true Christian priest, he bent to his supplicant again and listened. Hal and I exchanged glances. It seemed an age before Cedric and John came back with the hurdle.

"I have sent the lads on," John said. "No point in standing around in this."

"Good" I said. "Let us get Martyn onto it."

"What has happened?"

"He went off for a piss we think," said Johannes as he manoeuvered himself to take the weight of Martyn's torso, with its projection of hazel stick. "And the stick he was using, broke, spitting him in the groin as he fell."

John crossed himself. "Hazel doesn't break that easily," he said, puzzlement in his voice.

Crispin at last finished Martyn's confession and made the sign of the cross over the hunched man.

As we lifted him, the screams which came from Martyn would have woken the dead. Johnathan told me later that the boys who were nearing the village looked back in fear, and crossed themselves, when they heard him. He moaned and whimpered as we lay him down and screamed as we set off, the sledge catching the icy roadway and jolting him.

Gradually and thankfully he passed into unconsciousness and we increased our pace a little.

Johannes kept his eye on his patient. The wound had not bled further and the stick had plugged a hole in Martyn's groin. I know that Johannes was very worried about what would happen when he removed it.

Crispin lingered behind us. I kept casting glances in his direction but he was too absorbed in his own thoughts. I surmised I knew what those thoughts were.

We passed John's house at the very edge of the village. The falling snow had thinned a little but it still formed a screen between us and the further distance where we could just about see the other lads undoing the packs on the hurdles and storing the goods in Walter Reeve's outhouse by the village green. Later we would see to apportioning out the food.

We hurried our burden into the manor courtyard and Johannes shouted it would be best to go into one of the guest rooms. The hurdle was pulled to the door and Martyn was manhandled as gently as we could, into the room.

Crispin, Hal, Johannes and myself went in and as I shut the door I said to Alfred, "Send Cedric - he knows where the food lies and has the youngest legs; get Stephen and Peter to help him drag it home on the hurdle we used for Martyn. They are fresh."

Alfred nodded, touched his very wet and snowy forelock, shook his hood of snow and was gone.

Crispin made sure that Martyn was still with us and rushed off for his viaticum to do for a second time the hurried thing he had done on the roadway. Johannes took the small pack which he always wore on his back and laid it down, brushing off the accumulated snow and fetched out his doctoring equipment.

"I'll need light and heat and water."

Hal ran off to organise that.

Crispin returned at last. One look at me and he realised that I already knew what Martyn had told him.

"You know?"

"Aye, Hal and I know."

"Know what?" asked Johannes sorting out a bottle from his pack and pouring some liquid from the pale amber pottery bottle. He dropped a few drops very carefully into a wooden cup.

I sat down heavily on the stool in the little room and leaned forward, tired with the task of walking three miles dragging the food, and heavy hearted and weary with the knowledge that Martyn, my childhood friend and companion, was a murderer.

I told Johannes everything I knew.

"So I am attempting to save the man so that he can be hanged at a later date?"

"I can forgive him the killing of Glazer, though the law will not."

"He is absolved, Aumary," said Crispin sharply. "God forgives him."

"It's still murder Crispin, whatever we say. I cannot however forgive him the attempted murder of the poor peddler and for Hilda's broken head. He tried to kill her too. And he wounded Brice."

Crispin looked crestfallen.

"No, he has probably not told you of that. I think he tried to prevent young Brice from catching a glimpse of the oaken piece of wood with which he killed

Glazer. I am sure he built it into the roof beams of the stable and thatched on top of it. He is parsimonious with his wood and his leavings. It would have been gone forever, except Brice was thatching there that day and might have seen it. That is why he had to be pushed out of the way. He was quite right, Martyn did push him. I don't think he meant for him to fall and hurt himself so badly, though. It was an accident."

Hal returned and brought a lantern and two oil lamps. John and his son Peter wheeled in the brazier which we'd had in Brice's room and set about lighting it. Peter Devizes, my man at arms, brought more candles and soon the place was flooded with light. The snowy sky had made the day dark and the light was fading into evening anyway.

"I'll be off now, sir, with Stephen and Cedric. We'll fetch it all back."

I nodded. "Good man."

I stood. I did not want to be present when Johannes did whatever he had to do to poor Martyn. Hal said he would stay. He could see I was very upset. I moved to the door.

"I'll be in my office if you want me. Keep me informed. Whatever happens."

Hal opened the door for me and said kindly, "P'raps 'tis fer the best. T'would only be hard for you... if you...."

"Aye it would. It would be very hard, Hal."

"Maybe it's best he goes, eh, Aumary?"

He rarely called me by my name but he was one of the very few who felt they could. I nodded and I passed from the room.

With heavy feet I crossed the yard and mounted the steps. I could hear Hal following me but didn't't turn round.

I undid my office door, staggered inside and threw myself onto my daybed. I heard Hal come in, remove my boots, pull a blanket over me and then shut the door.

*****

I slept for the rest of the evening and when I woke, it was very dark. A brazier had been lit in the room, a candle had been left for me and a jug of watered ale. More blankets had been heaped onto me. My wife had been in to see me, it seemed. I stood and shakily downed the ale in one, for I had had nothing to drink since my breakfast of honeyed bread.

Hal was now in the hall. I looked in and he shook his head at me. No news.

I came back into my office, and as was my normal custom, I set everything I knew onto parchment. I scribbled and rewrote, scrubbed it out and started again. My writing grew more and more spidery as I tried to set out what I thought. Eventually satisfied, I put the resultant parchment into my chest and locked it again.

Peter and Stephen, along with Cedric, had come into the manor a little before I had awoken but Hal had not let them disturb me. Now they were in the hall; Cedric dozing, curled up on a bench by them. Poor lad, he had walked further than any of us. Peter and Stephen stood and gave their report in their usual efficient manner. All foodstuffs given to us by the town were now safe in the reeve's outhouse.

I approached Wilfrid and Hilda who were huddled together, chatting, their knees raised under one blanket in the corner by the solar stairs.

"Go home to your goats, Hilda, Wilfrid. You are no longer in danger." They stood and shook out their clothes.

"Have you caught him, sir?" asked Hilda, her eyes imploring me to explain.

"I have. You will learn in due course."

Wilfrid and Hilda looked at each other wide eyed and then fell to hugging.

"Thank you, sir," and they skipped off into the night.

The peddler and Janet Woodsman were sitting together on the chapel stairs sharing a beaker of ale.

As I approached they stood. Janet's practiced eye took in the state of me and my clothing. "Oh my, m'lord... you look as if you have had a fight with a demon in a dunkin' pool."

I think I smiled. "I feel as if I have Janet," I replied.

"Martyn," I winced at the name and vowed henceforth this man would always be 'Peddler'. "Can you come to my office, I have something to tell you?" The peddler handed the ale pot to his betrothed and slid from the step.

"Aye sir... lead on."

He closed the door quietly behind him.

"Do sit, peddler."

The man hooked a stool nearer to him with a foot and folded up onto it.

"I have found the man who tried to kill you, though like I said, it was a case of mistaken identity."

Martyn sat up straight then and fingered his scarred head. "Do I need to know who it was, sir?"

"Aye, I think you do. And I think you need to know why he tried to kill the person he thought you were."

"The glazier, sir?"

"Yes."

I told my story over again, leaving out the names of the victims; it would serve no purpose for him to know.

The peddler went white. "Holy Mother of God," he said and crossed himself. "And I shared an ale pot with the man. Many's a night I sat with him, talking of this place and that, places we had both been in, once my memory of them came back and all the time that man was...." He broke off, horrified at the images my tale had painted for him. "No wonder the poor carpenter wanted revenge."

"Yes, that is just what it was...revenge, redress for a wrong...."

He stared at the coals of the brazier. Suddenly his head came up.

"Will he hang, sir?"

"I don't know. At the moment the doctor is trying to save his life." And yet again I told a tale - this one was not a re-telling, though I would retell it again and again, later.

"I'll not accuse him sir."

I smiled. "You are a good man, peddler. Many's a man would be baying for his blood."

"It was justice sir...justice."

"Perhaps."

I saw in my mind's eye Martyn Carpenter gingerly coming into the hall the day he reported on the finishing of the stable woodwork. I saw his face as he took in the peddler and his injury. How shocked he was to find they shared a name. Yes, this was guilt and shame and regret. I recalled how he fled after he had spoken to me.

"You know it all now, peddler. Please, until we know what will... what will happen... can you keep it to yourself. Everyone will know, I suppose, soon enough."

"Aye sir. Rely on me."

"Oh… and here is the little book of poetry I promised you. Guard it well, for it belongs to the priory and they will have my balls for a bell if it is damaged."

The peddler chuckled. "Again sir... rely on me."

*****

I ascended the solar steps later in the evening. Lydia and Hawise were sitting together close on one bench, a rug over them.

"And the prince of the fairies, never again doubted his wife and they all....."

"Ah, another story?"

They both swivelled to look at me. "Dada, you're back!" cried Hawise wriggling from Lydia's grasp. She ran towards me but stopped when she saw how tired, dishevelled and dirty I was.

"Oh dear," she said, in a most grown up way "I don't think you are very happy."

"No, I'm not, and I am very tired and cold and wet and dirty."

"Come and sit here, I'll get Alice to prepare you a bath," said Lydia.

Hawise and I sat together under the same blanket on the bench in front of the fire.

"Did you get the things you wanted from the town?"

"Yes, my sweet, we did. We shall still have to be careful what we eat but I think we shall last into the spring with the stores we already had and this extra. Even if the weather is still unkind."

Lydia came back into the room, "We have run out of charcoal, Aumary - we gave our last to Hal for... for Martyn."

"None at all?"

She shook her head.

"Then we shall go out as soon as we can and look to our charcoal burners and see what we can do." Like the shepherds on the downs, I wondered how the families who made the charcoal deep in Savernake Forest were faring in this weather. They had special sanction from the King to use wood from the forest and to hunt small game. Deer were the King's own beasts and unless we had permission we could not hunt and kill them. We ate venison rarely.

"Is it true that Martyn Carpenter is sore hurt, Aumary?" she asked as she dragged the half barrel bath, to the fireside, from the corner of the room.

I passed my hands over my weary face.

"Aye, he has taken a hazel spike through the groin. It was an accident...none of us saw it happen, but Johannes was there almost instantly and…."

"Will he die?" asked Hawise in a whisper.

"I do not know sweeting. I hope not. But I fear he will."

"No," said my daughter with all the authority of a five year old. "He will not. Uncle Johannes is the best doctor in the whole wide world and he will save him."

Lydia looked up. Alice and the kitchen girls were bringing in the jugs of hot water to fill the bath.

"Off to your rest now, Hawise" she said. "Felice, will you take Hawise to bed please?"

"God save you Hawise," I said and kissed the top of her head.

"And you dada," she said. "See you in the morning," she added,

"If he spares us," I answered. It was our nightly ritual.

When everyone had gone, Lydia came to stand in front of me. "So what are you not telling us?"

I undressed, throwing my dirty and no doubt smelly clothes into a heap by the door for Joan the laundress to collect, and slipped slowly into the hot water.

"Not telling you?" I chuckled "Are you a witch that you know something is amiss even before...."

"I know you and I know your voice and your looks," she said.

I luxuriated in the heat of the bath. I dipped my head under the water and came up spluttering.

"Ah, this is hot!"

"It's good for you. So...what is it that is bothering you?"

I looked at her as I slicked back my curly black hair with two hands.

"Bothering me? Only that Martyn Carpenter is our murderer, that is all."

"Jesu defend us… no!"

And so naturally, I had to tell my tale all over again.

Before I retired to my bed, I plodded across the yard to the little room where Johannes was looking after Martyn and entered quietly. The room was in semi darkness.

"He lives?" I asked.

"He does."

Johannes yawned and threw a blanket over his shoulders.

"I removed the splinter. I was all ready for the artery, the big blood line in the top of the leg which runs through the groin, to be severed or at best damaged, but no, there was no gushing of blood. No pulsing."

"Is that good?"

Johannes made a moue. "Yes. If it had, I would be lying asleep by the fire in the hall now for I would have no patient to worry over."

"Ah I see. He would have bled to death."

"There is very little one can do if that sort of damage occurs."

"But…?"

"I fear that the damage is to his bladder. I cannot mend that. We can only wait and see what happens. I may be wrong. I have given him a poppy syrup. The strongest I dare brew. He slept through the removing of the spike… well, there were a few murmurs but no screams." He smiled. "I do so hate it when my patients scream. It makes me seem a bad doctor."

I returned his smile. "Hawise says you are the best doctor in the world. She has every confidence in your ability to save Martyn."

He bowed. "Then I must do my best for the little Lady Hawise's sake."

There was a murmur from the bed and Johannes was up in an instant. The blanket which had been around his shoulders fell to the floor and the doctor lifted Martyn's chin to check the pulse in his neck.

I came closer. My first name was whispered.

"Yes Martyn, I am here."

I hunkered down and put my ear to the man's face.

"Tired."

"I know."

"Confessed."

"Good. If you go to God it will be with a clean soul."

"You know - I killed him - Aumary?"

"Yes, I know. And you pushed the lad from the roof so he would not see the wood you used to bludgeon Glazer, built into the roof of the stable?" Martyn nodded almost imperceptibly.

"Couldn't burn it. Can't waste it. Good oak."

I took his hand.

"You always were a hoarder, even as a child."

And suddenly I was transported back to the riverside on a sunny July day. Crispin, me and Martyn, and a couple of other lads, splashing in the pools and learning to swim. My throat constricted. The back of my eyes prickled. I swallowed.

"Am an idiot," said Martyn.

"Where did you think you were going, taking off like that into the forest, Martyn? There was nowhere to go, especially in this weather."

"Aye… just thought… gotta go… go away."

"It was foolish."

Martyn licked his lips, "Aye. Heard Wilf…"

"You heard Wilfrid arranging to meet the glazier?"

"Aye. Din't come out."

"No..I don't suppose he did..So how did you get Perkin out there, Martyn?"

The carpenter grimaced.

"Treasure. Told him. Seen it."

"How did you know?"

"In wood barn… heard Glazer ask." He grimaced again, "Ask Dysig."

"Ah… I see," I said.

"Watchin' out Hawi…"

"You were watching out for Hawise?"

"Aye."

"That was kind."

Martyn whispered again. "Sorry to the peddler. So sorry…."

"I know. I told him. He bears you no ill will, Martyn. He is a remarkable man. He asks that should you go with God, he bears you no ill will, for he understands the reasons why you had to have revenge on the glazier."

The carpenter smiled and his eyes closed.

"The girl… I was foolish… stupid. Hilda. I should never… so sorry - tell her. Desperate. Not thinking straight."

"I will tell her," I said and I gave his hand a reassuring squeeze. "Sleep now."

*****

I woke in the darkest hours of the morning to a frantic screaming.

Everyone knew that Martyn had been taken, wounded to the guest room on the southern wall and so no one panicked at the yelling and the agonised pleading for death, for God to take him, now...no more please, but there were many who crossed themselves and made the sign against the evil eye, I'm sure. We all heard the screaming. Luckily Hawise, the furthest away and behind another door, did not hear but slept peacefully through the disturbance. Gradually the weeping and screaming passed. I lay listening, expecting a scratch at the door and for Johannes or Hal to come and tell me that Martyn had passed to his eternal rest, but no. In the early morning, just before dawn, another bout of screaming jolted us awake.

"The same," said Lydia. "Pleading for God to take him and not to torment him any longer."

She pulled the pillow over her head. "Oh, I can't stand to hear the poor man. Jesu, please take him as he wishes." And she wept into her pillow. I cradled her head until she fell asleep again.

And so on it went....

I looked in that next morning. Johannes was asleep on a chair, covered by a blanket.

I poked my head through the door.

" 'E still lives. Johannes said that the bladder is pierced and it won't be long. It's leakin', see, into the body. Can't go on like that." Hal shook his head.

Johannes woke at our voices. He rubbed his face and stretched his neck. Then he rubbed the side of it vigorously.

"Aw...."

Hal grinned. "Sleepin' with a cricked neck eh?"

Johannes looked up at me.

"Be prepared, Aumary," he said seriously after the small moment of levity.

"He is dying. I cannot do anything now. I have no more opium. No more pain killing relief."

"Does Lydia not have anything in her armoury?"

"Not as strong as we shall need but I will ask her… yes. I will ask."

"Hal tells me that his bladder is leaking into his body. Is there nothing we can do?"

"No. I am so sorry, Aumary," he said sadly. "He will go, it's just a matter of when. And he is in a great deal of pain."

All that day I listened to the bouts of screaming from the little room on the south wall. Everyone went about with a long face, whispering and hurrying to be out of earshot. It was horrendous. No man, however wicked, should have to take so long to die, in such pain. At last the screaming lessened to crying, the crying to whimpering and then, when there was only the odd sob, I poked my head into the sick room.

Hal was still there, staring into space half asleep. Johannes was once again asleep in his chair and snoring with his head back on a pillow.

By the bedside holding the wounded man's hand was Hilda. She looked up.

"He may have tried to kill me, sir, but as God is my witness, he has paid for it tenfold. Poor man."

"You know then… what it was he did and why?"

"Hal told me."

I nodded. "I'm sure it won't be long now," I said.

But I was wrong. It was well into the next day when at last Martyn Carpenter slipped into a permanent sleep. Johannes was there and came to me shortly afterwards.

"It's over."

I crossed myself.

"Thank God. I do not know how you can stand it, Johannes. You have my complete admiration."

He shrugged. "Sadly, you get used to it… ah, no… what am I saying? You never get used to it. It's just something you have to do."

"The end?"

"Was peaceful. He was quite lucid. I think the pain had more or less gone, for the part of him so affected had shut down I think. I do not know how it works and I wish I could know more but..." He yawned. "I'll sleep now."

I thanked him for his help.

He turned at my office door, "Do you know, at the last, his eyes opened, he breathed normally, there seemed no difficulty. He looked beyond me and lifted an arm. I thought to take it but it clenched as if he had already taken a hand."

"Oh?"

"Aye - as if he had taken an unseen hand and he said quite clearly, 'Maggie... you came.'

Who was she, Aumary - anyone?"

"She was his wife... his much loved wife. She died two years ago," I replied, and I shivered.

Chapter Twelve

The weather clutched us in an icy fist that did not relent for weeks. We had no more snow, thankfully, but the ground lay frozen and unworkable for weeks on end. We rationed our foodstuffs further and grew thinner. One more elderly person died, Old Giffard, even though he was well tended by his family. We used Martyn's house as a makeshift morgue and left the bodies there until we were able to hack the ground to bury them. Crispin would be busy come the thaw. We were beginning to run out of wood and so parties had to be sent out to forage under the snow and ice. I gave permission for some trees to be felled so that we might have larger pieces to burn, to cook and heat our food, what little we had. I and six of the men went out, to the charcoal burners' kilns. Their cottages were deserted. We knew not where they had gone. We brought back what little charcoal we could discover there. John and a few men went in search of rabbits for the pot and came back from the warrens, jubilant, swinging their finds by the legs, smiling and praising their small earth dogs' skills at finding and unearthing the small game. We ate the doves from the dovecote. We began to shoot with bows and arrows and cook the larger birds that circled the manor: the crows and the magpies, until they became wary and clever and came no more. We struggled up onto the downs and hunted for partridge and pheasant but they were scrawny fowl, for they too were starving. We had long ago eaten our poultry.

Then, one morning in late March we woke to bright sunshine and a drip, drip from the eaves of the manor. I watched carefully lest the drips froze again, but they did not and the thaw continued.

Slowly the snow receded, very slowly, for it had been hard packed for months. The place became waterlogged as feet of snow languidly dribbled into the flattened grass and earth and our boots churned up the mud. The fish pond thawed and we trawled the depths for any fish still living and counted our stocks. The river trickled at first and then became a rushing beast hurling itself headlong towards Ramsbury. A couple of homes were flooded, those nearest to the boggy meadows and the Salley Gardens: our stands of willows which stood by the river.

Johannes made his way home in the cart of Giles the Thatcher together with Brice, his arm supported with a light bandage and workable in short spells. They chatted happily in the back of the cart; Titus Johannes' horse tied to the cart tail. We waved them off and then turned to see to the damage done by the prolonged snow and ice.

Richard, my head groom, his foot now mended, looked over his new home. (He had bravely chosen to take over the now deserted house, previously lived in by the Brooker twins) and pronounced it fair and in need of a little work before he would take his new wife there. They would be married in May. There was time to repair, re-build and extend. Luckily, Martyn Carpenter's habit of saving every piece of building wood meant that there was a goodly stock with which to do so. We would also seek permission to fell some trees.

All was bustle and hurry, everyone had a role and a job. Everyone was smiling, relieved that the worst was over.

On the fine morning of the 26th April, St. Peter's Day, a Saturday, we buried our dead at last and gave thanks in our little church, for their lives and for our deliverance from the hell through which we had lived this past four months.

Martyn was buried in Durley on that day. Nothing was said about his role in the murder of the glazier. We put it about that a desperate wolfshead had come close to the manor from out of the forest and had slain the glassmaker and attacked the peddler and later on, Hilda Frithson. If the tale was met with skewed looks and disbelieving glances, no one took the slightest bit of notice.

That day too, in the afternoon, the peddler came to me, beaming with delight. "Well m'lord," he said," I reckon as I have done it."

I looked up from my work, "Hmmm?"

"I've solved your problem.....your riddle."

I put down my pen. "You have? How… what…?"

He put up his hand then and interrupted me, "Ah no....it's my secret for a while. Until tonight. If you would care, sir, to stay in the hall after supper, then you will know all."

I smiled after his retreating back. No matter how awful our situation, there was always something good to come from it. Martyn Summersete was definitely the best thing to come out of the horrors of the past few months; Martyn, and a reconciliation of the brothers, Wilfrid and Tostig Frithson. Nothing like adversity to bring warring parties together.

What was it I had heard Johannes say? "Behind dark clouds there is always a blue sky."

*****

We waited with bated breath in the hall that evening for Martyn the peddler to finish his beggarly supper. All knew that he would sing or tell a story that night. Only I knew that it was to be something wondrous and meaningful. Gradually the hall fell silent. The peddler stood. He slapped his sides. "Ah well, 'twas a good if meagre meal." He bowed towards Matthew Cook who accepted the praise with grace. "But one can't sing well on too full a belly, 'tis well known."

Folk laughed at that and fell silent again.

Martyn walked to the place before the dais on which we sat; Lydia, Hawise, Crispin, and I, and bowed.

"My lord. A while ago, you set me a puzzle. I despaired of ever solving it. 'Twas like no riddle I had ever come across before. However, I have solved that puzzle, that riddle, and I will now sing it for you, for I have set to a tune of my own making, those words which you put before me, as runes."

"Thank you peddler." I said, my heart thumping, "Pray sing."

He turned to the body of the hall and in his beautiful, sweet tenor voice, he began, what I liked to think of as my apple song.

Ic giefe mīnre lufestran þone æppele būton á þære heortan
Ic giefe mīnre lufestran þæt hús būton á þæm dore
Ic giefe mīnre lufestran þære palendsan þærin héo mōt libban
Ond héo mōt onlúcan hīe būton á cæge.

Mīn héafod is se æppel būton á þære heortan,
Mīn mód is þæt hús būton á þæm dore
Mīn heorte is séo palendse þærin héo mōt libban
Ond héo mōt onlúcan hīe būton á cæge.

And then he sang again so that all listening would understand it.

I will give my love an apple without ever a core
I will give my love a house without ever a door,
I will give my love a palace wherein she may be,
And she may unlock it without any key.

My head is the apple without ever a core,
My mind is the house without ever a door.
My heart is the palace wherein she may be
And she may unlock it without any key.

There was total silence as the last word faded. The tune was like none I had heard before, plaintive and unusual and the final words were so quietly sung, with such control of the breath and voice, that we all leaned forward to hear the beauty of it and dared not breathe. The hall erupted. There was a stamping of feet and a cheering and such a clapping as was deafening. They would, as Hal said later, have heard it in Burbage.

The peddler turned to me and bowed once more. I swallowed the lump in my throat.

"Thank you." I whispered. "Come to me later and I will reward you. You can also tell me how you did it."

I went to my office and took out the little gem of an apple. I found the first word and I followed the sentences round the golden circle. I sang the words the peddler had uttered in my head.

I took out my piece of parchment upon which I had written what words I had known and I filled in the gaps. It made sense. Martyn Peddler had done well. The first four lines were on the outside and unbelievably the last four, the solution, were written so tiny, on the inside of the gold apple.

I took out some coins from my chest and wrapped them in a square of linen and dripped wax onto it, pressing my seal, the seal of the Belvoirs - three tiny flowers surrounded by oak leaves onto it.

The peddler came in moments later. I smiled at him and uttered just one word. "How?"

He chuckled low in his throat. " 'Twas the book, the little book you lent me, sir."

I must have looked puzzled for he said, "It took me a mortal long time to plough through the poems, sir and my, my, aren't some of them naughty?"

I laughed out loud then, "Indeed they are and not the sort of thing..."

"...you imagine a bunch o' monks would be readin'," he finished for me.

"Anyway, I did a lot o' comparin' and guessin' and fittin' in words I did know. I used the words I did know from the little rune poems and worked out what some of the other letters might be."

"But how did you know they were right?"

"Ah...that's where I had a bit o' luck. Janet's Grand Uncle...."

I screwed up my forehead and thought. "Janet's Great Uncle..ah that would be, Old Giffard. The Giffard we buried today in the churchyard?"

"The very same, sir. Now his body was failing but his brain was as bright as a bird with a bean and when Janet went to see him - she's been visiting, 'cos she liked him see. I went too."

"How does Giffard...?"

"Do you know how old Giffard was, sir?"

I thought back to my childhood. He had been reeve before Walter and that had been well before I had been born.

"He was near on ninety....he could'a made a hundred had we had a better winter I think. Imagine that? A hundred."

I frowned, trying to catch where he was going. He saw that I was not following and went on. "He were born when folk were nearer to the old ways, sir. Nearer to the old language and he remembered quite a few words and so afore he died and got too wobbly to talk, we pieced together the runes and the words and made a whole poem, sir. That's why it took me so long. Giffard remembered some words I didn't't know."

I sat back in my chair beaming.

"Martyn Summersete" I said, "You are a remarkable man." I pressed the coins into his hand.

"You are a man with a brain like I have never known," (though I had known one other who was similarly gifted, Master Quimper, my brother's tutor. He too was a wizard with words.)

"May God always grant you a clear head to use your considerable intellect and talent."

"Aye, well sir," said the peddler, fingering the scar behind his ear. "I reckons if people will give over hitting me on the head and addling them a while, my brains will last till I'm ninety."

"I sincerely hope so," I said.

"Yes, Paul, Martyn Peddler is still alive and living in the village. He has two fine sons and two grand-daughters now, and I think a great grandchild on the way, though dear Janet passed away about oh... it must have been sixteen years ago now. He isn't ninety yet. But I bet you, he will outlive me...!"

I vowed that night to go out as soon as I could and search the river bank for further treasure.

*****

One day in late April, when the sun shone, and the great tits were singing their spring song, Hal, Crispin, Johannes and I made the trip out to the riverbank and paced up and down between the two alders. We searched the ground, four of us, walking six feet apart and scanned the turf for disturbance. We started about ten feet out from the bank and moved in slowly.

"There must have been some sort of movement here for Dysig to catch hold of the apple so easily."

"Aye, it must have been almost on the surface," said Crispin.

"But why?" asked Johannes. "Why would this one piece be in so shallow a grave?"

Hal knelt on the bank and peered over the edge of the river. "Nothing 'ere... the bank slopes down."

He got up and rubbed his wet and muddy knees. "Ah well... I am as wet and as mucky as I am goin' a get. Why not a wee bitty more," and he waded out about three feet into the stream and stood in the water where it almost reached the top of his boots.

Then he began to walk slowly up the stream from the alder tree at the pond end, towards the alder tree at the threshing barn end, scanning the bank as he went. We followed him on the grass.

"Nothin'." He turned and retraced his steps.

"Wait... what's that?" Hal fished about in the water for a while and brought up, dripping and dribbling, a manor lantern.

"Now we know where it went," said Johannes pointedly.

Hal handed the lantern up to the bank and as he did so his eye was caught by something in the mud.

"Nah. It's nothin'. Except…. Nah.' tis a bit o' rubbish."

"It may not be rubbish, Hal," I called. "Can you fish it out?"

We handed him a small trowel which the builders had left behind when they finished their work on the walls a few years ago.

He started to dig carefully. Hal swore. "It's devilish difficult to get out. I don't reckon as it was ever meant to come out agin."

I jumped down to help him. Together we freed the thing trapped in the mud at the side of the river. Hal bent to wash it in the water and when he straightened up, he almost dropped the small thing he held.

"Well I'll be bug… bent as a bloody bow… sir. It's a finger bone."

Indeed it was a finger and on it was a gold ring covered in mud and cemented to the bone with it.

Crispin was now down in the river with us.

"Lord above," he said. "We have a burial. The poor man has lost a finger. We must be very careful." He made the sign of the cross over the site of the supposed body, in spite of the fact that the man interred here was no Christian.

I handed the finger bone to Johannes. "Aye tis a man. This is his little finger."

"We need to cut back the bank to find the rest of him for he lies right under where you are standing, Johannes."

Johannes stepped back as if he did not wish to stand on a corpse. This man, however, was no corpse. He would be nothing but bones and those precious things with which he had been buried; those things he valued in life.

"Why so near to the river, Aumary?" asked Crispin once he had finished mumbling under his breath, some prayer he felt might suit the moment and I suppose, the man.

I looked round. "See here, the river bends round in an 's' shape. I suspect that the river was over there," and I pointed to the field, "when our man was laid in the ground here. It has moved over the centuries."

Hal chuckled." 'E wouldn't a wanted to be washed away now would 'e?"

"No but I think that is what has happened to some extent. That is why the apple was so easy to find. I think that Dysig must have been just over the edge of the river on the snow.

Our apple was almost in danger of being washed away before Dysig scooped it up."

I put up my hand and Johannes pulled me up onto the bank.

"We shall know more when we uncover him."

Crispin was wading to the bank a little further on where it dipped and he scrambled up.

"Should we disturb him, Aumary?" We all looked at him.

"I have no doubt that he was a pagan, Crispin, but I don't think we can leave him here, now we know he is here. Would God not thank us for lifting him and burying him in consecrated ground, then?"

Crispin shrugged. "I have no idea. I have never buried an six hundred or so, year old pagan before."

We all stared at the finger bone and then at the riverbank.

Hal broke the silence.

"We gotta find out what is buried with 'im. We none of us will rest till we know that."

"And whatever we find... will belong to the King," I said. "We must be agreed."

We all nodded.

"Right then... let's dig and dig very gently." I paced out the bank.

"If we think he is lying sideways on...and his head is..."

"To the west.."

"Yes, Hal, then he might be about here." I struck the ground gently with my soggy boot.

*****

We dug all the rest of the morning and part of the afternoon. Hal fetched us something to eat and drink and we ceased our labours only to consume them. Then we dug again. The man lay in a shallow scrape just about three feet down. He was lying on his front with his hands to the side and it was his left hand that was missing the finger. He had no coffin and all his vestments had long ago perished, along with his flesh.

Curious manor folk gathered close by though none would venture too near and many made the sign against the evil eye.

Hal fetched one of Hubert's tarred cloths and carefully we lifted the bones, mud and all, onto it. Johannes supervised us as I am sure our poor corpse would have been laid in the wrong pattern had it been up to us to put down the relics in the order we found them. Then, we dug around in a six foot circle which terminated with a squared edge at the river.

It was then we found what he had been buried with. There was no doubt, this man had been a wealthy person in life. It was hard to tell from the strange misshapen items we dug from the soil, but we could tell many were of gold and enamel, like our little apple.

We carefully wrapped each find in linen and as the light was fading, we trudged to the manor and fetched our man in through the sally port. We laid him on the bier in the mortuary and took the finds from his grave to my office. Only then did we clean ourselves and take some more food and drink.

I won't bore you with the details....

"What Paul? I must? You think my readers will be interested in all the little things we found? Oh very well then, if you are sure."

When we cleaned up what we had found, and it was a long task, I can tell you, we had an assortment of military equipment such as the cheek pieces of what we thought were helmets and the top of a sword mounting. We had beautifully chased belt buckles and tags, rings with gems which we suspected were garnets and carnelians; strips of work of which we did not understand the purpose - why they were made, except they were items of the utmost beauty. Some of it, we were sure, were for swords, for they were not unlike our own weapons, save that none of us owned such fine work nor items made of such precious materials. Each night I would lock them in my chest for safe keeping and then bring them out the following day to work at cleaning them with a thorn and sheep's wool.

Naturally I did not do this all day, for the work of the manor and the forest had begun again and we could not interrupt these vital labours for a few items of gold covered in mud.

We interred our Saxon lord, for so had named him, in the churchyard. He was a wealthy man to be buried with so much treasure, revered and honoured, and he lies there to this day, awaiting the last trump. What a shock the poor man will have when he finds himself in Heaven and not in the halls of his Gods.

May day came and went and at last we were done.

A letter was penned to the King telling him of our find and I waited for an answer, as the days grew longer and warmer, the martins returned to the barns and the flowers bloomed in the hedgerows once more.

*****

One morning, it was May seventh as I recall, when Hal and I had just finished our daily practice in the courtyard, one of the young lads from the village came hurtling into the yard. I had gone up the steps and into the passage-way, wiping my sweating head and neck with a towel, when I heard him. He quickly looked round and ran up the steps.

"M'lord." He bumped into me. "Oh sir...." He swallowed. "A party of horsemen sir, on the Marlborough Road, a large party."

"Thank you Robert. Don't worry, I don't think they are enemies," and I smiled as he backed off and disappeared through the door.

I hastily threw my gambeson, on top of my sweaty shirt, quickly combed my unruly locks and made for the manor steps.

A clatter of horses came though the gateway and ten or so of them milled around in the yard. The rest stayed outside or in the gateway itself.

John Brenthall, who happened to be crossing the yard, looked back and immediately went down on one knee. Folk in the courtyard followed suit and those coming from the outbuildings to take in the commotion, saw their fellows and also dropped down. I stood at the top of the steps, waiting. There was silence save for the jingling of harness and the snorting of the horses. A loud voice echoed around the stony enclave.

"Aumary Belvoir... where are you, you base born, boil brained pimple?"

I laughed. "Here, my liege."

The King looked up and shielded his eyes against the glare of the sun reflected from the glass windows of the manor house.

"Ah... there you are, you rascal!" He threw himself from his horse and took the manor steps two at a time and before I could fall down on one knee before him, he had embraced me in a bearlike hug and kissed me on both cheeks.

"It's good to see you at last, my King," I said.

John took off his hat and scratched his head.

"Ah yes well... the snow. Bloody stuff. Kept us from our plans at Christmas... but here we are now!" He stuffed his hat back on his head and turned a circle on the top landing, holding out his hands as if it were some step in a dance.

As he did so he took in the whole courtyard before and beneath him.

"Oh for goodness sake... Rise..." he shouted, "Or you'll all be as flat kneed as a Frenchman."

There was a general hubbub as people struggled to their feet.

"The Frenchies are always on their bloody knees for this and that...." said John jokingly.

I laughed. "Welcome to my home, sir. It's many, many years since you last came."

"I remember it well." He clapped his hands. "Right! In... in... and we shall no doubt have some of your famous ale."

"We have some newly brewed for Mayday just gone my lord. I reckon we can run to a dribble or two."

John laughed heartily. "Oh, Aumary, it does my soul good to see you again. You always were a natural with me. No ceremony, no fancy manners, no idiot bowing and scraping and two faced..." I interrupted him,

"Ah but sir, I am only a - what was it - a base born, boil brained pimple! I'm sure I have no manners at all."

John hooted with laughter and slapped me on the back.

"Gods. I had forgotten how much I love your company," he said. We moved into the hall.

There was Henry the steward down on one knee in the rushes; Hal too. Lydia gracefully fell into a perfect curtsy and Hawise taking her model from her step-mother, wobbled a copy of her obeisance.

"Up...up everyone," cried John. "While I am here, I am simple John Plantagenta - Aumary's good friend. We shall have no fawning and flattery. I've had my fill of that these past months."

I signalled to Henry to bring some refreshments.

"Sire, your men, would you wish..."

"They can do as they like. I've left most of them at Marlborough castle. I'd like to be here alone, with you...."

He strode to Lydia and lifted her up. "And your delightful lady."

He took her hand and kissed it.

As he straightened he saw Hawise looking a little put out, just behind Lydia.

"Who is this...? My, my, well, Aumary, you told me that you had some gems and gold for me to look at, but you didn't' tell me they were human and as beautiful as this."

John made an exaggerated bow. Hawise giggled and bowed back.

"This is the Lady Hawise Belvoir, my lord King," said Lydia.

"Hello Hawise," said John grinning.

"Hello King," said Hawise and they smiled sweetly at each other.

*****

The King and I retired to my office. I turned the lock behind us. Hal stood guard, his back to the door. I lit every lamp and candle I had, and opened the shutters wide. I unlocked my chest and brought out the items we had found with our mystery Saxon. I told John of the ancient body by the river.

Once again I related the story of the finding of the apple and the unravelling of the puzzle. John listened in silence, except to ask one or two pertinent questions, turning the beautiful little items over in his perfectly manicured fingers. He brought one or two of the smaller pieces to the candle and inspected every tiny detail of the patterning, the gold work and the fine enamel. I told him how the glassmaker had explained how these items had been made; I outlined the processes of enameling and engraving and at last I told him that if he would stay into the late afternoon and take meat with us, I would have Martyn Peddler sing for him the beautiful words which were inscribed on the apple.

"I will indeed, Aumary. I am as intrigued as you must have been. And all because your fool threw a snowball at your daughter. What a story!"

"Aye, if that had not been scooped up," I nodded to the apple in John's hand, "the window would never have been broken, and we should never have known what we had down by the alders."

I sat down heavily behind my table.

"And we should never have known what we now know about the glass-man, nor have solved his murder."

John's head came up from looking at the apple. "Another murder, Aumary?"

"Aye sadly my liege." I told him the whole story from beginning to end.

John listened, shaking his head at the sad tale of little Madalen and the assault on Cassie.

"So the foul culprit is murdered. May he rot in hell. And his killer is dead?" he asked soberly.

"Aye John, he is."

"Well I cannot say this is not justice. Sometimes God takes things into his own hands for his own purpose. What I shall say though," John slapped his knees and stood "I have the right man for my constable… yes indeed, the right man. You have a mind as sharp as a pin, Aumary."

He turned the apple once more in his hand. "You uncovered that mystery as easily as if it simply lay beneath a sheet and all you had to do was peel back the cloth."

"Oh no sire… I had a great deal of help."

I could see Hal smirking by the door, "Oh yes… your doctor friend… is he in the manor today?"

"No, my lord, he was called back to Marlborough."

John nodded. He grinned. "That is it then. It is confirmed. I confirm it… you will take on this role permanently, forthwith. No murderer is safe from your gaze, Aumary. I should not like to be the killer you are stalking. You would have me quaking in my boots."

"Thank you, my King." I nodded a bow.

"And something else I can confirm."

"Sire?"

"I am ravenous….let us go and see what your cook has managed to magic out of thin air. I hear that he is particularly good."

"Where have you heard this, John?" I asked, puzzlement in my voice.

"Ah… his cooking is legendary at the castle, you know. I have a mind to sample some of his magic."

***

We feasted on whatever my magical cook could find for us to eat. John was content. He knew the parlous state his realm had been in the winter of that year. He engaged Hawise, sitting between us, in jolly conversation. He was gentlemanly and polite to Lydia, seated on his left, though I grew concerned when I caught some of the looks he threw at her. His appetite for women was legendary.

When the meal was done, I motioned for the peddler to approach the high table. I could see that he was nervous. He had never been so before and was a natural performer, but I suppose singing for one's King is not the same as singing for one's friends or neighbours. However, I knew he would not let me down.

Martyn began by reciting those words in that almost unintelligible language which we had found on the bands around the apple. He promised that his song would be a translation.

He filled his lungs and out came that pure sound which we had all come to know so well over the past few months. John sat, his chin cradled on his hand, his elbow on the table top and listened, as rapt as the rest of us.

> I will give my love an apple without ever a core
> I will give my love a house without ever a door,
> I will give my love a palace wherein she may be,
> And she may unlock it without any key.

> My head is the apple without ever a core,
> My mind is the house without ev'r a door.
> My heart is the palace wherein she may be
> And she may unlock it without any key.

No one clapped until John did and he was fulsome in his praise. He turned to me.

"And that is truly what is written on that little thing?"

"Truly ,sire," I said.

"Amazing," he said shaking his head. "If I were a man with a mind for music... I'd filch your peddler and take him to Westminster with me."

"Ah my king," I answered. "It wouldn't be up to me. You'd have to ask his wife."

John bellowed at that and I could see poor Janet blushing to the roots of her hair, for she had heard what was being said about her husband. I nodded to Felice to take a sleepy Hawise to bed and John moved into her seat. He leaned conspiratorially towards me. He had drunk deep of my wine that afternoon and his eyes were a little glazed. He turned his back on Lydia.

"Talking of wives, Aumary."

"Yes sir...?"

He whispered in my ear. "I don't suppose you would consent to me, this night, lying with your wife? She is uncommonly beautiful and I have a mind to have her."

The buzz of the room faded. My head hammered. My heart raced. I had heard before that John had asked many a man for consent to bed his wife for a night. Some he had not even asked. They were always well rewarded and few denied him. No woman had been bedded without her own consent.

I thought quickly. "My Liege, my friend, John," I said. "I would share my last mouthful with you, I would share my last penny. As you know, I would give my life for you." I rubbed the place on my shoulder where I had taken a crossbow bolt meant for John, in the spring of 1204, just to aid his memory, "But I cannot, I cannot, share my wife with you."

So be it if he now called for my head, for my manor to be seized, for my role as constable to be rescinded, my right to the title of Warden of Savernake eliminated.

The gaiety went on around us. There was silence between us.

I waited for the blow to fall. John wiped his nose on his hand and snorted.

"Aye, well... forget it. I am horrible in my cups sometimes. Of course you won't, you have only been married months. Forget I asked. No, no, forget it."

And he slapped me heartily on the back but I could tell he was miffed.

However, I was able to breathe once more.

*****

The afternoon grew into evening. John sobered up. He called his men around him and prepared to leave us. "I shall be at Marlborough for a while Aumary, much of May I think, come and see me."

"I shall, my lord," I said.

"I have a mind, before I leave, to stop by your little church and see where you have laid this Saxon prince of yours, and give him my thanks. Yes, I shall."

He swept out of the hall. John paused by the office door and Hal offered him a large leather bag into which we had carefully put all the finds from our diggings, our little apple and the gold rings and sword mounts, the strips of gem encrusted enamel work and the belt buckles. He took it with a nod. We followed him outside to the manor step.

Lydia and I stood together, our arms locked.

John kissed me on each cheek. "God keep you, John," I said.

The King reached over and whispered something in her ear then pecked Lydia on the cheek so demurely that she flinched and blushed and didn't't know what to do. In the end she curtsied low, letting go of my arm.

"Guard her well, Aumary. She is a gem worth dying for."

"I know," I said. His eyes met mine and he smiled.

I did not see him reach into the bag but when he was gone, I saw Lydia looking at the hand he had grasped as he left us.

There, in her palm, was our little apple.

"What did he say to you?" I asked.

She looked up at me with those beautiful violet eyes.

"He said...he said..'And she may unlock it without any key.' What do you suppose he meant by that, Aumary?"

I chuckled.

I have absolutely no idea my love," I said. "No idea at all."

"Pardon Paul my scribe? Did I ever tell her what the king had asked me? No... Paul, no, I never did."

AUTHOR'S NOTE

Savernake Forest lies at the southern edge of Marlborough town in Wiltshire and can still be visited today. Access is along the A4 to Newbury or the A346 to Salisbury. It is much smaller now than in the 13th century when it was at its most extensive, covering some 150 square miles. Today the Forestry Commission manage it but there is still a hereditary warden, the Marquess of Ailesbury, and it is Britain's only privately owned forest.

Today Savernake is a forest of mixed woodland but in the thirteenth century, it had for example, few of the large beech trees we see today. They were planted, in the seventeenth century, and sadly are coming to the end of their lives now. The oaks though are of considerable age. Big Belly (ied) Oak, is one of the oldest, already being about two hundred years old when King John rode past it!

In the days of John, the L'Estourmi family were the wardens of the forest. Geoffrey L'Estourmi fell foul of King Richard, having to pay a huge fine for supporting Count John in his uprising against the King. In my tale, I have changed the family's name. Unless we know who they really were and what they actually did, I'm loath to make them do anything, so I'd rather make it up and have fictional characters, though the names of some of the minor players are to be found in the annals, if you look.

Now to Aumary. He is a minor lord, not terribly wealthy and more a business-man than pure aristocracy. As warden of the forest he has quite a practical job and needs to know about the forest and its trades. He is a knight - yes, but first and foremost, a forester. I have made him a sympathetic character as so many folk of his class in novels are portrayed as proud, haughty and nasty. I fail to see how many of them could be so. They were dependent upon their peasants for their livelihood. If the peasant didn't't prosper, neither did they at this level of society. Grander folk perhaps could be less amenable. Aumary takes every man as he finds him and isn't averse to rolling up his sleeves and getting on with it.

The name Belvoir is pronounced Bell voir and not 'Beaver' as it is nowadays. The English pronunciation 'Beaver' was built up over many centuries through the inability of the Anglo-Saxons to master the French tongue. It's the name of a small town in eastern France and there is still a castle there once owned by a noble family of the same name. Aumary's family must have been a Norman offshoot.

Durley, now a small hamlet on the edge of the fores, was once well hidden in the trees. The manor can no longer be seen but there is a farm and a house called Durley House though this manor wasn't founded until the 1400's. The manor most people know about of course, is the one in Hilary Mantel's Book, Wolf Hall, (originally Ulfhall) probably a timbered building very near Burbage. The manor belonged to the Seymour family in the sixteenth century (who were also the hereditary wardens of the forest) and was the childhood home of Jane Seymour, Henry V111's third wife. I didn't't want to go anywhere near there.

The Regalia existed. It was extant until the seventeenth century when it disappeared. It was very likely broken up and melted down in the Civil War, however the ivory and silver horn is in the British Museum but is not on display.

The manor I have 'invented' is a walled courtyard house with a stone hall of two storeys and a mezzanine floor, accessed by a staircase of stone and an under-croft below, very much like Boothby Hall in Lincolnshire, the finest surviving mediaeval house of its type in the country. The village around it owes much to Sheila Sancha's portrayal of Gerneham (Irnham near Grantham) village, again in Lincolnshire, in her wonderful children's book The Luttrell Village - Country Life in the Early Fourteenth Century.

This is a depiction of the home of Sir Geoffrey Luttrell in the thirteen hundreds, so wonderfully documented in the Luttrell Psalter (now in the British Library) and considered one of the richest sources for visual depictions of everyday rural life in mediaeval England.

Salerno in Sicily was one of the finest medical schools in the known world from the tenth to the thirteenth centuries. It was the most important source of medical knowledge in Western Europe, both of the Arab and ancient world and people of both sexes flocked from all over to study there. Books were the mainstay of the school, hundreds being translated from Arabic, Greek and other languages. As a result, the medical practitioners of Salerno, both men and women, were unrivalled in knowledge and practicality.

Sadly the school declined in favour of Montpellier later in the thirteenth century and then as the church tightened its grip, medical research came to a grinding halt, not to be resurrected until the seventeenth century.

I have tried to follow the Patent Rolls (in the form of the Rotuli Litterarum Patentium) by Thomas Duffus Hardy in 1835, to show where King John was known to be on certain days in his reign. I hope I have it right.

As to King John's character, I have never thought the portrayal of this much maligned monarch quite fair. He did have bad press. He annoyed the church so they were less than kind to him in their writings. He annoyed his barons of course, so they too were less than complimentary about him.

Many of his critics were hardly snowy white themselves. The thirteenth century is a very shadowy time and much of what is written is ambiguous. We know King John was good to his friends; he did have some. His half brother William Longspee was a life long supporter. William Marshall, that octogenarian, larger than life character who bestrode the twelfth and thirteenth century mediaeval stage like a colossus, thought him worth backing, with a few reservations, and kept faith with him to the end of his days.

Life as a monarch in those days was a tough one and decisions had to be made which we would find utterly distasteful today. I know John was probably a bit of a baddie but he certainly was not the out and out baddie of the legend of Robin Hood, (which incidentally antedates the reign of John by almost a couple of hundred years.) I have tried to make him a little more human.

The winter of 1204/5 was one of the worst and longest ever recorded over the whole land. Many people died; starved or frozen to death. Crops failed, cattle died, illness and starvation followed.

The crimes against children such as we find in this book, were not against the law in the thirteenth century but neither were they 'turned a blind eye to'. They were often 'policed' by the community at large. It took until the late eighteenth century to become against the law and into the twentieth to be more fully understood; to this day having a sexual attraction to children is not illegal. Practising it is. Rape however was and is a crime, though in the past it often went unpunished. The age of consent was twelve for girls and fourteen for boys.

The Saxon treasure buried on Aumary's land is based on the Staffordshire Hoard. Discovered in a field near the village of Hammerwich, near Lichfield, in Staffordshire, England on 5 July 2009, it consists of more than three thousand five hundred items that are nearly all martial or warlike in character. Many feature beautiful garnet inlays or animals in elaborate filigree.

GLOSSARY

Abjure the Realm - The person taking the oath swore to leave the country directly and never return.

Beowulf - One of the oldest poems in the Old English language.

Bliaut - Voluminous over garment worn by both sexes (but mostly women) and pleated to the waist or under the bust.

Burntwine - Brandy

Capuchon - A hood which goes over the head and shoulders.

Chamberstick - A candlestick which has a handle for carrying.

Cordwainer - A shoemaker

Coroner - The man appointed by the crown to deal with unexpected deaths. The coroner was the man who drew up the jury of twelve men to decide the cause of death and if need be, impose fines.

Dais - A raised platform at one end of the hall upon which the lord sits for meals and to pass judgement at manorial courts.

Daub and Wattle - Building material used for making walls, in which a woven lattice of wooden strips called wattle is daubed with a sticky material usually made of some combination of wet soil, clay, sand, animal dung and straw.

Earth Dogs - Terriers

Evil Eye - is a curse believed to be cast by a malevolent glare, which is usually given to a person when they are unaware. Many cultures believe that receiving it will cause misfortune or injury. A hand gesture was made to counter it.

Freeman - A person not tied to land as a villein or serf.

Goodwives - Ones female friends. Sometimes a man's mother-in-law.

Hue and Cry - A loud cry calling for the pursuit and capture of a criminal. In English law, the cry had to be raised by the inhabitants of a hundred (area of land), in which a crime had been committed, if they were not to become liable for the damages suffered by the victim.

Irons - Leg restraints which can be locked so that miscreants cannot walk far or so they can be shackled to a hoop in a wall.

Marchpane - Marzipan

Mummers - A band of men in disguise (also called guisers) who performed a little play, which may have come down from pagan times, the origin of which is much disputed.

Palliasse - Straw filled mattress.

Parish coffin - A coffin always in reserve for emergencies.

Pumpion - A smelly unkempt person.

Rebec - A primitive violin.

Reeve - An official elected annually by the serfs to supervise lands for a lord and act as the go between.

Rites for the Dying - are meant to prepare the dying person's soul for death by providing absolution for sins by penance, sacramental grace and prayers for the relief of suffering through anointing.

Runes - are the letters in a set of related alphabets known as Runic Alphabets which were used to write various Germanic languages before the adoption of the Latin/Arabic alphabet.

Salley Gardens - Collection of willow trees.

Sally Port - The small door in the wall of a town, castle or manor which allows one person to enter or exit at a time.

Sanctuary - A sacred place, such as a church, in which fugitives were immune to arrest recognized by English law. They had forty days to make up their mind to either plead guilty and go into the hands of the law, or Abjure the Realm.

Scrip - A pouch worn on a belt at the waist.

Slickstone - Primitive iron/smoother made of metal or glass.

Solar - Generally on an upper storey, a room designed as the family's private living and sleeping quarters. The room was usually situated so that sunlight would be caught for the maximum amount of time in the day.

Stave (Quarterstaff) - Staff made from hardwood of a tree split or sawed into quarters.

Take the cowl - Become a monk.

Town Reeve - Forerunner of the mayor.

Undercroft - Lower part of a house used as a storehouse.

Yule log - a specially selected large log burnt on a hearth at Christmas. It should last the twelve days.

ABOUT THE AUTHOR

Susanna, like Aumary Belvoir has known the Forest of Savernake all her life. After a period at the University of Wales studying Speech Therapy, she returned to Wiltshire and then moved to Hampshire to work, not so very far from her forest. Susanna developed an interest in English history, particularly that of the 12th and 13th centuries, early in life and began to write about it in her twenties. She now lives in Northamptonshire with her husband and a small wire haired fox terrrier called Delphi.

TITLES IN THIS SERIES:

Belvoir's Promise
She Moved Through the Fair
Down by the Salley Gardens
I will Give My Love an Apple

Please visit the website for further information.
www.susannamnewstead.co.uk

or the Facebook page
The Savernake Novels.

Printed in Great Britain
by Amazon